Dead Cell

Chris Johnson

Johnson, Chris,
 www.facebook.com/ChrisJohnsonAuthor
Dead Cell

Cover design by Chris Johnson
Internal design by Chris Johnson
Typeset by Chris Johnson
ISBN: 154040112X
ISBN-13: 978-15-1540401120

DEDICATION

To my wife Katrina;

To my wonderful readers

Thank you for your encouragement
and support

All parts of this story are fiction, except for the true parts.

Contents

Chapter 1

Dylan Byrnes didn't know her name, and neither did she know his name. This was his first time at "dogging", meeting a random stranger for anonymous sex. The idea excited him when a workmate joked about it to him, showing him websites for it. "But you're married to a great lady, so you needn't do that," his work mate told him, slapping him on the back. But it was too late. The idea intrigued Dylan, and he thought about it often enough he experienced a permanent erection. He imagined what it would be like, flesh meeting anonymous flesh; he'd need a condom to avoid diseases. Then he shook off the idea. It wasn't worth fulfilling that dream. So it lived in his head for months, like an impossible fantasy, until tonight when the dream came true.

It started when he argued with his wife over something stupid. He couldn't remember the reason behind it, but he remembered feeling pushed so much he needed air. So he drove to a neighbourhood park, parked his car, and sat in the dark with his thoughts. An adulterous meeting was not forefront in his mind, but that's how it started.

He wasn't aware of the other car's headlights washing his car's interior as it turned into the parking space. Angry flashbacks of the argument still flickered across his mind, making his heart thump hard in anger. Then knocking at his window broke him from the dark memory and he looked up to see her, sex dripping from her silhouette and the moonlight glancing off shiny skin. His mouth dried, and he wiped his eyes when he saw her. Her voice bewitched him, easing his worries with her sympathetic voice, and her eyes glistened from the streetlights. The mood overtook him, and he soon found her delicious mouth engulfing him, his fingers tangling in her auburn tresses. He almost reached the point when she turned around, quick as a practised dancer. Her clothing rustled, underwear dropping as she raised her skirt, rubbing herself up to him. It felt good, but also bad. He didn't want to be there now he felt aware of others watching, their hands stroking themselves. He wondered why the woman used no condom; they didn't know each other. But then he realised   too   late   he   was   about   to—

Bile rose in the back of his throat as his conscience spoke its mind. He pushed the woman away, stepping back, and stumbled almost tripping on his pants wrapped around his ankles. What had he done? He hurried to pick his pants up, doing up the button, but forgot to zip up. His fingers fumbled for his car keys, and he heard the woman ask him what was wrong. He mumbled some kind of apology, said he is married, but he couldn't get his words right. Another man stepped forward to the woman who accepted his advances, and they started a new dance on the bonnet of her car.

But Dylan didn't care. He needed to leave, clear his head, and think. What had he done?

After escaping the scene, Dylan felt a horrible tightness squeeze his chest, head and neck. It made him want to vomit, and another part of his mind screamed suicidal thoughts in his mind. How could he face his wife? What would he say when she asked how it happened? His breath caught in his chest, and he wanted to cry again. Memory of the soft warm wetness around his member charged through his brain, and he let the tears flow. He needed to think, and then he saw the fast-food restaurant ahead. Dylan steered the car into the last parking spot, stopped the car, and rested his wet face in his hands for a moment. He paused, realising where his hands had been, and he felt dirty. Leaving the car, he rushed towards the restaurant's toilets.

The tap's cold water shocked him back to reality, helped him clear his mind. A wretched man's tortured eyes stared back at him from the mirror, filled with redness, as he looked at his reflection. He tried to control his emotions, his mind wondering where he could stay. Vicki wouldn't take him back if she knew. She'd smell the stench of sex on him. He had to wash. As fast as his guilt could take him, he dropped his pants and put soap on himself down there, washing it off the best he could. Panic filled his mind, and he fumbled to wash faster. Dylan wondered about his anonymous lover's cleanliness; how long would it take spots to show up if she carried infection? What if he showed no visible symptoms and passed it on to Vicki? What would she say?

His hearing, sensitive from guilt-ridden shame, picked up approaching voices, and his fingers fumbled in desperation to finish. He had just re-zipped his fly when the door opened and a man entered with his young son. The father looked with suspicion at Dylan as he guided his son to a private stall. Dylan swallowed; he must have looked creepy right now. Once the stall's door closed, Dylan hurried outside.

Dylan strode out the door toward his car, aware that the teenagers behind the counter knew he had used the toilet without buying food. He could hear their indignation as the cold air breezed over the wet skin. Food. He needed to eat. Maybe that would mask the guilty taste lingering in his mouth. A few minutes later, he chomped on a chicken nugget while driving away from the drive-through counter. It wasn't the best tasting food, but it would do. His thoughts turned back to his wife and the argument. She was right as usual. Maybe he could smooth things over before he arrived home.

He picked up his phone, writing a text as he chewed the salty fries.

Police received the call at 9:38pm of 28th May 2016. Witnesses reported that Dylan seemed to lose control of his car. It weaved a few times before heading straight for the side of the road. His car engine roared at full acceleration as the vehicle wrapped itself around a telephone pole with a sickening crunch. Its engine continued to roar like a feral lion, but the car otherwise remained still.

Dylan died before the first person arrived to find him in the car. Fries overflowed from his mouth, filled beyond bursting, and his eyes stood open wide as though in terror.

Chapter 2

Their unspoken questions filled the darkness that enveloped the room's occupants, tingeing it with a tense anticipation. Ramsey smiled to himself, his own mood much more humorous than everyone else's, and listened to what the others were less likely to hear. The woman sitting next to him in the darkness squeezed his hand, maybe without realising it, as she tensed. Ramsey turned his head in her direction, remembering her attractive profile before someone turned the lights off. It wasn't often that he held hands with a beautiful stranger in the dark, and he enjoyed what the touch told him.

The guest speaker spoke in a solemn voice. "Would everyone please keep holding each other's hands? The circle must remain unbroken. Never break it under any circumstances."

A slight mumble came from another direction as a guest shifted in his or her seat, scraping wood on carpet. Ramsey could not see who it was.

"Quiet, please." The man's voice spoke, regaining control. "We need silence."

Silence came over the room again as the man, a medium called John Angel, began by muttering a prayer. Such a thing wasn't necessary, but Craig Ramsey knew showmanship's importance. Ramsey could not hear it all but heard the words-blessings, love, light and spirits-and figured the words were part of a prayer before the real show started. He chuckled in silence, knowing it made little difference.

Angel stopped praying aloud for a moment. Ramsey could imagine Angel pretending to be concentrating while feigning the expression under darkness so that his acting could carry more conviction.

A friend, knowing Ramsey's background, had invited him to this evening's performance because they felt suspicious of the medium and wanted Ramsey's expert opinion. People in Ramsey's circle, both friendly and unfriendly, knew him well for his uncanny ability to weed out the fake from the real. This was thanks to his background, both as a real psychic and stage magician. He could appreciate the difference, even if his balanced stance upset people on both sides of the fence.

The medium in question, John Angel, was one of the over-confident ones who appeared from nowhere. Posters and pre-publicity had appeared in various places across Statton, announcing his arrival several weeks beforehand. People, some on Angel's staff perhaps, shared and posted YouTube videos from his social media pages. Some appeared convincing but smacked of editing and staging to Ramsey, just like other magicians who claimed to be psychic. Craig had seen them before and felt that Angel was more dramatic and fake than fey.

In one clip, Angel appeared with Anja Williams, one of the top celebrity TV hosts, and gave her a reading. He made a few statements, some general enough to fit most people, but Anja nodded at them with enthusiasm. Others struck like a lightning bolt that left Anja stunned. But that wasn't all. Angel said he had something else to impart to Anja, something meant only for her ears. Was it okay for him to whisper it to her? The talk show host laughed, assuming flirtatious Angel only wanted to kiss her, but Angel's expression showed him to be serious.

Whatever he said must have been true. Anja appeared

shocked, looking at Angel with a worried expression, and asked him if he was serious. Angel only nodded, leaning forward to whisper more to her. His words, known only to Anja, must have been comforting, as Anja seemed to relax with a relieved expression. But there was still a look of worry behind her eyes.

It turned out that Anja had to visit the hospital. A close friend of hers had suffered a terrible fall from a ladder at that moment Angel was telling Anja about it. How could he have known? He could not have set it up himself or even with help, could he? A week later, Anja gave Angel more airtime again. This time other celebrities attended, and some audience members picked earlier at random, and Angel was happy to read for them too with the help of his spirits.

That had happened a year ago. Now Angel was coming to Australia, visiting its capital cities, and a few of the larger towns and cities in the rural areas. Statton was part of that tour.

Under normal circumstances, Ramsey would not have taken part. He stayed away from most psychic shows. Having worked as a stage magician and mentalist in the past, he found many performances crude and substandard. They lacked theatrical merit and entertainment value. Then there were those who believed themselves psychic when, in reality, they suffered delusions of grandeur with a mild Messiah's complex. But the friend who invited him, a past client who still passed referrals for him, had insisted he come along to see Angel's work. He refused at first until something changed his mind, which made his friend happy because the expensive tickets were non-refundable.

Angel spoke out loud again to everyone. His voice

sounded disembodied in the darkness. "Does someone here know Albert?"

Another voice, a guest's voice, responded. "Yes."

"Who are you?" Angel asked.

Silence dominated for a moment, and the voice, a woman's, answered. "It's Doris."

"Albert is your husband?" Angel asked. "I mean, he was your husband?"

"No, he was - "

Angel interrupted her. "You don't have to answer. I know. Albert is here. He says you need to look behind the nightstand beside the bed. His ring is there and -"

"His what?" A male's voice responded from next to Doris.

Doris' voice answered, sounding upset in the darkness. Ramsey had to stop himself from laughing as he sensed the obvious drama unfolding. Doris started, but Angel's voice interrupted.

"It is not what you think, Trevor," Angel asserted, emitting a sound of authority in his tone. "Be calm."

"But he - "

"But he what?" Angel interrupted. "Screwed your wife? Is this the time for you to cast stones right now?" His tone seemed to carry an accusation there while carrying enough ambiguity to avoid libel charges.

Whatever the truth, it helped Angel regain control. Trevor went quiet, and Ramsey's eyebrow cocked a little as he listened.

"I told you my name is not Albert!" A hoarse whispering voice spoke, heard by no mortal ears other than Ramsey's. It sounded angry.

"There is no Albert here," a harsher whispering voice

said. "But I know *him*."

Ramsey heard the voice emphasise the word, him, but could not tell who it meant. Angel seemed oblivious to the voices and answered Trevor. "Albert is innocent of any cheating," he explained. "He came by to fix the pipes in the en-suite."

Doris confirmed. "Yes, he did because you never fixed them yourself, Trevor. You kept finding something else to do."

A voice next to Ramsey's ear, belonging to a woman, whispered. "Can you hear the others, Craig?"

Without moving his lips, Ramsey answered by his thoughts, telepathy. "Sure do, Emily."

Angel continued making his quick readings for the audience who responded with sounds and replies of approval. Meanwhile, the other disembodied voices in the room became louder and more insistent.

"Why are you not taking notice of me? I know you can hear me!"

"What does this one have to hide perhaps? Perhaps he is not such an Angel as he claims."

Ramsey silenced his thoughts, wondering if the disembodied voices had heard him instead. It made no difference.

By now, the voices thundered and a new one joined in, sounding even louder. This new voice-arrival seemed more insistent, ominous, and more than capable of getting what it wanted.

"I'm here for Thomas," it said, in a matter of fact tone. "Which one is Thomas?"

Ramsey looked up with surprise at the voice's tone. He felt no doubt. It came from Angel, but it wasn't his voice speaking.

"What? Who is this?"

Emily's voice whispered in Ramsey's ear. "Did you hear that?"

Ramsey nodded, leaning forward to concentrate so his vision could focus better with his psychic senses.

Angel sounded distracted when he responded. "Thomas?" he said aloud.

A man sitting near Victor, who had invited Ramsey, responded. "I'm Thomas."

Everyone, not just Ramsey, could sense Angel's movements and that of another being they could not otherwise hear. Ramsey knew it was a real spirit being this time, much meaner in temperament than the others who insisted on Angel's full attention. This one had Angel's complete attention when it spoke.

"I have names that will interest Thomas."

Angel relayed the message and mentioned a name aloud. "Bradley Harris."

Thomas responded with a gasp. "What?" he stammered.

Angel's voice sounded stunned; Ramsey thought it was because he heard a voice that did not belong to his hidden assistant who had been whispering information to his hidden earplug's receiver. "Bradley is here with us." He paused. "And so is Emma Gent, David Han, Jason Craig and - "

"Stop!" Thomas' voice cried, betraying a sound of fear he tried to hide in vain. "What are you doing? I don't know those names."

"Ah, but you do!" the spirit intoned through Angel's vocal cords, having possessed his body.

The lights came on with a pop and everyone gasped in surprise to see Angel's face had taken on the pallor of a dead man. His California tan had disappeared, replaced by a pale porcelain colour, and a spider web of veins criss-crossed his features. His eyeballs had also withdrawn in their sockets, sinking back, and glowing from within their cavernous recesses with a brilliant red.

Ramsey felt a pain in his left hand, realising the woman beside him was holding a tight grip on him from the initial fright. He saw no one near save for the handful of spirits who he guessed had competed for Angel's attention while he gave fake readings earlier. Breaking her hand's grip on him, Ramsey moved forward to get a closer look at Angel who was several feet away. Angel showed all the signs of possession.

Thomas also showed strange signs, reacting with growing fear with each name Angel rattled with machine gun speed.

"Jenny Queen. John Fraser. Oliver Frank."

As each name came from Angel's mouth, a new voice seemed to speak up in the room until Ramsey realised the room seemed crowded. Children, or rather their spirits, filled the room until it seemed like there was no room to move. Each child cried their name aloud until such a hullabaloo rose in the room that Ramsey wanted to cover his ears. But, the voices spoke in the mind more than in the ears.

The man named Thomas stood, pushing people out of the way, as he backed away towards a wall. Each child's spirit moved towards him, cornering him. Sweat gushed from his face, shining with pure panic, as he heard each of their names, and even saw the spirits rushing towards him.

The other audience members turned to watch what was happening, some panicking as they saw the spirits too.

"Where did all these children come from?" one of them asked.

The woman who had held Ramsey's hand earlier in the circle cried out, "They're after Thomas. Why would they be after him?"

Possessed Angel's voice boomed. "Thomas, your victims have named you and is time to take your punishment."

A fierce gusting wind came from nowhere, blowing with the speed of a hurricane, and pushed at Thomas. His long blonde hair, exposing itself as a fake hairpiece, blew away like a dead creature's skin, landed on a woman's head, and she screamed. Picture frames, furniture, and any other loose object flew towards Thomas. He did his best to fend the flying articles away with his hands and arms, with little effect, as the children continued crowding about him and chanting their names.

At last, it became too much and Thomas ran, pushing past the living and running through the intangible spirits. Everyone else stayed where they were, watching Thomas flee like a madman, except Angel whose features reverted to his normal tanned flawless self as he fell into a heap. Ramsey noted the spirit form that left Angel's body at that moment. It resembled a man he had seen somewhere before but he was not sure of when or where.

The spirit wore a leather jacket over a t-shirt and casual jeans with a brown Calvin Klein belt, its CK insignia visible in the leatherwork, and Nike shoes. Whoever the spirit was, he could not have died over ten years earlier, but Ramsey felt it was more recent. The spirit moved past

Ramsey, appearing to ignore him, save for an eye movement that acknowledged his presence but showed no recognition. Ramsey felt the being's energy and interpreted it to be angry by its reddish tinge, but it was also a good spirit. It was not evil, just driven and vengeful, and it enjoyed scaring the living daylights from its targets.

Emily appeared beside Ramsey, speaking in her Scottish brogue to him. "Does he look pissed to you?"

Ramsey replied, "Just a tad. I'm going after him."

"I don't think you will stop him," Emily called after him.

Ramsey followed the avenging spirit, which was flying after Thomas who was trying to get to his Mitsubishi Pajero. The children's spirits milled about the adult spirit as though he was the pied piper, cheering on their avenger who followed Thomas without distraction. Ramsey had heard something about this thing before but could not place what it was.

Thomas reached his vehicle and fumbled in his pocket for the remote. At last, he found it, just as the avenging ghost reached him and grabbed his neck from behind. He screamed in terror as the spirit pushed him hard, so hard, that his face hit the car's window with a sickening thud. Astral fists crashed into Thomas' body and he felt the wind knocked out of him. Somehow, he ducked another fist and dashed off down the street, throwing the remote to the side as he ran.

"Wait!" Ramsey called to the male spirit. "Who are you?"

It paused a moment to regard Ramsey, sizing him up to see if he was a foe or not, and bellowed back at him. "My name is not important to anyone but him right now."

In a blink, it seemed to fade into a wispy cloud before it gained mass and rushed off after Thomas who was halfway down the street.

Ramsey made ready to chase when he noticed that the children spirits were vandalising Thomas' Pajero. Random scrawling and graffiti appeared as though done by invisible spray paint cans on the vehicle's once pristine exterior. One of them, appearing to be a teenaged boy, manifested a large knife in its astral form and stabbed the tyres until it deflated.

Ramsey snorted, pulling a helpless smile, before chasing after Thomas and his pursuer. He couldn't see them by this time, but Thomas' screaming was a dead giveaway leading Ramsey straight to a playground. Ramsey huffed down the street, approaching the park where a single streetlight illuminated the scene enough for him to see what was going on. The avenging spirit had caught up to Thomas and was now proceeding to rip the clothes off him as though they were paper. Garments and pieces of cloth flew about in all directions, ripped and torn. The leg of Thomas' jeans landed just in front of Ramsey as he stopped to take in the scene in disbelief.

"Holy shit," he whispered.

The spirit now had Thomas pinned face down to a playground roundabout and Ramsey wondered what it was doing to him. A smell of burning flesh reached Ramsey's nostrils, almost making him gag, and Thomas screamed louder. As he approached them, Ramsey felt an invisible force holding him back and all he could do was watch and wince at the smell of burning flesh.

At that moment, Emily appeared beside Ramsey. Distracted, he looked at her. "Can't you stop it?"

Emily shook her head. "No, that would not be my place to do. That gentleman has unfinished business with him."

Ramsey looked shocked. "Unfinished business. I'd say it's more than not splitting the lunch bill."

Thomas stopped screaming and Ramsey looked back again to see the spirit stand again from its victim. Turning to face them, the spirit approached Ramsey and Emily, looking them both in the eye.

"I am not done with him yet."

Ramsey looked past the spirit. "He looks finished. What is your beef with him?"

Thomas called out with a pathetic voice. "Has it gone? I've had enough. I'll talk. Just keep it away from me."

The spirit, a hint of a smile on his face, turned back to Ramsey. "It was not just him. It is his kind. He's not the first, and he's definitely not the last."

Ramsey felt a flash of recognition. "You're Gerard Hohn, aren't you?"

The spirit reacted to the name, stepping back. "I am not known by that name any more."

Ramsey realised what had caused the burning flesh smell and knew what he would see tattooed across Thomas' shoulder blades and the small of his back. He also knew what word Hohn's spirit had burned into Thomas' forehead, and the man deserved it. All who had contact with the spirit world knew Hohn's obsession with hunting down paedophiles and child traffickers. He looked back at the vengeful spirit; it was concentrating upon the helpless man, one powerful hand holding Thomas to the roundabout's platform while the other did its work upon him.

"Hohn," Ramsey said, holding up handcuffs from his jacket's pocket, and walking around to Thomas. He snapped one cuff over Thomas' right wrist and the other over one of the roundabout's metal handholds. "I'm a private investigator. I can take him to the authorities. You're done with him."

Hohn turned to Ramsey, paused a moment, and was about to say something but Ramsey's mobile phone rang, interrupting them.

"Wait right there," Ramsey said, holding up a finger, as his other hand answered the phone for him. He was not on the phone a long time, but he didn't need long to listen to what the caller said and to answer. "I'm on my way."

Looking back at the roundabout, he gasped in surprise to find just his handcuffs swinging from its handhold. Thomas and Hohn were gone.

"I told you to turn that phone off before," Emily quipped, floating across the ground to him. "Do you see what happens when you let it distract you?"

Ramsey shrugged, knowing police officers would find Thomas "gift-wrapped" on either the police station's front doorstep on in one of their watch-house cells. There Thomas would blabber about the ghosts of the children he had molested, trafficked and killed in the past twenty years before telling them about his still-living victims. The psychic community, the real one, know Gerard Hohn's spiritual journey for justice well.

"We've got to go," he said, walking past his spiritual companion who felt increasing sadness from him. "Something's wrong."

Chapter 3

Blue and red lights flickered across the scene as Sergeant Hohenhaus examined the carnage before him. A camera flashed as the police photographer took pictures of the damaged vehicle and its unmoving occupant. The other vehicles passing the scene slowed down, slower than necessary, as they passed.

Blasted rubberneckers, he thought to himself as he watched one car slow down to less than a crawling pace. Its occupants, a family of five, gawked at the twisted metal frame of the car as it passed. Another camera flash popped through the air and Sergeant Hohenhaus cursed. Some police officers had placed a shield to obscure the public's view of the body in the car. But a lucky photographer could find the right angle, snapping a photo of the corpse. He hated to think what would happen if that picture made it to Instagram or Twitter.

"Hey!" he called out to a uniformed officer. "Divert the traffic down that other street, can you? We still have a body in that car, for Christ's sake. Do you want that ending up on the news?"

The ambulance had taken away the surviving passenger but the deceased driver still sat there, waiting for its trip to the morgue.

Detective Cogan appeared beside the Sergeant. "What is it with this corner?" Cogan asked, tossing her empty coffee cup in a nearby bin. "I've never seen so many accidents here."

Hohenhaus looked back towards his colleague. "It's too many," he replied. "Ten accidents in one week on this same corner, fifteen on East and Turbot."

Cogan stood back as the police photographer finished taking photos of the damage. "There must be a pattern here."

"But what is it?" Hohenhaus replied, sounding frustrated. "The visibility is so perfect here. You can't miss seeing a thing here that blind Freddy wouldn't know about."

He pointed to a second crumpled vehicle. Everyone from that car survived. "That car was in front, and the area is well lit. Even if its tail-lights were not working, the other driver couldn't miss seeing that. The intersection is lit up more than Kings bloody Cross."

Cogan just looked about, thinking, her eyes searching for something. She didn't know what she would find, but she felt certain she would know when she saw it.

"The passenger from this car," she said, indicating the corpse's vehicle. "What can you tell me?"

"A young guy, early twenties, I think. Samoan kid. He's taken away already."

Cogan looked up from checking the passenger's seat and walked around to check an angle from the front. "What did he have to say?"

Hohenhaus shook his head. "The kid's unconscious, or at least he was when we arrived. He was still out when the ambo's came for him."

Cogan's blue eyes narrowed, checking the cracked windscreen before turning back to Hohenhaus.

"What about the driver?" Cogan examined the driver's side, eyes moving and noting details.

"She must have been dead upon impact," Hohenhaus replied, pointing a thick finger at the driver's side window. Cogan saw the impact mark upon the glass, near the door frame.

"Looks like her head hit the side of the car," she said, noting the bruise mark on the victim's temple.

"Poor thing," the sergeant said, shaking his head. "Too bloody young, even if she was in the wrong."

Cogan ignored the sergeant. "But the other car was in front of her, and she drove straight into it."

"Yeah, and?"

Cogan looked him in the eye. "If you hit something straight on, where do you expect your head to go?"

The sergeant stopped a moment to think. "Straight into -"

Cogan interrupted. "Yes, straight into the steering wheel. No air bag either. Her head should have hit the steering wheel, not the side window."

"Who knows how these things can happen in an accident," Sergeant Hohenhaus shrugged.

"Simple physics," Cogan said, calling the photographer back. She explained that she wanted more photos, pointing out the angles for them before turning back to Hohenhaus. "When a body is moving in a particular direction, it stays on that path until another force pushes it in another. It's called inertia."

"So how do you explain this?" Hohenhaus asked, nodding at her explanation as he showed the bruise and its position. "Could she have looked in another direction before the collision?"

"No," Cogan replied, walking away from the scene. "Someone or something forced her towards the car door. We need to speak with the survivor."

***

Cogan walked into the patient's room, almost

expecting the patient to be asleep. The doctor who gave her permission to speak with the accident victim also advised her to keep it short. She knew the patient needed rest, given the circumstances, but it was important Cogan gained the information she needed while it was fresh in his mind.

"Tyrone Manson?"

She looked at him, noticing that Hohenhaus had been wrong about the passenger's age. He was a well-built Samoan boy, large enough to be mistaken for a young adult, but Cogan recognised the looks of youth in his face. The teenager's eyes opened to regard Cogan, his eyes bleary and unfocused. She hoped the sedatives he received had minimal effect upon his ability to recall things.

"Yeah." He found speaking difficult, but it wasn't fatigue.

The doctor had warned Cogan to not tell Tyrone of his sister's death yet, due to his shock from the accident. Cogan disliked being dishonest to the poor kid, but seeing his extensive injuries, she didn't want to make things worse just yet either. Bruises, black and purple, darkened his brown skin in patches and his nose looked as though broken. He had been through too much to learn of her demise yet.

Cogan offered her hand, but he felt too whipped to take it. "Tyrone, I'm Detective Brianna Cogan," she told him. "I'm here to learn about the accident. Are you up to it?"

Whatever friendly light had been in Tyrone's eyes disappeared like a candle's flame in a breeze. "What about it?"

Cogan found a chair, pulled it closer to the bed, and

sat on it, facing Tyrone. She tried her best to be as friendly and supportive as she could. "You're looking pretty banged up there. Are you in much pain?"

She knew it was a stupid question, but she didn't know how else to lead into things. It didn't seem to faze Tyrone though, and he responded. "I think I hit the dashboard, but I had my seatbelt on." He mentioned the last part as though trying to convince her he was good.

Cogan smiled and rested her hand on his. "It's okay. I'm not worried about the seatbelt and I am sure you were wearing it. Can you tell me how it all happened?"

Tyrone hesitated a moment before shrugging. "I guess Debbie couldn't stop the car in time. Are the people from the car we hit okay?"

Cogan smiled in a way designed to relax him. "Yeah, they're fine, maybe a little shaken but they're okay."

"What about Debbie? She's dead, isn't she?"

Cogan tried her best to stay calm without faltering. Something told her Tyrone was perceptive, most teenagers are, and she didn't want to lie either. "She's sleeping at the moment."

Tyrone looked at her a moment and Cogan let her best poker face show while letting her eyes work to keep his trust.

"I like you," he told her, "but you're not a good liar. My uncle Craig would see through you even better than I can."

"What do you mean, Tyrone?"

Tyrone looked her straight in the eyes. "You said Debbie's asleep. But you didn't say if you had seen her, if you were going to be seeing her, or if she was fine or not. When my mother and father died, they told me they were just sleeping because I was a kid. I know what it means."

Cogan opened her mouth to respond, and Tyrone held up a hand to interrupt. "I know they drugged me, but I can still see through you and I know that you're trying to make things easier."

Cogan hesitated, measuring her words before responding. "Of course I am interested in your welfare, Tyrone, and Debbie's. I - "

Tyrone would hear nothing off it, and he raised his voice a notch. "Listen, I know you think I'm a dumb kid still, but I'm sixteen, and I know what I'm talking about. What do you really want to know?"

Cogan wasn't sure if she was regaining control or if Tyrone had played her; she suspected the latter. "I want to know what happened, Tyrone. Will you tell me?"

Tyrone's features turned stony as he went silent. His hand, relaxed earlier, now tensed into a fist and his eyes closed. Cogan looked at him and noticed the closed eyelids, but not for sleeping. He felt anger and emotional pain, but was he angry with Cogan or was he angry after the accident? Then she saw a tear forming in the corner of his eye. It trickled down the side of his face towards his ear as he lay back on the pillow.

"I wish I could take it all back," he said, his bottom lip quivering.

"Take your time," Cogan reassured him, her hand over his balled fist. She felt it relax. "Tell me about it please."

Tyrone opened his eyes, and he tried to sit up but gave up in frustration. The sedative must have affected his motor skills. Cogan stayed silent, watching him with an open expression. Her other hand held the iPhone closer, its App recording the whole conversation to save Cogan from writing notes, which she hated doing.

***

Debbie and Tyrone had been out that night, watching the latest young adult movie with Jennifer Lawrence as the heroine. Although the two of them were close, the three-year gap between them made it difficult. Tyrone was in his senior year of high school. It was a tougher year than usual for him with studies although he had picked his favourite subjects in mathematics and the sciences. On a similar note, Debbie was studying at the University of Queensland in Brisbane to be a dentist. That meant she was away from home and could only catch up when their holidays coincided.

This week was one of those times and Debbie had driven the eight-hour drive to Statton just three days ago.

Debbie negotiated the car out of the cinema's underground car park and onto the street. A few spits of rain hit the windscreen, and she flicked the wipers on.

"So what did you think of Jennifer's bum?" she asked Tyrone, grinning.

He laughed. "Yeah, she's got a nice one all right. They just don't show it enough in the movie. What did you think of it?"

Something Tyrone missed most with Debbie away at Uni was when they used to always talk about girls. Tyrone was happy with his sister being lesbian as long as they weren't pursuing the same girl. That irked him, and he didn't like the competition either, but it was a double-edged sword. His sister was gorgeous herself, but he liked how she served as a good wingman, and he did the same for her.

"She's not too bad for a white chick," Debbie laughed.

Her mobile phone beeped as it received an SMS, and Debbie picked it up without thinking to read the message.

Tyrone looked horrified, seeing someone crossing the street in front of them. "Hey! Eyes on the road, sis!"

Debbie looked up, slowing enough to let the pedestrian cross between the parked cars at the side. "Stop stressing, little bro," she said. "You worry too much for a sixteen-year-old. Has anyone told you that?"

"That's because I want to live to be seventeen, bitch!" he said.

She slapped him with the hand that held the phone. "Don't call me a bitch, you little bitch. Besides, I can multi-task. I'm a woman."

"Still," Tyrone answered. "You shouldn't be doing that. You could kill someone."

"You need to get laid," Debbie quipped, brushing off his comment by changing the topic.

Tyrone looked out the passenger window through the raindrops, noticing two girls he recognised from school.

"Which one of them do you have the hots for?" Debbie asked, looking back for herself.

The phone beeped again before Tyrone could answer. Debbie picked it up, read the message and began thumb-texting an answer back. Tyrone was unsure what happened at first; Debbie's scream caught him by surprise. When he looked, he saw someone else in the car with them; it was a man dressed in a kind of black robe. Where had he been hiding?

The man was sitting in the back seat, reaching between Debbie and Tyrone. A loud slapping noise came to Tyrone's ears through Debbie's screams, and he thought he felt something hit his foot. He looked and saw Debbie's phone, its screen lit up on the Facebook App, and then he looked back at the man. The stranger gripped Debbie's right wrist, forcing it to the console behind the handbrake, and his other hand gripped the top of Debbie's head by her long hair.

Tyrone heard the sound of Debbie's hair ripping as the stranger pulled it by its roots. He steeled himself, her screams of pain filling his mind, and he reached around to fight the man away. He noticed the blank expression on the man's face, and he heard the steely voice from his grey lips, which remained still. But he couldn't catch the words. The stranger spoke again, words just as intelligible, and forced Debbie's fear-contorted face to the steering wheel.

Tyrone punched towards the man's head, impeded by his twisted position in the passenger's seat, and felt surprised when his fist passed through the man's head. Instead his fist slammed the driver's seat, wracking his wrist with daggers of pain. He didn't even see the stranger retaliate or flinch from Tyrone, but Tyrone sure felt the impact as his nose exploded with copper-flavoured blood. The stranger moved that fast. Tyrone pushed through the pain, and kept flailing, trying to reach the man's body to force him away from his sister. He had trouble seeing from the punch, but Tyrone discovered the car was out of control. He could hear Debbie's screams. They were now screams of pain, punctuated by the hard impact of her head against what must have been the driver's door and window. The stranger was slamming Debbie against them.

"Leave her alone," Tyrone roared out, trying to grab Debbie's shoulders to keep her away from the door. But it was too late.

A loud cracking sound filled his ears, paralysing him with a knowing dismay. Debbie slumped in the seat, unmoving. He couldn't remember what happened to the man. The next sound he heard was the car hitting another car.

And he blacked out.

***

Cogan watched Tyrone as he finished telling the tale. Tears streamed down his face as he told it all, recalling how he tried to save his sister.

"I knew she was dead when I heard that loud crack, Detective Ma'am," he said. "That was her neck breaking, wasn't it?"

Cogan felt the waves of compassion rush over her. She had seen action in Afghanistan herself during her time in the Army before joining the police. The pain of losing friends, and even family, felt familiar to her, and this kid had seen more than he should have seen by witnessing his sister's death. But she also knew no one else had been in the car apart from Tyrone and his sister Debbie. Witnesses had not mentioned seeing anyone leaving the scene, and that was not a detail likely to escape notice or mention. Either shock was affecting Tyrone's recollection, or he was lying. She had seen teenagers lie before, having been one herself, and she believed this was more likely to be shock.

The detective nodded, not wanting to say the words to answer Tyrone's question. Cogan was about to stand and thank him for his time when Tyrone's next words startled her.

"You won't be able to catch him, you know?"

Detective Cogan hesitated, measuring her response.

"We usually do. Why do you say that?"

Tyrone's eyes remained closed and his voice confident when he answered. "You don't catch men like him."

Cogan stood, taking in his confident words, and walked out the door with the boy's words playing on her mind.

Chapter 4

It was Friday morning and half an hour had passed since the sun first poked its golden head above the horizon. The early morning traffic was in full swing as people made their way to work to start the day. But the observer was working already, watching the traffic with eagle eyes as it passed him. He watched each of them; some of them looked awake and others looked half-asleep still. One caught his eye, and he moved to get a better look at a beaten up Toyota Corolla hatchback across the street. It seemed to move much slower than the rest of the traffic, much slower than the limit. He focused on the driver and felt no surprise when he saw the damning evidence. Why don't they ever learn?

He took in the car's details as it slowed a little more before turning left. Its turn was too sharp, and its rear left tyre jumped up on the footpath's edge. Pedestrians waiting at the corner had to jump back to avoid it, yelling at the car's jerk driver to watch what the hell he was doing. But the car's ignorant driver took no notice and kept driving. The car's rear wheel crunched back to the road as it left the footpath.

The car looked like it had seen better days. A blanket of pockmarks covered its faded black paintwork; signs of being in a hailstorm. Another car had crashed into its once, leaving a sizeable dent in the right-hand back passenger's door. A criss-cross patchwork of faded silver duct tape covered the dent, holding something together. Even the duct tape was lifting from the car as it peeled. The engine sounded like it needed professional tuning too. So the driver could not afford repairs or was too lazy to take the time to visit a panel beater.

The silent watcher's eyes, like those of a hunter, narrowed as he took in the car's registration number from its dented plate. He almost felt sorry for the driver who had signed his own death warrant. The observer didn't know the driver, not enough to decide if he liked him, but he knew enough to decide this was the next target.

Inside the Toyota, Marc seemed oblivious to the man who slipped into his car while he waited at the traffic lights. Thoughts about the latest online video game he planned on playing with his "Clan" were foremost in his head. Secondary to that thought was the argument he had with one of his housemates. Marc held the lease on the house and he had taken on two housemates, a young married couple who were saving money to buy a house of their own. The husband was a pain in the arse, he felt. Sure, there were lots of things wrong with the house he rented. It's an old house but Marc didn't have time to be seeing the landlord about the things that needed fixing. He only cared about the video game he played online; that is where his friends were, his real friends. He had never met them before, but he considered them his friends because they loved playing the same war game. Besides, if he spoke with the landlord about the repairs, the landlord would chase him for three months of unpaid rent. The last time the landlord asked him about the rent, Marc lied by telling him the housemates hadn't paid their share yet. It seemed easier to blame them, but he hadn't expected the landlord to suggest getting the money from them or face eviction. That meant he had to go without buying another video game, just to pay the rent. Why did life have to be so unfair? Marc knew he couldn't evict the housemates because they always paid their money on time. He only hated that they were so responsible with things, and he wasn't. The threat of eviction scared him too because he had stored almost every possession accumulated in his life under the house. No one could walk under there without tripping on something. The housemates called him a pack-rat for keeping so many things he didn't or wouldn't use but he couldn't bring himself to part with things. Anyway, he never knew when he would need them again at some point.

Maybe he needed to plan a budget? Nah, that could wait until later after his next meeting with the Clan online.

Marc's phone rang again. Why couldn't his mother just stop ringing him? He picked the phone up, checking the caller ID. Shit. It was his mother... again.

Marc didn't get to speak. His steering wheel jerked about in his hand, and he felt an icy sensation on his wrists as though something had gripped him. He fought to grip the steering wheel and pull it back straight, but the icy feeling had numbed him so much that gripping the wheel proved difficult. His mother's voice floated to him from the phone's speaker but distractions made it difficult to understand her words. He needed to concentrate so he could control the car.

He pulled the wheel to the right, trying to keep it from moving to the left where the bridge's railing waited for him. The bridge was old and needed repairs, maybe as much as his home or car did. He doubted it would stop him. The wheel jerked back to the left again.

Marc screamed, "Mummy!"

Her voice answered from the phone's speaker, sounding worried. "Marc. What's happening, honey?"

Then he felt the unseen fist hit his head. He saw stars, felt dizzy.

He tried to take his foot from the accelerator. It was no use.

Something was making the car hurtle faster, its car's engine roaring as it brought him up on the verge. Marc's heart beat faster as he fought the invisible thing that now controlled the car. He could do nothing, but scream, as he felt the impact when the car scraped on the bridge's rails.

The car's steering wheel twisted more and then he felt his stomach drop. The car's radio turned on and Marc heard the dark voice through its speakers.

"Bye bye, Mummy's boy!"

Marc was dead before the car splashed in the hungry river with the crunching force that broke every bone in his body. He didn't hear his mother's voice crying through the phone, asking him to talk to her. He may have been in his thirties but he was still her little boy.

The assassin watched from the bridge as the black Toyota sank into the murky river's brown depths. Its swift current, from the recent floods, carried the car away. A hint of satisfaction welled inside him but nothing showed on his face. He turned to leave. Traffic was slowing to stop, and people ran from their cars to investigate the scene. One onlooker removed the mobile phone from her pocket to call the police. Another took photos and video of the carnage. A siren wailed in the distance, about ten blocks away, getting louder as it approached. It was slow, due to the traffic choking its progress.

***

By Friday afternoon, Detective Cogan felt knackered

on both physical and mental levels. The previous night's interview with the Samoan boy Tyrone kept playing in her dreams, despite walking to the toilet and drinking water before going back to sleep. It came back again with Tyrone's voice saying, "You will never catch him."

She didn't believe there was a "him" to catch unless it was Tyrone himself who had killed his sister. Cogan wasn't putting that past him either. Although he seemed a tame enough kid, and well-mannered, she wasn't a shrink to know if he had split personalities either. By the afternoon, she had a report on her desk to confirm no history of mental illness existed for Tyrone. Her dreams still disturbed her; one involved Tyrone's features melting away like hot wax as he told her she would never catch "the man".

As if the dreams were not enough, Cogan's phone woke her when the Superintendent called her. Another accident had happened just before the early morning commuter rush. Why did they call it a rush when the traffic had slowed or stopped? She didn't know, but that accident was the second strangest she had seen, and there had been plenty of strange traffic accidents in the past week. The only thing different was it wasn't at East and Turbot Streets but at the bridge crossing on Cale Street. A car had jumped the verge with such speed it rammed through the bridge's railings as though they were ribbons. Witnesses reported it was so fast it flew through the air, appearing to hover a moment, before somersaulting to the river.

"It executed a perfect tuck and pike before inward-twisting to the water with a belly flop," one elderly witness told her. She had to stop herself from laughing at that.

The old man had the darkest sense of humour, and it came close to matching her own sarcasm.

Cogan and her team had just finished with that scene when she received a call to another accident with yet another fatality. That one was even stranger than the diving car. For no clear reason, the car's hood had crumpled as though it had hit an immovable force, like a stationary truck, only there was nothing in front of it. The woman who called that accident in had been jogging at the time along the side as she did every morning. There were no sounds of brakes and the jogger saw the Mitsubishi's hood crush in on itself with a loud noise. It was so abrupt the driver's body smashed through the windscreen, landing ten metres away amidst showering glass, before rolling along the bitumen like a limp store mannequin. The cars behind it could not stop in time and soon there was a pileup of rear-enders. In the meantime, the Mitsubishi rolled forward further, stopping just short of crushing the driver's injured body. Cogan believed, or hoped, the driver died without suffering. She had not received the coroner's report on it yet.

The first traffic incident involved only the driver, no other victims. But the jogger from the second incident mentioned seeing someone dressed in black sitting in the Mitsubishi's back seat. She couldn't give a full description as the other cars had piled into it, distracting her. When the jogger looked again, the man in black was nowhere to be seen.

Cogan and her team found no evidence of a second person in the Mitsubishi.

Why is it the worst accidents seemed to happen during commuter peak times? Redirecting the traffic was murder enough for the uniformed officers, but it was just a pain in the arse trying to negotiate packed traffic in her own vehicle; people can be so ignorant of police sirens.

The morning was hectic and the rest of the day seemed not much better. Detective Cogan felt glad she had one of the administration staff who could transcribe her interviews for her. That gave her time to mull over the other things related to the incidents. The Inspector let her focus on them since Cogan convinced him there was a connection, considering the times and frequency at which they happened.

She stretched at her desk, reaching up towards the ceiling, her fingers interlaced, and took a long deep breath before releasing it. A knock at the door surprised her.

Cogan looked up toward the sound. A man somewhere in his late thirties with bright lively eyes and straight brown hair gelled to create a spiky look stood grinning at her. His face's skin looked smooth and his mouth formed a wide smile that made his eyes sparkle more.

"Yes?" she said, taking in the sight of his attire - black dress jeans, dark blue Ralph Lauren long-sleeved shirt and black leather slip-on shoes. He was on his way somewhere but she wasn't sure where.

"Detective Brianna Cogan, I presume?" he asked, grinning more.

Cogan stood to approach the office door, but the stranger invited himself in and offered his hand to her. His straight teeth seemed to glow. "I'm Craig Ramsey."

Cogan didn't know how to take this personality right now although, after seeing so much recent chaos, she felt she could use the distraction. His cheeky demeanour showed he could provide welcome comic relief. She took his hand, noting its firmness, and replied, "How can I help you?"

Craig Ramsey tipped his head a little, as though listening to something, and then returned his attention to her with solid eye contact. He smiled at something, not Brianna's words but more likely his inner voice. "I'm here to learn more about my niece and nephew's accident."

Cogan released his hand, although she didn't want to as he felt good, and invited Ramsey to take a seat. "You have me at a loss. I don't remember any Ramseys although your name -"

"Yes," Ramsey interrupted, looking about the office. "It is familiar but not for the reason I once enjoyed. You see, my niece was in -"

"Last night's accident," Cogan replied. Ramsey's mouth curved a little at the end with another smile, his eye flicking to the left, as though he was smiling at a private joke. "What is it?" she asked. "Did I say something funny?"

Ramsey was about to smile but let it slide. "You thought it was funny we were finishing each other's sentences."

Cogan looked amazed, faltering a little. "Yes, but I -"

Ramsey shook his head, looked to the side again, and answered, "It's not why I'm here. Finishing sentences, I mean. You see, I want to know what you have on my niece's accident last night."

Detective Cogan hesitated. Who had let this guy in without at least paging her so she could prepare for him? The office looked a mess from the different reports and she felt she looked just as bad too. "How did you know to come ask for me?"

"Are you the Detective Sergeant Brianna Cogan who spoke with Tyrone Manson last night?" he asked.

"Yes, I am," she responded and then the penny dropped. "You are 'Uncle Craig', are you?"

He nodded and Cogan apologised. "I was expecting you to be -"

"Samoan?" he asked, grinning. "Well," he said, elongating the word, "yes, I believe most would, but, you see, I adopted both Debbie and Tyrone some years back. I used to be friends of their parents who worked with me. They have since passed, and the kids always knew me as Uncle Craig. I don't like them calling me Mum. Tell me what you know." He said the last sentence with a more serious tone.

Cogan shrugged. "There's not much I can tell you at this point as we haven't received all the reports yet. I assume you have seen Tyrone already this morning. His story doesn't quite match the evidence we have, and I believe that's the result of the concussion or the shock."

"Would that be the part about the man in the car with them?" Ramsey said, his voice sounding almost like that of a commanding officer as he leaned forward. His hand touched one of the report folders on Brianna's desk. As he did, his expression changed, and he appeared as though lost in another world. It only lasted for an instant before he refocused his attention upon her.

Brianna was about to tell him to relax and sit back when he did just that and looked at her. She took a breath. "Yes, there is the matter of a man allegedly sitting in the back seat. What Tyrone says does not add up for a few reasons. No other witnesses saw a man leaving the scene after the crash. And how he reported the man in the back seat hit Debbie's head against the side window does not match. The amount of force needed to do that is not possible to muster while hindered by the driver's seat. It's impossible."

Ramsey looked like he was blinking tears back as he listened to her words and Cogan felt sorry to have to tell him this. Perhaps with better preparation and advance notice of his arrival, she could have worded it better. He lifted his hand, wiped his stubbled chin, and replied, "Impossible? Not for an ordinary man, that's right, and not everyone can see a man leaving an accident or a murder scene."

Cogan wheeled her chair around to the side of the desk so she could be closer to Ramsey before answering him. "I checked the security camera footage, Mr Ramsey. We watched it at least three times because we caught it all on camera, thanks to the city having a network of them to keep the streets safe. No one left the car's back seat."

"No one you saw," Ramsey made it plain he didn't believe her, and he worded it so she could not argue his point either.

Cogan shook her head in sympathy. "No. We saw people running to help, but no one left the car's back seat. I would have seen it myself."

Ramsey paused, thinking, and then looked back at her. "How could you see when the video footage had a slight distortion just before the first people arrived to help?"

"What are you talking about?" Cogan asked. "There was no such thing."

Ramsey studied her when she responded. "You didn't think of that, did you?"

Cogan took a deep breath, realising the mixed tension she felt, and released it. "It was just a second or two of distortion at the most, not enough to show a door opening and closing, or to hide one either. What makes you think there was distortion or someone else in the car?"

"You just told me then." Ramsey looked at her and he seemed to have an idea. "Can I hold your watch please?"

"What?"

"Your watch," he said. "You want answers."

He had reached across the short space. She reacted, pulling her wrist back before he could do more than touch the watch. Angered, she kept her voice low in response. "Mr Ramsey, it is time you left."

Ramsey stayed seated, calm as a quiet lake, and looked her dead in the eyes. "I'm sorry about that. I needed to touch something that belonged to you to show you how I know things."

"How you know what?"

He looked straight at her, into her eyes, and she noticed the strong brown colour of his eyes. They were like a puppy dog's, but deep as the earth and its secrets. He looked through her as though she were glass, and he spoke with a monotone voice as though reciting from memory. "Your middle name is Sophia, named after your mother. She's still alive but your father passed away when you were away with the Army. You were twenty two. They are not your real parents, are they?"

Cogan felt shaken as she had never told anyone about her adoption as a little girl. To have a stranger tell her this much was disconcerting and eerie. She tried to control her voice, but it still quivered. "How did you know that?"

Ramsey softened for a moment. "I am a psychic and I

know all sorts of things by touching your possessions. It's called psychometry. I wondered at first if Tyrone was telling me a wild story too when I saw him last night. But Tyrone never lies and, when I touched his hand, I saw everything that happened in that car. There was someone else in the car with them." His confident and assertive tone had returned by this time.

Cogan moved her chair back behind the desk, letting it be a shield between herself and Ramsey. "I don't know what to say. What else do you believe you know, Craig?"

She didn't believe him. Her sceptical side was already trying to rationalise things, trying to prove him a fake. Could he have Googled her and run a check on her through public records? No, he never had the time for that, and she didn't even have Facebook. Cogan nodded to show Ramsey had her attention, and he continued speaking.

"There was another man, someone they didn't know, in the car with them. Tyrone didn't get a clear look at him because things happened so quickly, but the man broke Debbie's neck. The blows to her head didn't do it. You are right that no one could have mustered that much force from behind the driver's seat to kill by blows alone. The angles would not allow the murderer to gain enough leverage to do that. The laws of physics wouldn't allow it."

"It's strange to hear a psychic talk about physics," Cogan responded. "But you made a mistake. There's nothing about Debbie's neck breaking."

"Not yet," Ramsey stated, standing up to leave. "You still haven't received the coroner's report but you will see I'm right when you receive it. She died before the car crashed."

"Thank you for your time," Cogan told him, standing as well to mirror him. She stepped back when he produced a business card at his fingertips. Sleight of hand, she thought. That convinced her he was not a real psychic, just someone good at looking up public records to bamboozle people.

Ramsey stood there, holding the card for her. "Take it. You will want to call me again soon."

Something in his tone convinced her to take it but she still responded. "I doubt it, but I will call when they finish the autopsy."

"And you will find it was not a blow to the head that killed my god-daughter," he responded with a steely voice. He paused a moment before turning to leave.

Cogan stood there, watching him walk out of the office and then down the hallway as though he belonged there. He came in, saying he wanted information, and yet he seemed to give more than she gave. What a bombastic bastard, she thought to herself, before looking at the mountain of paperwork and folders on her desk. Just the same, Ramsey proved a good distraction from this.

There was another knock at the door and the detective turned to face the new arrival - a constable who looked like he had news for her.

"There's been another two accidents, Detective," he said.

"What? And no one told me?" she boomed. Although she felt tired inside herself, she moved to get her jacket.

"They happened at the same time just now," he replied.

"Oh?"

"Opposite ends of town," the officer replied, as Cogan passed him and hurried down the hallway. "What are the odds of that?"

Cogan looked at Ramsey's card which she still had in her hand, before slipping it back in her jacket's pocket. "Yes," she muttered, "what are the chances of that?"

Chapter 5

"That was exciting, wasn't it?" Emily said, floating alongside Ramsey as he stalked along the hallway.

As a spirit, invisible to most people, Emily Fraser enjoyed watching interactions between the living. She had been listening to the whole conversation between them, and made side comments to Ramsey while he was talking to Cogan too. This had distracted Ramsey, making him appear flaky to the detective. It is so easy to distract a man when he is trying to concentrate on one thing at a time.

"You always find it exciting when you embarrass me in front of a woman," Ramsey answered. He did this through telepathy because they were passing a few police officers. He didn't want them thinking he had an imaginary friend either.

"Of course," Emily replied with a cheeky smile, taking a moment to eye off a well-built police officer they passed. "It's how I keep you on your little tippy toes. But what was all that in the office?"

Ramsey paused for a moment outside the police station, looking at his watch as he answered. "What was what? I went in, looking for information. She told me what she could, and I found out the rest another way."

Emily laughed, sounding sure she knew there was more than Ramsey admitted. After all, she could tell things he couldn't know, him being a mere male. "What did you find out?"

Ramsey's features clouded for a moment as he considered his words. "I wish that Samuel and Ginetta were still alive, Emily, because I don't know how to handle this. But I'm glad they aren't here to see this. Debbie is too young to die."

Ramsey didn't speak the words aloud, because it hurt too much to admit, so Emily received his thoughts instead. Her hand reached out and touched his shoulder gently as she understood what he meant. In a past life so long ago, Emily Fraser once had a family, lots of children, and some of them died too young too. She remembered promising to protect them, to raise them to be strong and clever, and to be of great use to their clan and community. She believed living to see the young die was the greatest curse God could have placed on her.

A couple of people approached and Ramsey looked up, moving to the side when he realised he was blocking their passage into the building. The two women looked at Ramsey with concern as they passed, noting the tears he held back, and looked away. They had business of their own.

Emily bethought her answer for Ramsey's benefit. "You have done a great job with Debbie and Tyrone, better than I thought you would. Do you remember what little devils they were when you first became their guardian?"

Ramsey grinned, remembering the games the two children used to play on him. Debbie used to have an air of authority, enough to make someone believe her to be a responsible person. She and Tyrone used to take great advantage of that. One time, Tyrone came home from school, telling his "uncle Craig" that the next few days were "pupil-free days" and that he had those days off. Ramsey knew what those days meant, having heard of them when Sam or Ginetta mentioned them in the past, so he did not blink an eye at it. Debbie backed Tyrone's story up as well; being the older, and presumably most responsible one, she convinced Ramsey. They took the subterfuge further. Knowing Ramsey's psychic ability to know things through touching people or their possessions, the children took great pains to ensure he didn't touch them or their things. By doing so, they /could make sure Ramsey did not realise the truth. At least, that was their theory as he found out - when the school's principal called to let Ramsey, as their guardian, know they were absent.

Ramsey smiled at the memory, laughing to himself as he played it in his mind. It had been embarrassing for him when the school's principal who had seen Ramsey perform asked him, "How can those two children trick you? I thought you were a psychic." Ramsey knew exactly how they did it and he knew what to do about it too.

Unfortunately, he wasn't able to send the kids to school in time due to an important performance interstate. And knew he could not trust them to turn up at school if he sent them by plane back to Statton. But he had ample time to think of a suitable punishment their principal was happy to implement upon their return; detention during lunch times to make up for the time they had away from school. Ramsey felt tempted at the time to go further but he felt they received the message.

Although they were little devils, they were still good kids, and the only other real shenanigans came about from practical jokes they used to play on him. One time, he came back home to take a shower. Ink had sprayed out all over him from the shower-head they had sabotaged. Ramsey's response was just as simple. The children returned home to find that Ramsey had wrapped all their possessions in aluminium foil. Their beds, their pillows, their books, and their toys all received the same treatment. Debbie had screamed with dismay to find her teddy bears wrapped. It took Craig the whole day, with the help of a few other spirits, to help him out with that.

Brakes squealing and horns blaring interrupted Ramsey's reminiscence. He looked up in time to see a car run up onto the footpath and smash into the brick wall next to a lawyers' office. Ramsey noted the irony as the lawyer was a known ambulance chaser; he specialised in road accidents.

What he saw next surprised him. A dark robed spirit stepped through the car's door and surveyed the damage. Ramsey thought it seemed odd. It was not because the spirit dressed like the Grim Reaper who he knew from a long past encounter. He thought it odd because the spirit stepped from the front passenger seat where there was no body. Someone else sat in the driver seat and was not moving.

Ramsey looked towards Emily, motioning with his head. "Are you thinking what I'm thinking?"

They both hurried towards the scene, which was already gathering other spectators. A few pedestrians who had managed to dodge the runaway car approached as well. Some pedestrians were living, the others long dead. The spirits wore the clothing of their different time periods and a few still showed the traumatic cause of their death.

The "Reaper" spirit ignored them all, taking the time to touch the driver who remained completely still. Ramsey could see that movement came from the driver but it was driver's spirit exiting its body.

"Hey! You!" Ramsey called out. "Stop!"

The "Reaper" stopped what it was doing and glanced towards Ramsey. A deathly chill enveloped Ramsey as he approached, an obvious sign of anger from the spirit, and he slowed a little. Emily also slowed but kept a steady gaze upon the dark spirit as it fled the scene.

"Are you all right, Craig?" Emily asked him, noting his chills.

Ramsey nodded. "Yes, I'm fine. Follow him, Ems! Don't let him get away." He coughed, unable to stop as if something wanted to vacate his body, and Emily paused, but he waved her on. "Move!"

Emily, now certain Ramsey was fine, nodded and melted away as she hurried in pursuit of the Reaper. Ramsey coughed a little more, spitting up some phlegm before concentrating on his breathing. He cursed to himself for letting his psychic defences down lately. Under normal circumstances, he could have shaken that off without batting an eyelid. But Debbie's passing had been a shock to him and he had not even slept that night or allowed himself time to grieve. There had been so much to do, and he had neglected his meditation too. It was only through his years of conditioning that allowed him to recover as fast as he did now. But, just like physical exercise, the discipline still required persistence. Having finished coughing the negativity out as a green ooze, he stood up and felt better.

Craig Ramsey ran the fifty metres towards the accident scene and looked things over. The smashed car, a dirty blue Camry, faded by years of sunlight exposure, looked terrible and its driver looked worse. Craig was careful not to touch anything. He stood back, knowing the woman behind the wheel was dead and she wasn't capable or resurrecting as he did so long ago. Her slack-jawed mouth hung open in what must have been a scream of terror and her glazing brown eyes reflected nothing. Ramsey scrutinised her fingers, still gripping the steering wheel in vain, and noted the wedding ring on her finger, holding back a vision from his past. That was from another time and another Ramsey, a memory not worth reliving, but he knew how this woman's husband was likely to feel.

"Such a waste, isn't it?" a whispering voice said from beside him.

Ramsey turned and saw an old man looking through the window at her. He was about to reply when he noticed the man had no shadow; the old man was a spirit, wearing the work clothes of a labourer from the 1950's. Long trousers, long sleeved work-shirt with the sleeves rolled up to the elbows. The man must have been in his late forties when he passed.

"Yes," he replied, surprising the spirit with his direct response as he looked at him. "Did you know her?"

The spirit-man took a step back as though uncertain how to respond. "You can see me?"

Ramsey nodded, "And I can hear you too."

The man smiled, revealing teeth like tombstones, and appeared glad that someone could communicate with him after so many years wandering the streets in death. "You have no idea how it feels to be able to talk with someone these days!"

Ramsey tried his best to stay patient. "I understand more than you know," he smiled. "Did you know this woman?"

The spirit shook his head and took a step closer

towards the car, his head passing through the car's window to look closer at the dead driver. "I wish I did. She looks like one gorgeous dish, doesn't she? She must have upset that other guy though."

"Other guy?" Ramsey questioned, feigning ignorance. "What do you mean?"

"There was another guy in the car with her when the car lost control. All dressed in black, he was," the man said.

"He isn't here now," Ramsey said. "Do you see him?"

"Are you kidding?" the man said, wiping his brow with his cap. "He took off. I thought at first he must have been with her somehow and would wait for her to leave her body. I've seen it happen before when a husband waits for the wife, or the other way around. But, no! He took off so fast. I thought you would have seen him as he heard you call out to him before."

"So, he was a spirit then?" Ramsey asked.

"Yeah, but not like any I have seen, mate," the spirit replied. "Didn't you see how his shape seemed to change? I thought he was Death coming but I've never seen the Reaper kill someone before like a mad man would."

"I don't understand," Ramsey said. "You said you thought the spirit and the victim were both connected, yet you mention he was trying to kill her. What did you see?"

The working man's spirit thought for a moment, scratching his chin as he recalled the events. "When I first saw them coming over the intersection, he was in the seat beside her. They looked like married couples do. Do you know what I mean, how you can tell they're having a lover's quarrel or a domestic, as they call them these days?"

"Which car seat was he sitting in?" Ramsey asked, almost demanding the answer.

The working man's spirit thought for a moment. "You know what? I think he moved. At one point, he was in the back seat and then he moved into the front seat. That's no surprise though as some of us can just move through solid things, right?"

Ramsey listened to the spirit witness' report and thought to himself. Could the "Reaper guy" could have been the same who killed Debbie?

"Do you know who he is?"

The spirit thought for a moment. "No, I can't say I do, BUT I have seen him around before. There's been other times here that -"

Cogan, who had just arrived on the scene, interrupted at this point. She had been watching Ramsey talking to thin air as though he was having a one-way conversation with no one in particular.

"Is everything okay?" she asked, showing concern.

Ramsey spun around to face her, fielding a disturbed look on his face. "There's been another murder," he blurted without thinking first. Turning towards the crumpled car with its bonnet in the brick wall, he pointed. "See?"

Cogan looked at the scene, following the direction of his finger pointing. "What makes you think this one is murder?"

Ramsey still felt a little shocked, putting facts together in his mind, and answered. "It was a man in black."

Cogan paused, looking at Ramsey, thinking to herself and flicking hair from her face as a winter wind blew past. "A man in black? Seriously?"

Ramsey nodded, knowing how silly it sounded but he

said it, anyway. "Yes, a black robe, just like the Grim Reaper. He disappeared quickly after the car collided with the brick wall."

The detective looked again at the crumpled mess, feeling a mixture of frustration and even a little anger well up inside her. Believing Ramsey was just a grieving parent looking for things to blame for his daughter's death, Cogan felt frustrated that she could not tell him what she thought. He had to stop interfering. She felt angry with herself for not being able to tell him that and empathetic at the same time. Other police officers had arrived at the scene and were closing off the street. So she grabbed Ramsey's sleeve, guiding him away from the car and its deceased occupant.

As the detective guided him away, Ramsey's dark sense of humour came out to play. "You're closing this street off so often, have you considered we may as well turn it into a pedestrian mall?"

Cogan eye-balled Ramsey, stopping him with a deadly stare. "Are you sick or something? Your niece died here last night too, and you're making jokes as though nothing happened."

Ramsey hesitated, making an inaudible gulp. "Sorry, coping mechanism I have." He removed Cogan's hand from his elbow and released it.

The working man's spirit, who had been watching the whole time, laughed, saying to Ramsey, "Mate, I think she likes you."

"What?" Ramsey said, distracted by the spirit.

"I didn't say anything," Cogan responded.

"Not you," Ramsey told her then turned his head back to the spirit.

"If you could see what I see," the spirit laughed. "This is amazing. How long have you known her?"

Cogan waved her hand in front of Ramsey's face. "I'm right here, just me. Here. Who are you talking to?"

Ramsey's attention snapped back to Cogan, looking into her eyes as he felt himself drawn to three things at once. He found it difficult to concentrate under the circumstances. "Excuse me a minute," he apologised, holding up his right index finger while he gripped the upper part of his nose, closing his eyes. "There's a lot going on right now."

Cogan's voice was stern, almost like a mother would use. "Mr Ramsey, perhaps you should go home. You have had a lot happen with your family and you have just seen this accident now."

"Hey! She's talking to you in that tone, mate," the working man's spirit laughed. "She's got it for you."

Ramsey looked towards the working man's spirit, telling him by telepathy to be quiet, as he wasn't making things any better. The spirit only just laughed back at him. Cogan was saying something else to him as well which he couldn't make out. It was like trying to listen to many conversations at a party, difficult to do with the interference.

"Well?" Cogan's voice cut through to him.

"What?" Ramsey said.

"How about you leave it to the professionals if you have nothing else to contribute as a witness?"

"There's not much more to say," Ramsey stated. "The car came from past Woolworths, and there were car horns blasting as it cut through the intersection. Someone thought they saw someone in the back seat of this car here, moving into the front seat, before appearing to argue with the driver. It veered to the side and -"

Cogan spoke over Ramsey, interrupting him, "And where is this person, or is that the hooded figure you're telling me about?"

Ramsey replied, exasperated, "Exactly!"

"Do you realise how this sounds? I can't chase after ghosts over town or any other hallucinations you may have had."

"But I saw it too," the working man's spirit answered with annoyance. "You tell her, Mister Ramsey."

Just then, Emily appeared at Ramsey's side, saving him from an embarrassing explanation. "You would never guess what I found," she said, ignoring the working man's spirit and Cogan. "Craig, there's been another killing! It is the same rascal as this accident. I saw him myself."

"See?" the working man's spirit blurted. "The pretty lady saw him too."

Emily looked at the working man's spirit, "Oh, you saw it too?"

"Sure did," he replied, looking back at Cogan again. "And are you seeing what I am seeing here?"

Ramsey felt distracted by Emily and the working man's spirit, feeling their gazes upon him and Cogan. "What? Can't you see I'm working here?"

"I don't see what could be working here, Mr Ramsey," the detective told him, noticing other officers on the scene glancing in their direction. She ignored embarrassment and faced back to Craig Ramsey. "We have another accident here and, if you have nothing further to contribute here, I feel you need to go home and rest."

Ramsey fumed. He found it hard enough to convince

sceptics to take him seriously. It was even harder when spirits kept talking to him, and interrupting, at the same time. Turning away from Cogan, he clenched a fist, took a deep breath, and ran his fingers through his brown hair. He let the breath out before turning to face the detective.

"You know what? I have more to contribute, Detective Cogan." He emphasised her name to show his frustration. She tensed when he spoke, looking her in the eye, staring into her soul. It unsettled her. When he was certain he had her attention, he spoke. "You obviously want information you don't have already. Before you came out here, you received a call. No, sorry, you didn't receive the call. An officer visited you with the news and he told you about two recent accidents. They happened at the same time, correct?"

Cogan opened her mouth to respond, but Ramsey held up a finger, waggling it to stop her. "Uh uh! It's your turn to listen as a detective with manners. You think I'm a flake, someone you can't take seriously, but here's something you don't already know. A third accident happened," lifting his watch to check the time, "in the last five to ten minutes."

Cogan opened her mouth and Ramsey cut her off again. "And you're about to ask how I know that, right? I assure you I am not responsible for the accident. Nor did I plan it. Nor did I arrange it. I did nothing that your closed-off sceptical mind could believe. I know because that is what I learned just now while you patronised me."

Cogan felt stunned and stood in silence, aware that one of the other officers tittered to himself. She didn't have a comeback. "Where was this third accident?"

"Did I say it was an accident?" Ramsey enquired,

taken aback. "Oh, yes, I did. I should have said 'murder', but your teams will conclude that it's an accident. Your over-glorified CSI teams won't be able to come up with anything else."

He turned around and strode off. Cogan couldn't see or hear her, but Emily still stood next to her. She and the workman spirit had been watching and listening the whole time with smiles on their faces. Emily smiled at Cogan, "Don't worry, love. He gets this way when he hasn't had a proper nap," before hurrying off after Ramsey.

Cogan, a little stunned by what she saw as Craig Ramsey's defensive passion, was about to move after him when her mobile phone rang. She stopped walking to answer it. "Yes?"

She paused, listening before thanking the caller and hanging up. "Guys, there's been a third one on the other side of town at Hospital Hill."

Cogan looked down the street, just catching sight of Ramsey as he walked around the corner, still talking to himself. "How did he know?" she wondered aloud.

Chapter 6

The rest of the Friday and the weekend following had been tiring for Craig. In the afternoon, he received a call from Tucker's funeral home. They were picking Debra's body up from the medical examiner's office on Monday morning. Craig thought that was a good thing. At least he had something to tell family and friends when they rang to ask about the funeral. Debra had a lot of friends, especially from high school and university, and there was her family as well. They all wanted to call, to convey their wishes, and ask about any funeral plans. Thankfully, they rang the landline phone, as they didn't all know his mobile number, but it was still tiring on his energy. He hated to think of how many were coming through on her Facebook account. He loved that people felt so much for Debra and her passing, but he felt drained on a physical and emotional level.

In the end, wanting nothing more than to hide away and rest, he brought out his old answering machine. It could relay the latest news for people with its opening greeting and take a message at the same time. He could have hired a Virtual Assistant to do it, but he knew the relatives would not like talking to a stranger. The machine seemed the better idea.

It would be easier to call a few key people back with detailed news as it happened, asking them to pass it on to the others.

Tyrone was home too; Craig had picked him up earlier that morning not long after meeting Detective Cogan. The teenager, still tired and sleeping off the sedatives, couldn't answer the phone either.

Samuel's brother, Michael, dropped around on the Friday evening after his work. Michael was a large man, just like Tyrone's father, with the same impish sense of humour; a big kid at heart. He visited on most weekends after the children's father passed, and he often took them to the theme parks or wherever their adventurous souls wanted to go. Ramsey welcomed his company on this Friday night; it gave him a chance to tell Michael everything that he knew about the traffic incident. The large man knew Ramsey's psychic gifts and his past as a magician and mentalist, so listened without judgement. Ramsey appreciated that.

Possessing a logical mind, Michael also asked a lot of questions. What connection did Debra have with the spirit assassin, or even his other victims? Could Ramsey pick the assassin's identity? What motive did it have for killing anyone?

Ramsey had no idea about the spirit assassin's motive but he knew it was one that felt a lot of anger. The cold feeling of burning anger that emanated from the creature had almost paralysed him that morning. He had felt it a few times before, but this time it surprised him before he could defend himself.

Although Ramsey felt tired enough to drop, he and Michael talked until the wee hours of Saturday morning. Michael ended up staying the night in the guests' room of Ramsey's large house.

The next morning, Michael helped with the phone calls. They made a list of a few key relatives, those who Michael knew would call all the others for them. The efforts of many would help lighten the burden. By 4pm, every Samoan relative knew the plans, and so did Debra's university friends.

On Saturday night, Ramsey received an unexpected but welcome visitor. He awoke from a dream, aware that something was happening. He usually kept the room pitch-black at night, drawing the curtains, but a soft blue light bathed the room with a shimmering glow. It looked like he was underwater. Peering from heavy eyes, he noticed a young woman standing at the foot of his bed. At first, he thought it was Emily floating there until she moved closer to the head of his bed. Then he saw her coffee-coloured skin and large expressive eyes.

"Debra?" he said, a bit surprised. "I wondered if you had moved on or not."

Debra's spirit smiled, saying nothing, but he could hear her words in his head. "I had to come see you, Uncle Craig, before I do."

"Had to? As in unfinished business or because you wanted to, Deb?"

Craig sat up in his bed out of habit to allow Deb to sit on the edge, but she remained standing. He looked at her, knowing this could be the last time he saw her, and he wanted to remember everything. Debra raised her arm, holding it towards him, and he touched it; his palm rested against her astral palm, and he could feel its slight tingle.

"I wanted to see you, Uncle Craig," she smiled, sitting beside him with a loving look on her face. "They told me I will be seeing Mum and Dad before I move onto my next stage."

Ramsey felt his eyes well up with tears and he was just aware of Tyrone knocking on the bedroom door before entering. Tyrone made a noise upon seeing his sister sitting on the bed and Ramsey looked up to see him.

Debra appeared to be aware of Tyrone's presence but held Ramsey's gaze. "Thank you for all you have done for me and for Tyrone," she said. "I never told you and I didn't think I would have to so soon."

Ramsey sniffed, wishing he could hold Debra in a hug but settled for trying to pat her hand. "I'd do it again without hesitation. I'm sorry I couldn't save you from what happened but I will catch the spirit that did this."

Tyrone was watching his sister, tears streaming down his eyes. "I'm sorry too, sis."

Debra turned to her brother. "You be good, little bro." She held her fist out towards Tyrone who did his best to fist-pump her back. But his hand went through hers, much to his mixed reaction. Debra's expression showed her sympathy. "Aw, Tyrone, I don't know how to become solid. I wish I could hug you both."

Tyrone tried his best to hug her, and Debbie's face betrayed a hint of sadness. "Oh, wow," she said. "I can feel that!"

They hugged, holding on despite the lack of complete tangibility, and Ramsey stood to hold them both. The hug was a long one, and they wished it could last longer.

"I'll meet you again, Tyrone," she said to her brother, "but not until you are a very old man. Take care of Uncle Craig and say hi-bye to Uncle Michael for me too, okay?"

Debra's spirit turned to face her adoptive uncle. "I'll see you again but sooner," she answered. "Try to forgive the one who did this to me, okay?"

Ramsey felt surprised but also proud of Debra. "I'd kill him if I could."

Debra shook her head at him. "No! You can't do that.

You'd do the same in his position. Please treat him with compassion; do you understand?"

Curiosity at Debra's passionate appeal overcame Ramsey. "What do you mean?"

But Debra was already fading away. The blue light illuminating the room shrank away with her, encapsulating her until she finally vanished before the two men's eyes.

"Debra?" Ramsey said, reaching for her as the last fragment disappeared. "Damn! What did you mean by that?"

***

That was five night ago. Now Ramsey sat with Tyrone at Debra's funeral service. Most of Debra's relatives and friends made it for the occasion.

He looked at his adopted nephew, half-listening to the service while he thought about the things Debra had told them. Although he knew it was Debra who visited, he still wondered about her message. Be compassionate, she had said. Her message sounded enlightened for a teen-aged girl's spirit. It shocked him with its simplicity, but he couldn't let go of the wish for answers or some kind of justice.

Tyrone, Michael and Craig were the only living people who knew Debra's death to be more than a mere traffic accident. They decided between themselves not to mention it to the other relatives or friends, and Ramsey felt certain that Detective Cogan wouldn't tell others either.

Ramsey snorted to himself gently when Emily, invisible to all but himself and Tyrone, whispered in his ear. He looked in the direction Emily pointed and he saw Detective Cogan sitting in the back row, watching him. Their eyes made brief contact, and she gave a sympathetic nod to him. Ramsey allowed himself to give a quick smile in response before turning back towards the front where the preacher spoke about Debra's life. The preacher made a mistake in his speech, but no one corrected him. Preachers rarely had their facts straight when talking about the deceased anyway, Ramsey thought to himself. That's how they turned the story of Jesus Christ into a money-making lie for the masses they bled and deceived.

Then he noticed a plume of smoke appear from behind the preacher and squinted to look closer. The smoke changed form, transforming into a human shape wearing an Australian Army uniform, and Ramsey smiled. The spirit, puffing upon a cigar clenched between its teeth, looked about until it saw him and floated through the congregation towards him. Ramsey knew the soldier as Colonel Ryan, the resident spirit guardian of the cemetery behind the church.

You wanted to see me, Ramsey?

Ramsey nodded towards Colonel Ryan, thinking his answer back. *After the service, Colonel, yes.*

I'm sorry to hear about your niece, mate. I'll see you then. Ryan faded away as soon as he finished bethinking.

"I hope you don't want me hanging around for that conversation," Emily whispered in Ramsey's ear.

"He's not so bad," Ramsey whispered back, smiling. "You just don't know if you can handle his charm, being a man in uniform and everything."

"Ha!" Emily scoffed. "He's incorrigible and foul-mouthed. My ears are too delicate for that kind of talk!"

Ramsey smiled, knowing he had heard much worse from Emily, and resolved to stay silent through the rest of the service out of respect for anyone else there.

When the service finally finished, Ramsey leaned towards Tyrone, letting him know to head to the wake with his uncle Michael. Tyrone nodded, understanding that his Uncle Craig was on a mission still and what that entailed.

Ramsey shook a few people's hands, knowing those who were Debra's high school friends and a few relatives although he couldn't recall their names. Those he didn't know he soon knew by the mere shaking their hand or touching their sleeves. Psychometry can be handy at such times. Just as he thought he could move towards the cemetery, he caught sight of another familiar figure.

"Good morning, Detective Cogan," he smiled. "I didn't expect to see you here today."

Cogan shook Ramsey's hand, her hand feeling warm and soft in his. She responded with something he didn't quite hear as he picked up some impressions from the contact. Ramsey understood that Cogan had a soft heart despite her hard exterior and she didn't want things to be bad between them either. His eyebrow moved when he realised that Cogan had not visited funerals for the other victims either.

Cogan repeated what she said to Ramsey. "I'm sorry for your loss, Mr Ramsey."

"You can call me Craig," he said, softening a little himself.

"I have things I need to share with you," Cogan replied. "Can we talk?"

Ramsey looked around at everyone else. He wanted to talk with her too, but he didn't want her seeing what he was about to do. The detective already thought him to be strange.

"I don't mean now," Cogan corrected herself.

"Perhaps tomorrow?"

Ramsey smiled, keeping it low-key. "Yeah, tomorrow is fine, but I need to go now."

Cogan nodded. "Of course," she answered, handing him her card. Ramsey looked at its simple design, removed his black leather wallet from his pocket and placed the card inside it. He exchanged one of his own.

"I'll come by at 10am," he replied, before turning and walking off in another direction to speak with other friends who had turned up. "Thank you for coming."

***

Ramsey excused himself from the other attendees. After checking to see no one was following him, he hurried along the pathway from behind the chapel and past the walls of cremated remains. As he moved closer to the graves, he felt aware of phantom eyes watching him. He looked at some of them, recognising some of them from previous visits but no one he knew. Phantoms of all kinds, dressed in a range of clothes from different time periods, floated about the graveyard with their business. One of them, a man Craig who knew as Oliver, called out to him as he passed. Craig would have stopped to talk, but he was in a hurry. He waved to the man as he passed, whispering, "Next time," and Oliver went back to chasing away birds.

At last, he came to the section reserved for those who died serving in the armed forces. Phantoms, dressed in different uniforms as though they were still active in duty, marched or carried out drills. In a way they were on active duty as they now served the Spirit Force. He looked at Colonel Ryan's tombstone, beside the spirits, but saw no sign of him.

"Over here, Ramsey!" Ryan's spirit called from the

side. "Come into my 'other office'."

Ramsey turned towards the disembodied voice that sounded like a mix of John Wayne and George Peppard, only with an Australian accent. Ryan's ghost, no longer dressed in the ceremonial uniform, was now in battle fatigues and smoking a cigar that Ramsey could smell. As Ramsey approached, Ryan gestured towards a seat sheltered from the sun by frangipani trees. They sat down on the seat near a small pond with a family of ducks, a mother and her ducklings, swimming in a line across its calm surface.

"It's the family I left behind," Ryan murmured, watching Ramsey with concern. "How are you holding up, civilian?"

Ramsey shrugged. "The worst of the grieving is gone. Now I want to stop this character before it happens again."

Ryan nodded, turning the cigar in his mouth with his fingers, before blowing another plume of smoke out. "What do you want from me?"

Ramsey sat forward in the seat, looking Ryan dead in the eye. "I must know who this spirit is."

Ryan let a smile flicker on his visage before removing the cigar from his mouth. "Ramsey, I don't know who the spirit is. He's creating a few ripples for me too, in case you hadn't guessed." Ryan motioned something to the other armed spirits and continued. "This is the most activity I have seen since Vietnam when you weren't even an itch in your father's undies." Ramsey lifted an eyebrow in curiosity and the phantom colonel explained. "At present, we have a situation from the downstairs people, meaning Density. You know the place; bad people go there. Some of my scouts, those who have returned, tell me trouble is brewing down there. The administrators down there are having trouble keeping people in for their full rehabilitation. We have caught a few of them and either disposed of them or sent them back."

"What about the hooded one?"

"Well," Ryan answered, chuckling to himself. "He is inadvertently helping recruit for both sides. I don't mind the people who come to me sooner than needed, but I'm not happy about those he sends downstairs. Do you get my drift?"

Ramsey listened, feeling the enormity of the situation. "So you want him just as much?"

Ryan shrugged. "What happens to the living isn't entirely my business, but I don't need the complication either."

Ramsey smiled. "Does that mean you will help me track him down?"

Colonel Ryan appeared to take a deep breath, considering his answer before looking Craig in the eyes; meanwhile, the living man shielded himself from the coldness in Ryan's mood.

The Colonel felt impatient with him. "Listen, Ramsey," he asserted, throwing his cigar into the pond where it splashed despite being immaterial like himself. "Chasing after a dip shit like that spirit is not my problem. I have no men to spare, and any information I give will be what I or my unit trip over. The man you seek is not mine, and although he seems capable, I assure you I didn't train him. I am not even sure if he belongs to our other units across the town."

"How can you be sure he's not?" Ramsey asked,

thinking Colonel Ryan knew more than he would have him believe.

The Colonel found another cigar in his pocket, lighting it with a finger which seemed to catch fire. "Because their commanding officers asked me. He's causing headaches for them too."

Ramsey allowed that information, or rather lack of it, to digest for a moment before standing. The Colonel added, for his benefit, "Ramsey, I understand Debra meant a lot to you and those kids are the closest you've had to family in a long time. I still remember when I first met you, and I think highly of you, even if you can be a stubborn boofhead sometimes. Do you mind if I give you some advice?"

Ramsey looked at him, nodding.

"Don't turn your back on the living for the sake of the dead."

Ramsey acknowledged Ryan with another nod, as though considering the soldier's words, but the Colonel knew he was considering something else.

He called after Ramsey who was already walking off down the path towards the car park. "Oi! What are you going to do with him when you catch him? How can you gain revenge on a dead man? Did you consider that?"

Ramsey didn't respond and Ryan shook his head. "Damn mortal bastard never listens."

***

Colonel Ryan removed the cigar from his mouth, spitting a glob of ectoplasmic goo in the grass at his feet. Another soldier, a spirit with a hole in his chest that allowed a view through his body, approached.

"What is it?" he growled at the soldier.

The spirit, a private with half of his left leg missing below the knee, saluted. "Sir! Bad news. There have been deserters!"

Ryan's eyes opened wide in surprise. "What? Who?"

"Some of the new recruits, sir!"

The phantom colonel swore loudly. "Send out a couple of the special ops to track them down." As the soldier ran off to carry out his orders, Colonel Ryan wondered to himself, contemplating if he should tell Ramsey as well but changed his mind. Ramsey had enough on his plate already. With what was happening for Colonel Ryan's unit and the escalating conflict with Density, Craig Ramsey would realise what was happening soon enough.

Chapter 7

Linda Crandon terminated the phone call, letting a heavy sigh escape her tired self. Why do all the crazy and angry people call up during a full moon? One of the other banking consultants in the call centre told her five years ago that it always happens. She didn't believe it then, but she did now. The previous call, the first since she started her shift, left her craving time away from the workstation and she had barely started her shift. The caller was an unemployed customer; she preferred to wait ten minutes in queue, rather than two minutes on an automated service, to learn if her pension had arrived in her account. She blew her temper because it had not yet arrived. Was it because she needed to buy food for her children crying in the background? No. She wanted to buy grog and cigarettes; she said so herself. Linda used to feel sorry for the Centrelink pensioners, being a single mother herself after her deadbeat husband left for some blonde bimbo with more boobs than brains. After receiving so many calls from the unemployed, she realised how many of them were mostly beyond reason or the capability of budgeting. Linda's bank deposited the pensions into their accounts up to twelve hours earlier than other banks, but their customers believed it was their "right" to have it sooner. When it was not provided before its due time, they became seething illogical creatures filled to the brim with bubbling venom and screamed through the phones like spoiled children.

The phone rang again, barely four seconds after the last call finished, demanding Linda's attention. She wanted to cry from mental exhaustion already but sucked up the feeling and answered the phone, introducing herself as the bank's representative. Was this another Centrelink customer who wanted money to feed her kids at the fast-food restaurant instead of cooking healthier and cheaper food at home?

"Hello Linda," the caller's voice, familiar to Linda, said to her. "Is it a busy night tonight?"

Linda recognised the voice, and she wished it was another angry Centrelink customer. It would be even better if it were some nice elderly person asking for help to use internet banking; those calls took forever, but those people were polite - most of the time. Anyone would have been better than the Customer Service Department's manager, Marnie Aniston. Linda used to be friends with Marnie, another single mother, when they first started together. Their friendship and close bond continued even while Marnie rose through the ranks although Linda always recognised the sociopathic tendencies behind Marnie's apparent workaholism. She used to forgive that until she learned what Marnie had done behind her back, leaving Linda feeling dejected and angry with her.

Linda took a breath to reply and terrified screaming cut her off.

"Marnie?"

Linda thought she heard a man's voice say something viciously, something like "cock" and "bitch", above Marnie's screams.

A soul-wrenching scraping and crunching sound added its sickening voice to the cacophony of noise torturing Linda's ears.

"Marnie!" Linda almost shouted into the phone. "What's happening? Are you okay?"

For all the ways Marnie had betrayed their friendship and her trust, Linda felt concern and fear her now.

She heard brakes squealing.

A massive thump.

Crunching.

A blood-gurgling whimper.

Silence.

Another thump. Louder this time.

Metal screeching and crushing.

Longer silence.

Linda's lower lip trembled, and a tear stung her eye before she wiped it.. Her heart beat so fast and she felt sick in the stomach. She could still hear something. Some kind of wind noise. She didn't know what it was.

A dying breath?

Linda choked back something that tasted like reflux or vomit, swallowing hard

"Marnie?"

Silence filled the phone line, and Linda strained her ears trying to pick up anything. She thought she heard something but wasn't sure if it was her imagination.

The phone rang again, making her jump with a surprised scream.

A part of Linda wanted to answer the call, pure force of habit, but she couldn't. The phone kept ringing until it stopped on the seventh ring, the call automatically diverting back into the queue to wait for another consultant to answer it. Whoever answered that call would receive an angry voice asking why they had to wait after hearing the phone ring. Her phone flicked into Not Ready, so it wouldn't ring now.

Linda could not care less as she continued processing

the recent events. What could she do? On the one hand, she still felt angry with Marnie for what she did to Linda behind her back, sleeping with her boyfriend. But Marnie was still a human being, a dumbarse at times, but still human.

Serves the bitch right, Linda thought to herself, and then wondered if she should report it. What if her call was recorded tonight? She could not hide it under the carpet as anyone who listened to the call would hear the impact.

Linda picked up the phone, dialled Marnie's number. It went straight to voicemail without ringing. She hesitated, not knowing what to say to the voicemail, and left a short message, letting Marnie know she had tried calling.

It had been so long since Linda showed friendly concern to Marnie. She did not know what to say if she was okay although she had a sneaky feeling that Marnie was dead. Linda recalled the background sounds she heard earlier before Marnie's terrified screaming. She must have been driving while talking on the car.

At least Linda had covered her arse now. Her workplace would see that record and know that she had cared enough to try calling.

Her phone rang, surprising her, but she picked it up.

"Is everything okay there, Linda?" It was one of the supervisors and, better still, he was one of the cool ones.

"Yeah, Neil," she replied and hesitated.

He picked up on her uncertainty and asked her again if everything was okay.

She thought for a moment, recalling her previous phone conversation and imagined what could have happened and the consequences if she did nothing. "No, I'm not okay, really. I just had a call from Marnie. Yeah, our

Marnie Aniston. I think she had a car accident while talkingto me."

The supervisor felt no love lost for Marnie. The other consultants knew how Marnie had screwed up his career path within the call centre. However he still paused; either because he had a heart and recognised Marnie as another fellow human being or because he respected Linda's feelings and past friendship with Marnie. But then his sarcastic humour kicked him.

"It serves the sadistic bitch right for calling while driving, eh?"

"Yeah, right." Crandon laughed. It wasn't funny, but Neil always highlighted the truth in a way that shocked with honesty. "But what do I do? I tried calling her back and there was no answer."

Neil paused, thinking, and Crandon felt what he could say. "Did the phone ring or go to message bank?"

"Straight to message bank without ringing."

"Probably her calling the cops, do you think?" Neil enquired. "That would explain why you can't reach her. I'd think differently if it rang for ages before voicemail took over."

"I don't know, maybe," Linda answered.

Neil paused again and Linda could hear him thinking before he responded. "I'll call her check and that will cover both of us. You have done all you can. If it was any other customer, we couldn't do any more with it as we wouldn't know where they were. Whatever. It serves the bitch right anyway, and you weren't being recorded, so relax."

Linda Crandon laughed, "I knew you would say that."

"Great minds," Neil chuckled back. "Relax and take a short breather. The queue's dropped a little anyway as the pensions have finished processing."

***

Marnie's limp corpse hung from the driver's side window. She wore no seatbelt at the time of death when her killer forced his astral finger through her skull, stirring it in her brain until her motor functions stopped. Death was not instant. He had put his face in front of hers, making himself visible to her so she could recognise his face before she died. Marnie's look of horrified recognition was worth it although he didn't like looking in her eyes then. The assassin recognised Marnie from a distant faded memory. He must have known her well, he thought, to feel the tinge of remorse biting his conscience. But anger exploded from his mind, and with a wave of his hand, he psychokinetically flung the compressed gas cylinders from the service station into the car. He had hoped for an explosion, but it was enough the car and its driver were now out of commission.

Now he stood there in silence as he watched Marnie's body in the blue Mini Cooper. Marnie's body shimmered, a double image forming, blurring for a moment before separating.

He allowed a smile to edge across his face as he watched Marnie's spirit leave its physical body.

At last, Marnie emerged with a lurch, looking back at her inert corpse. A moment later, she gasped, realising she had died, and then with a desperate cry she tried in vain to re-enter her body.

"You're too far gone, Marnie Aniston," her killer murmured.

Marnie turned around to face him, recognition crossing her face. "You?"

He nodded. "You deserved it, just like the others."

Shocked, Marnie looked back at her body before facing her killer. "Why?"

Marnie's phone flew from where it landed straight to the killer's waiting hand, and he shook at her. "Because you're a thoughtless sadistic bitch like the others. People like you did this to me, not caring about what you are doing when you talk and text on these things while driving a fucking guided missile."

Marnie thought for a moment. "I went to -"

"Shut the fuck up, bitch! You and everyone else were warned by others, not just me. You can't say you didn't know this could happen. But you let your own festering addiction to mobile phones, their pretty pictures and sounds, take you over," the killer boomed. "It's my job to remove you like the cancer you are."

"What about my own daughters? Who will care for them?"

The killer hesitated for just a second but didn't get the chance to answer.

They heard a sliding sound to the side and turned to see a doorway of bright white light appear. Marnie's killer stepped back, holding a hand up to shade his eyes, and he thought he saw another familiar face there. He couldn't enter there yet and he knew it wasn't for him.

"Damn it!" he cried, as Marnie floated towards it. "Why does she get to go there? She doesn't deserve it."

Marnie's spirit passed through the doorway which promptly closed, disappearing and leaving the killer on his own with Marnie's corpse staring at him from its place.

He heard sirens and turned to see the police cars and ambulances arriving. Sniffing back an astral tear of anger, he took off into the air and stood on the nearby roof of the service station.

Marnie's voice still lingered in his mind and he felt his anger growing to explosive force. Flicking his hand toward Marnie's car, he diverted the psychokinetic force towards the gas cylinders still embedded the vehicle's doors.

The explosion filled the night, spewing a ball of flame in the air and shattering windows with its shock wave. He watched, thankful only Marnie's corpse suffered, and smiled.

"Karma's a bitch, Marnie," he murmured before flying into the air and looking down upon the traffic.

Flying along the streets, he scanned each of the cars and trucks below before seeing another potential victim. Anger filling his being, the spirit dived into the passenger's seat of the silver Mercedes.

It was a clean car, maybe new. He looked at the driver, seeing her to be a young woman, mid-to-late twenties. Watching her, he took the time to take in her features, gazing at her beautiful features which reminded him of someone else he knew but could not quite remember. The driver was talking on the phone to someone, the words sounding full of hope and love. This woman was happy, and it triggered a vague recognition within; he just didn't know what. The woman possessed a special presence, something precious. Then it came to him, and he realised why she glowed with life, and conflict invaded his mind. He needed to stop this woman before she could kill someone else, but he couldn't kill her either; something in his conscience prevented it.

So he stood there weighing up idea after idea until inspiration struck. Feeling happy with his resolution, he reached towards the steering wheel, closed his eyes, and a thought popped from his mind. In response, the car shuddered, its engine coughing, and the dashboard lit up with warning signs.

"Oh, damn," the woman cursed, looking at the engine lights blinking. "Listen, I have to go. I've got some car trouble here." Hanging up, she indicated and stopped the car at the side of the motorway.

The spirit smiled to himself and then waved his hand over the windscreen which fogged before the driver's eyes. He smiled more when he heard her gasp at reading the words appearing in the fog, illuminated by the street lights.

"For your unborn's sake, stay off the phone while driving."

Chapter 8

It was 10am Thursday when Ramsey arrived at Cogan's office door. As with his first visit, Cogan felt surprised to see him there; somehow Ramsey passed the other police officers without being challenged.

"How do you do that?" Cogan asked in disbelief.

Ramsey only smiled, sitting down opposite her. "You said you had something to speak about?"

Cogan acknowledged his question but took a different subject first. "How are you feeling?"

Knowing what Cogan meant, Ramsey shrugged and paused a little before answering. "I've felt peaceful since Friday night, actually. I had my chance to say goodbye to her but I still want to catch the one responsible for this."

Cogan's brow furrowed, noting Ramsey's matter-of-fact tone. "I see. How are you hoping to do that?"

Ramsey shrugged. "I haven't figured that part out yet. Someone else asked me the same thing yesterday," he told her, thinking about his conversation with Colonel Ryan. "Am I picking up a drop in your scepticism or are you taking the mickey out of me?"

Cogan kept a straight face, looking Ramsey in the eye, something she found easier to do now, and challenged him. "You're the psychic. You tell me."

Accepting the challenge, he looked the detective in the eyes, deep enough so that Cogan felt as though he was staring through her skull and into her brain; it unnerved her enough she wanted to look away, but she kept the gaze. After a pause that made Cogan even more uncomfortable, Ramsey grinned. "Are you going to let me hold your watch this time?"

Cogan didn't answer, but kept a raised eyebrow as she looked back at him, so Ramsey added, "Please?"

She smiled, "Good boy," removing the Casio G-Shock watch from her wrist and handing to him. "That's much better."

Ramsey laid the watch upon his upturned left palm, holding his other hand an inch or two above it, and waited. After half a minute of that with his eyes closed, Craig took a breath and allowed the information to flow through him. His eyes fluttered a moment, and a ball of sweat clung to his eyebrow as he breathed deepening his trance. At last, he settled and opened his eyes to look at Cogan. "This watch has been through a lot with you, Detective, and seen a lot of death and action. You have toured overseas as a lieutenant?"

Cogan had been reading about how fake psychics used cold reading. His question seemed to be fishing for clues, yet he had mentioned something specific. Was it a blind shot or was Ramsey genuine? She paused, considering her response with a poker face. "Tell me more."

He nodded, continuing his impressions. "You were orphaned young, have vague memories of your real parents, and your adoptive mother is still alive - she lives in Banksia Grove - you should visit her more often."

Cogan laughed. "I bet you say that to all people with elderly parents. How many other parents want the same?"

Ramsey answered with a nod. "True, but once a year, Brianna? Banksia Grove is just two hours drive from here. You could at least visit her. She has only seen you once since you returned from Timor and she doesn't like using the computer to check your rare emails."

Cogan felt shocked; she was not sure how Ramsey knew so much about her unless he was a skilled private investigator as most of that information could probably be found thorough legal means. He was convincing, but Cogan believed Ramsey needed to be tested more.

"What colour underwear am I wearing?" she blurted, not knowing what else she could ask.

Ramsey looked surprised, his eyes jerking a little to the side before returning to her. Cogan thought she had embarrassed the poor guy, as the question seemed forward, even if she meant it as the obvious challenge; the colour of her underwear was not on public record.

He allowed a smile to cross his face. Cogan looked into his eyes again, wondering if she could throw him off the scent, and waited.

"You already know what colour underwear you're wearing, Brianna," he responded, "but you really want to know how much I can pick up on your cases. I see you have spoken at length with your Inspector Myles. Although you don't believe in psychic powers or - oogedy boogedy" - his right fingers wiggled in the air as though casting spells - "you still want someone to prove you wrong. The question is, will you be willing to change your beliefs when you are shown proof of it otherwise?"

Cogan leaned back in her chair, and her brow furrowed as she processed his dialogue. How did he know about Inspector Myles? The Inspector had called her into his office after she returned from the funeral and asked her about Ramsey; he even related something of his own experiences with the psychic who helped him on a case the previous year. Wait! Craig and Inspector Myles knew each other. That's how he guessed it.

"What else can you tell me?"

Ramsey smiled, handing the watch back to Cogan, and their hands touched briefly; she felt something almost like electricity at his touch. "I'm not going to tell you about tall, dark strangers," he started. "There have been three deaths this morning. Two in the same incident. You madly want to tell me it's not related to a spirit, and you want to watch me squirm. In fact, you want me to claim again that it is a spirit, so you can tell me I'm wrong, right?"

Cogan's mouth opened in a broad smile. "So you admit to being a convincing fake?"

Ramsey snorted, paused, and looked at her. "It's not fake, and I am as real as the watch you hold in your hand. Three more have died since yesterday, and you are wondering if I will blame a spirit for these. Why? Because they are victims who were shot while driving. Detective Sergeant Cogan, as you know, that means we have a different killer. You're right that spirits don't use guns. Snipers don't leave tattoos on their victims either."

"What?" Cogan raised a quizzical eyebrow as the tattoo remark surprised her. *What tattoos?*

Ramsey's voice raised a notch, the rich bass increasing with volume, and his hand swept across her desk towards all of her folders. Although they were closed, he somehow knew their relation to all the road deaths that happened under strange circumstances. "Your Inspector is no fool either. Have respect for him, and the dead, and study the evidence under your nose, Brianna! You will find your tattoos there."

Cogan raised her own voice, standing up and leaning on her desk to look at him. "I have looked at the evidence, Mr Ramsey! That is my job, to look at the physical evidence to solve matters."

"Then do your job!" Ramsey's bellowing roar echoed from the office's walls as he stood there, leaning forward across the desk to mirror Cogan, their faces inches apart.

Cogan's sharp commanding tone rang back. "Stay out of my way then!"

Both Ramsey and Cogan fell silent, apart from their heavy breathing from the shouting, each aware of their proximity and the growing tension; neither dared make the first move, and they continued staring into each other's eyes like two cats ready to pounce. Then the phone rang.

"Awww!" Emily moaned with disappointment at the interruption and pleaded, "Don't answer it!"

Cogan and Ramsey pushed away from their face-off positions, each of them straightening their clothes. She picked it up on the third ring.

"Detective Sergeant Cogan," she responded, trying to slow her angry heartbeat down so she didn't sound too terse. Her expression turned to mild surprise and shock as she listened to the voice on the other end.

"Yes, sir," she nodded, listened and nodded again, feeling the uncomfortable awareness of Ramsey listening from the chair with a smug grin growing across his face. "I am speaking with him now - Oh, you heard - All the way down the hallway? - oh, okay, sorry, sir - yes, I understand, but -"

Ramsey stopped his smug look, seeing Cogan's mood drop as her superior continued speaking. His finger toyed with the cord leading to the telephone and he gathered information, using his psychic ability to eavesdrop on the other half of the conversation. He felt Cogan's embarrassment, it matched his own, and he took a deep breath before letting out his own tension. At last, Cogan hung up from the conversation. Ramsey stayed silent, letting Cogan recover, until she looked back at him with a controlled anger behind her eyes.

"That was Inspector Myles," she confirmed. "He asked if you will collaborate with me on the case."

Ramsey tightened his lips so he could nibble the skin inside his cheek every so slightly; it looked to Cogan as though he was pursing his lips.

"Well?" she asked.

"I'm waiting," he answered.

Cogan felt exasperated. "For what?"

"You haven't apologised, for starters."

Cogan inhaled, cursing inside herself, and Emily whispered, "Oh, you really are a meanie, Craig."

Ramsey ignored his ghostly companion and waited for Cogan who ran long fingers through her blonde hair before looking at him.

"I'm sorry," she told him. "I should not have insulted you when I am wanting your help."

Ramsey waited, sitting back in his chair with an ankle resting on his knee and his fingers steepled. His eyebrows raised as he waited.

"What?" Cogan asked. "I apologised. Isn't that enough?"

"You forgot to say, please."

Cogan sighed to herself. Was he kidding?

A few seconds passed with the apparent speed of a tense minute. "The Inspector would like you to help on the case please," Cogan finally stated.

"And?"

"Oh, you are pushing it, Craig Ramsey!" Emily

huffed. "You have made the poor girl work for it already. Don't be such a bastard?"

Cogan was fit to explode when Ramsey grinned, stood and turned to walk out the door. "I'll think about it."

As he approached the door, Cogan called after him, "It's the Inspector who wants you to help. I don't believe in your oogy-boogy bull, Mr Ramsey."

Ramsey stopped, just outside the door, and looked at her with a piercing stare. "One more thing, Detective Sergeant Cogan," he announced. "I have an answer for your question."

"What? Will you?" she asked.

He paused, answering, "It's blue. Red would suit you better," and left before Cogan responded in surprise.

Chapter 9

Brianna wanted to scream, to throw something to release the frustration and anger building up inside her, but she could not do that so she slammed the door hard. The walls shook and her detective certificate fell off the wall; its frame smashed on the cabinet, overbalancing, and dropping to the floor where the wooden frame and glass disintegrated. She turned her head towards it, upset with herself for losing control, picked up the damaged pieces and examined it. Her fingers passed over the paper, still intact, and felt the embossed letters, remembering things from the past. With a sigh, she placed the broken bits aside, making a mental note to have it repaired later.

Thoughts of Craig Ramsey flew through her mind, and she mulled his words like mincemeat in a grinder. Somehow, his impressions about her were correct. The personal things he told her were spot on: her adoption, her adoptive mother's name, and even about her tours with the Army. That impressed her, even if he neglected to name where she served - Afghanistan and East Timor. But she was glad he didn't; that could show his depth of knowledge about another man she once loved and lost on duty; she didn't need old ghosts returning. Oh! What if Ramsey *had* seen that?

Cogan jumped track to other thoughts, these relating to the road deaths. How did Ramsey know about the gunshots? They were not public knowledge yet.

She shook her head as even more thoughts tumbled through her fatigued mind. It was time to leave the office for an overdue break. She reached for the sports bag between her desk and the wall and slung it over her shoulder. Closing the office door behind her, she ignored a snide comment from a passing detective about slamming doors.

Ten minutes later, Cogan, dressed in her black tank top, black tights, and gym shoes, faced the large Everlast wall-mounted punching bag. She took a breath, centring herself, and took a short jab at the bag, feeling its resistance, before starting her first combination of straight punches, hook punches and then uppercuts. When she felt warmed up, she executed more combinations, mixing them up for each set. She grunted, feeling each blow jarring her arms as her gloved fists crashed into the bag, never relaxing the strength or speed at which she delivered them.

***

Meanwhile, Ramsey left Cogan's office with a head full of new knowledge, each little piece screaming to be understood. He hurried down the hallway and heard a loud slamming noise from the vicinity of the detective's office.

"Do you think she wants to scream?" he asked Emily, not concerned if anyone saw him speaking with himself.

His spirit companion smiled with a knowing look. "I bet you want her to scream too, Mr Ramsey!"

He turned to face Emily, holding the headquarters door open for a couple of officers to enter before he walked into the bright sunshine. "I don't know what you mean, Emily."

Emily Fraser's ghost hurried forward, facing him but staying two feet ahead of him as he strode along the footpath. She crooned in sing-song fashion. "She loves you, wants to kiss you, and you want to -"

"It looks like we have two killers out there," Ramsey interrupted, pretending to ignore Emily's gentle teasing; he didn't dare admit he felt aroused around the female detective. Other priorities filled his thoughts.

"A second killer?" Emily's features changed as she considered the idea. "Is that sniper you mentioned? I wondered if it was something you picked up from her past."

Ramsey remained silent, making his way towards the car park where his car, an ash-grey 2015 Jaguar XE, waited. He unlocked and entered it in one fluid motion, starting the engine with a roar. Emily sat in the front seat where she could watch him, but he stayed quiet, meaning he was processing information. By the time they arrived home, twenty minutes later, Ramsey was heading to his own workout.

Stepping out of his back door, Ramsey followed the gravel path leading through a lush Japanese-styled garden, dotted with Bonsai and a koi-filled pond. At last, he reached a building resembling a small cottage, unlocked its door, and entered, shutting the door to keep out the winter winds. Movement sensors detected his entry and turned the lights, illuminating a high-ceiling gymnasium and martial arts studio. Three large, heavy canvas bags hung from the building's high timber crossbeams; the rest of his workout area comprised a Wing Chun dummy in a corner and a wall-mounted rack of weaponry. With light sensors, a large curtain drew itself aside to reveal a window framing the outside Japanese garden. This was Craig Ramsey's haven from the outside world and a place he used often for meditation and exercise.

Now dressed in long black pants and white t-shirt he wore for martial arts training, he faced his Sifu Jing Yong, a Chinese spirit who lived in the kwoon. Ramsey and Jing

Yong had been friends for twenty years, almost as long as Ramsey had known Emily. Jing Yong, sitting in a meditative position with his back to the weapons, looked up at Ramsey and stood, his robes flowing about him.

They bowed off and moved into position, circling each other like territorial cats. Ramsey watched his spirit sifu's eyes, which proved useless - Jing Yong's expression remained blank - before focusing on his shoulders instead; he was looking for anything signalling Yong's first move. Jing Yong burst forward, faster than Ramsey expected, delivering a flurry of furious fists, the first five hitting Ramsey in the chest before he could side-step. He twisted, catching Yong's next strike, deflecting it and stepping around to deliver a fist to his teacher's jaw. Yong who had died centuries before, now existing in spirit form, felt the strike; he ignored the pain, recovering in time to stop Ramsey's next strike with an eagle claw move, locking Ramsey's elbow joint. Yong deflected Ramsey's force, using it to throw him to the hard floor.

Yong resumed his tall stance, his expression serene as he watched Ramsey flip upward from the floor to take a cat stance. "Empty your mind," he chided his student before jumping forward and lashing a foot out. Ramsey ducked, blocking the leg and pushing his Sifu off balance. Yong's other foot struck Ramsey's shoulder with the force of a hammer, knocking him over so both were on the floor. Regaining their stances with quick reflexes, they regained their stances and faced each other like warring tigers before resuming the fight. They continued sparring, Ramsey sweating from the effort. His Sifu also sweated but Ramsey knew it was all an illusion Yong manifested for effect. Each of them matched the other's strikes with an effective lock, block or evasion until Ramsey gained another advantage by backing his master up to the wall. Ducking down and stepping under Ramsey's punch, Yong appeared three steps away, and pulled a hair from his chest, blowing upon it.

As Yong's breath passed from his pursed lips, the hair split into the air, like the seeds of a dandelion, each piece transfiguring into another version of Yong. Ramsey's eyes opened with surprise as he spun around to survey the twelve opponents surrounding him.

"That's unfair, Yong," he panted, dodging his first opponent. He ducked a fist, feeling its breeze on his cheek, turned, grabbed the Yong clone's wrist with a twist, and smashed a fist into his elbow. The joint cracked like a gunshot, but Ramsey's opponent screamed louder before a punch to his throat silenced him. Still holding the man, Ramsey threw him in the path of a second opponent, and kicked the knee of a third. Ducking down, he twisted, spinning to deliver a hammer fist to the kidney of a fourth. Two more approached him from different sides as he felt another grab him from behind in a bear hug. Ramsey thrust his buttocks back hard, bowing a little as he winded his opponent, and took advantage. He grabbed the hugger's hand and elbow, applied a joint lock and swung the hugger into the path of two other opponents; flowing in the moment, Craig dropped to bow stance, blocking a downward strike with one hand while punching the second opponent's gut. A fourth Yong took him in a headlock, squeezing hard on his throat and punched his face. Ramsey tasted his blood's coppery tang but ignored it. Turning his head, face burying itself in Yong's body, he grabbed the fourth Yong's right leg with his left hand; simultaneously, his right hand snaked upwards to grab the hair on the back of his opponent's head. Then in one synchronised movement, he pulled on the hair, taking the fourth Yong's head off balance while lifting his leg and flipping him over onto the wooden floor. With eight opponents down, Ramsey turned to face the remaining four, each armed with swords.

Mouthing a swear word, Ramsey retreated, flipping somersaults towards the wall where he found his own sword - a black katana. He faintly knew of Emily's spirit sitting to the side, munching on something that could have been popcorn; she loved watching martial arts. Grabbing the katana, he blocked two swishing blades, the steel ringing in his ears, as he kicked behind him; his foot planted square in the stomach of a Yong double, winding it. Dodging a second blade stabbing from the side, he side-kicked, missing the opponent's head. He felt the wind of steel, ducked, and twisted away, not noticing the sharp blade had sliced off an inch of his hair that fell to the floor.

Ramsey side-stepped, manipulating the fight's layout so that his final three opponents could not reach him from different angles. His throat burned, sweat stung his eyes, and blood rushed through his ears with a thumping drumbeat. Centring his thoughts, he took a long controlled breath, focusing upon them. Yong's long black beard drew his attention, and he released a blood-curdling yell as he launched his attack. Ramsey's sword whistled through the air three times, each stroke cutting through defences before removing the first Yong's left hand; the next stroke of the katana's handle knocked him unconscious. The remaining two Yongs looked at each other, backing away in surprise, but Ramsey refused to fall for the ploy. He picked up a fallen sword and now held a katana in each hand as he faced the remaining pair. A bead of sweat trickled down his skin as he assessed their positions. Before they could attack, Ramsey he pressed forward, his sword a glittering wheel of strokes that disarmed the second-last opponent and "killed it". Breathing hard, he turned to face the final opponent.

Jing Yong's spirit looked at Ramsey, their eyes locking, and threw his sword to the side. Ramsey replied in kind by relinquishing his weapon.

Armed with only their fists, the two warriors rushed at each other in a dance of death; their fists flew with furious precision only to be blocked by the other. It was a fight between two equals - master and student - that moved as though by choreography. Block, punch, counter-attack, kick, parry, grip, throw, reverse. Neither of them gave ground to the other as they circled in a hail of blows. At last, Ramsey overcame Yong's defences and flipped his Sifu to the floor, pounding his head five times in quick succession to win the contest.

Yong's spirit proved to be the ultimate punching bag and sparring partner as he could take damage without suffering. His bruised body healed in seconds, and Yong stood to face Ramsey. Facing each other, they bowed, right fist held by left hand in the Chinese martial artist's way.

Smiling for the first time since Ramsey entered the kwoon, Yong took Ramsey's hand in a warm grip. "You did well, Ramsey, but your technique still needs to flow better."

Ramsey smiled back. "Thank you, Sifu."

***

Although they didn't know what the other was doing, Cogan and Ramsey each finished their workouts feeling satisfied with working their aggression out. If asked, they would have admitted to picturing the other person as their target while working out. Each showered at the same time as well and, although they were each thinking of the other as they washed, their thoughts ran over the earlier argument at the police station and how they could work together.

So it was a pleasant surprise to Ramsey, who was lazing in his living room and listening to Pearl Jam tunes, when the phone rang. Picking up the phone, and muting the music with his remote in the other hand, he answered it. "Hello, it's Craig Ramsey."

"Mr Ramsey? It's Detective Sergeant Cogan."

Surprised, Ramsey's eyes widened, and he sat up expecting another verbal onslaught from Cogan. "Yes, it is. How can I help you?"

Her voice paused on the other end for the merest moment, and Ramsey grinned; Cogan still felt anger from the argument. "About before," she started. "We need to discuss how you can help with the investigations."

"Do you need my help?" he asked, trying to not sound arrogant, as he leaned across to a coffee table and lifted his mug of green tea to drink.

There was the briefest pause, but Ramsey could still sense it. "The fact is there seems to be a change with the recent shootings of random people," Cogan answered. "As you mentioned, they have the tattoos in common, numbers that increase sequentially with each killing - except for those who are shot."

Ramsey nodded. "Yes, indicating a second killer."

"*Indicating*," Cogan stressed, "that we have people dying by non-accidental means. Normally that shouldn't be a detective issue. Since you claim this is by supernatural means, is there any reason you can't investigate that while I go after the shooter?"

Ramsey thought for a moment; something didn't seem right. She seemed to mix her sentences or thoughts as though using double-speak. Craig believed Detective Cogan wanted to investigate something more tangible - the sniper, for instance - leaving him to chase something she felt to be a wild goose chase. He felt like saying that but changed his mind. It fit what he planned proposing anyway before she pre-empted him. "Okay," he told her, "on one condition."

Cogan seemed surprised. "What's that?"

Ramsey grinned as he replied. "I will follow up on the spirit killer, which I have been doing already; You can chase your sniper, but only if I have access to your records from those I believe related to the spirit-"

"Done!" Cogan answered, eager to move things forward. "I will -"

"I haven't finished yet," Ramsey insisted. "Since I am cooperating with the police on this, and you have been a key investigator so far, I also need to be in conference with you so you can stay up to date."

"What?" Cogan's voice sounded shocked and deflated. Ramsey couldn't help smiling at that.

"You do want credit when the killings stop, don't you, Detective Cogan?"

He could almost hear Cogan's thoughts of

exasperation, confirming she hoped to have him out of her hair in the investigation. Her voice came back through the phone. "I'm not sure that's necessary. I'm happy to -"

"Great!" Ramsey responded with a cocky tone. "I'll talk to you later. Bye!"

He pressed the button on his phone, hanging up without giving Cogan a chance to respond.

Emily's laughter came to Ramsey's ears, surprising him as he didn't realise she was there and listening. "You two are so funny, Craig!"

Chapter 10

Black hatred filled the disconnected soul as his vision spotted three more people - three more fools who deserved to be culled like weeds from the human gene pool. The pickings here were good since coming to the Statton Motorway. A metaphor came to his thoughts, making him think of a billiards game, as he surveyed the scene with calculated precision. He used to enjoy billiards, but this would be his favourite game. The assassin landed in the Mitsubishi's passenger seat and stared hard at its driver, a tradesman according to the equipment in the utility's tray. He didn't favour tradesmen for some reason he couldn't remember, especially those driving utilities like this one. He felt they weren't good for much in society; they failed at mental skills such as mathematics of science, but they excelled as thoughtless hoons driving trucks and utilities. This ignorant specimen continued using the mobile phone, pressed to his head, the spirit assassin forced his immaterial finger into the driver's skull. Stirring his semi-solid fingertips through the frontal lobe, the assassin felt exhilarated as the victim's fingers went limp, dropping the smartphone to the floor of the vehicle.

The spirit knocked the driver's dead hands away, twisting the steering wheel, and the vehicle mounted the traffic island, crossing into the oncoming traffic. The orange Porsche's driver, a woman tanned from frequent beach visits, managed a choked scream before the collision. Metal screamed in torture punctuated by shattering glass as the runaway Mitsubishi crushed her car into the heavy semi-trailer behind her. Glass exploded from the semi-trailer's cab as the driver rocketed through the windscreen. The driver should have worn a seatbelt. His lacerated body shot through the air and stopped, impaled on the piping in the Mitsubishi's tray. A phone dropped from the truckie's twitching fingers, its display blackened as he died.

It all took thirteen seconds Traffic slowed. People stopped to leave their vehicles and help. Others took photos from their car as they passed. The spirit assassin finished marking the third victim's neck and turned to look at those who still drove by at a crawling pace. This would be too easy.

Picking one driver, he reached through the window, squelching her brain with his hand as she passed. The dead driver's foot relaxed on the brake pedal, and the car veered to the left before crunching into the guardrails. That car had no sooner stopped than another car crashed into it, followed by more collisions in a long line. At a sauntering pace, the spirit continued along the road, stabbing his hand either into their brains or into their chests to play with their internal organs. The highway transformed into a killing field of death and mayhem, a macabre spectacle for those who remained. Survivors beeped their horns and complained from their cars, most of them screaming in fright to learn they were looking at a growing number of fatalities.

The assassin flew from the motorway and landed on a nearby footbridge to watch the mayhem. What a lovely scene of destruction. If the mortals didn't understand his message earlier, this would surely reach through to them. Subtlety was no longer suitable.

His head turned around, something prickled his consciousness, stirring a memory. What was it? The assassin couldn't help feeling drawn to something, something that controlled his hunger, and he followed the compulsion until he saw her. Exerting his will, he appeared in the ash-grey VW Golf's front passenger seat. He watched the driver, as she drove, casually holding her iPhone to her ear, and he listened to her as she spoke, oblivious to his presence.

"I have to take a different direction, Stacey," she said, listening to the other person on the phone. "There's been another accident on the motorway. Yes, it's a pain. People should take more notice of what they're doing on the road."

The spirit assassin smiled to itself at those words. Yes, people should pay attention to what they are doing and their surroundings. He poised to strike, ready to raise the morning's body count more, but stopped. There was something about this woman. He couldn't take her eyes off her, the way she watched the traffic in the suburban streets, even while driving. She appeared to know something, did she know he was there?

"I'd guess it to be about fifteen minutes before I can pick you up." The woman continued talking and stopped at a stop sign to wait for a passing string of cars. "Others have the same idea of avoiding the motorway. The back streets are filling now from diverting traffic."

Mustering his discipline, the spirit assassin moved towards his victim when a sound caught him off-guard. He turned his head and saw a little girl in the back seat, her eyes looking straight at him, and he stopped. Recognition hit his thoughts.

"Daddy, you are not supposed to be here," the little girl told him, looking him in the eye. "We are coming to see you."

Coming to see him? To visit his grave? Did they really do that? He turned, looked at the woman driving. If a spirit could gasp, he did then. Shocked, he realised he could have murdered his own wife, the mother of his daughter! How could he have not recognised her?

Conflict overtook him, tearing at his insides, as he felt pulled between his obsession - killing the people who deserved to die - and the love for his wife and off-spring. Wasn't that what forced him forward, the pain of not being able to touch them as fate had pulled them apart? Memories flowed through his thoughts like a river flood, flashing images like debris and flotsam on the banks of his consciousness, causing him to hesitate, falter and then cry. How could he continue his mission, without taking the lives of the family he wanted to protect? The spirit assassin recalled the pregnant mother he met a few days ago, and how he could not kill her either without taking another innocent life. He had to do the same now, give his wife a reprieve to save his own daughter.

He yelled at his wife. "Get off the phone!"

"Get off the phone, Mummy!!" his daughter cried, knowing that her mother could not hear her father.

Her mother turned around to reply. "Mummy's on the phone, honey. Please be quiet."

"But -"

"But nothing."

The spirit assassin moaned, feeling the panic and inner conflict, and then inspiration struck. Pointing at the phone, he concentrated, it beeped in her hand and she moved the phone in front of her eyes to look.

"Nooo!!!" he cried, realising his mistake. Sending her

a message while she drove was the wrong thing! He darted his hand out, gaining enough mental force to knock the phone out of his wife's hand. The phone bounced to the car's floor, between his wife's feet, coming close to the brake pedal. Taking one hand off the wheel, she edged down, trying to reach it with her fingers.

The spirit cursed again. How could he have been so stupid? Panicking more, he tried to lift her up to view the road, but it was too late. She missed the stop sign, the car continued forward and an unnoticed car from the right blared its horn at her. Brakes squealed.

She had no time to apply her own brake.

Silence. There was no collision.

The car floated upwards, carrying them in the air out of harm's way, avoiding the oncoming car that stopped underneath it, missing a collision by a hair's breadth. The mother screamed, and her young daughter called out, "Wheeee," unnerving her mother with the noise. Like a miniature plane, the car continued flying before landing gently on the green lawn of a house opposite the cross-intersection.

The mother's heart pounded. Realising they were safe, she stopped screaming and unbuckled her seatbelt so she could check on her daughter. The little girl was laughing, looking towards the passenger seat; but at what, the mother wondered.

She heard a noise on the car's controls, and she glanced to see the radio's tuning changing through different stations until it came to a point of silence.

Her blood froze, and her heart wanted to stop when she heard it. That voice.

"Rachael... Stop using your phone while driving. I

love you." Static blurred the scratchy voice, but both mother and daughter recognised the voice unheard in so long.

"Daddy is on the radio," Rachael heard her daughter tell her.

She looked at her daughter, Rebecca, with wonder and awe at what she could not believe, and then back at the radio as it continued. If she didn't believe its first message, the second confirmed it. "Rebecca. I love you too. Be good for your Mum, okay?"

Rachael heard Rebecca reply to her father's voice from the radio but it didn't register. Her thoughts filled with shock from the strange events. Something tapped on the window, she jumped, screaming, and she saw someone at the window; it was the driver of the car she somehow avoided.

"Lady!" Rachael jumped with a start, heart thumping hard again, and she turned her head to see the man calling through her closed window. "Are you okay in there? Are you or the girl hurt?"

Rachael turned back to the radio, looking at it, but it remained silent. The man tapped upon the window again, trying the door and opening it.

"Damn," he exclaimed. "I don't know how you did that. The car doesn't even have a scratch. Lady, are you okay?"

Rachael picked up the mobile phone, surprised when she realised it was in the console now, instead of the floor. How did that happen? She turned, facing the fifty-something-year-old man. "I'm fine, thanks. I need to call the police. Are you okay?"

The man looked inside the vehicle. "I'm good,

unhurt, but wow! I don't know how your car flitted through the air like that - seen nothing like it." He checked the back seat. "Hey, there, honey, are you okay?"

***

How often do you see the news happen right in front of your eyes?

Sally Green brushed the long wind-blown honey-coloured hair from her face, positioning herself so that Drew, the television cameraman, could manage a better shot; the wind continued messing her hair. Drew repositioned the camera's tripod and turned the camera to a suitable angle, and lifted the boom microphone over her, before nodding towards her.

Sally smiled into the camera lens then, changing her mind, adopted a solemn expression. "There has been another serious accident on the Statton motorway this morning with an orange Porsche crushed between a semi-trailer and a utility. Inbound traffic has all but slowed to a halt and outbound traffic is congested as well. Witnesses report the Mitsubishi utility jumped from the outbound lanes, across the traffic island, and rammed head-on with the Porsche. The semi-trailer ploughed through them from behind, crushing the woman inside the Porsche. The occupants from all three vehicles died on impact."

Another camera shot showed the remains of the three-vehicle carnage. Police officers could be seen directing traffic around the scene.

"More tragedy revealed itself with the discovery of another twenty-nine fatalities, all of them within fifty metres of the original accident scene. Some of the cars were passing the scene when the drivers appeared to expire on the spot. Authorities have not yet commented on the

100

apparent cause."

Looking into the camera, she concluded, "This is Sally Green from Channel 90 news."

Sally waited a few seconds for Drew's signal and relaxed, letting her hand holding the microphone drop to her side as she looked around the scene. "Drew," she said, "I've seen nothing like this before, and I've seen some strange things over the past twenty years."

Drew nodded, using the camera to take shots of the police directing traffic, inspecting the damage, and a few took photos of the victims. "That is one heavy death toll. I don't get it. Were they all using mobile phones and texting or something?"

Sally shook her head. "I'll find out from my contact later, but this is the biggest thing I have seen since I worked for BGQ-8."

Drew, still taking shots, remained silent a moment before replying. "BGQ-8? Wasn't that the Banksia Grove station in the 1990's?"

"1987," Sally responded. "That was the year I met Predator. At least, that's the name we gave him."

"That long ago?" Drew blurted then kicked himself for his tactlessness. Sally's was in her mid-fifties although she never admitted it and it didn't always show due to her fitness regime. "I was just a kid back then."

Sally laughed. "I know, I'm getting older and no wiser." Something caught her attention, made her look at the outward-bound traffic. Call it instinct. Before knowing why, Sally jumped, narrowly avoiding a vehicle veering off the road and onto the traffic island before its crunching collision with a thick-trunked tree there.

Picking herself up from the ground and untangling

from Drew, Sally hurried to the crumpled vehicle. She thought she saw two people inside, but the tinted windows obscured the interior. Wrenching the driver's door open, she looked inside to see if she could help.

Sally stopped, her heart jumped in her chest, and bile rose in her throat. She couldn't control it. Vomit rose, ejaculated, and landed on the boots of the policeman who had come running to help.

That image would stay with her forever, looking into the horrific stare of a dead man.

***

The spirit assassin floated unseen from his latest victim's car, watching the journalist throwing up on the policeman's shoes. Did the reporter see him? He remembered seeing her eyes connect with his through the car's tinted window. Could it be? A grin floated through his awareness for a moment before a tiny sense of accomplishment flickered through him.

Maybe this time, people would take notice.

Chapter 11

Rachael tapped her foot, waiting for the police to arrive. Marty, the other driver involved, had said the police station told him a car would be out in twenty-to-thirty minutes; that was eight minutes ago. She didn't want to wait that long, needing to pick up her sister-in-law, in particular with Rebecca still in the car with her. She felt embarrassed and did not want to be waiting around. In a manner of speaking, there had been no accident. The car appeared to be in good working order, with no damage to it; the front lawn where the car landed could be a different story as the tyres left some muddy tracks where it gouged the grass. But Marty, the driver of the other car, insisted they should wait. He'd suffered no injuries, unless one counted the speeding heartbeat from watching a VW Golf flying through the air and landing safely on the other side of the road, and his car didn't have any damage either. Neither vehicle required towing.

Rachael had tried to convince Marty of those very reasons for not needing the police. But he insisted.

The previous events still played in her mind, creating an inner turmoil, and perhaps that is the real reason Marty insisted they wait. She must have appeared strange or lost, and why wouldn't she, after hearing the disembodied voice of her incapacitated husband coming through the radio, talking to her? Marty appeared to be in his seventies, maybe a widower; how would he feel if his dead wife spoke to him through the radio? She could bet he'd be distracted as well. But it wasn't really the voice alone that distracted her. She felt the shape of her phone through the cloth of her jacket's pocket, not daring to pick it out to look again, in case it reminded Marty. Rachael was unsure if he saw the mobile phone in her hand before the strange event, she couldn't call it an accident, and she didn't want to remind him. For now, it was best she kept that from his mind. If it had slipped his mind, it was best it stayed away; out of sight, out of mind.

The ambulance arrived first, pulling up on the street next to Rachael's car, and its driver stepped out to walk around towards her. The other bearer moved to the back of the ambulance to retrieve a bag of first aid equipment. Smiling, the driver approached. "What's happened?"

Marty started, piping in quickly with his old crony voice, his eyes bright. "This lady came through the crossing from over there," he pointed to the intersection, "and her car flew through the air, and plopped down on the lawn here."

Rachael shrugged. "Things happened so quickly. I had a sneezing fit from my hay fever and something else distracted me." She said this in a lowered voice, not wanting to Marty to pick up on how she down-played it. This could work out to her benefit.

The bearer arrived with the bag and the driver placed a stethoscope around his neck and put the ends in his ears, before checking on Rachael's vitals. The ambulance driver looked from Marty back to Rachael again, before asking, "How are you feeling now?"

Rachael's hay fever claim was true, but she had taken something for it that morning; the worst of it was over, but she still had a red nose and slightly weepy eyes. "Still an itchy nose," she answered, "but that's all."

"But the car flew through the air and landed here," Marty insisted. "See? How else could it get there?"

The bearer looked at the ambulance driver. "She seems okay."

By this time the police car finally arrived, having found its way through the back streets from a local station. The other cars were at the motorway still, trying to reach the other accident scene.

A burly officer, chewing gum in his oversized mouth, stepped out of the police car and approached the scene at the ambulance, looking at the VW Golf and Marty's Holden. "What's happened here?"

Marty, feeling excited, stepped in, relating what he had seen. He told the officer all about how he was travelling along the main road, how Rachael's car had sped out across the intersection and somehow started flying through the air to avoid colliding with him, before landing on the lawn. The police officer looked at Marty, trying to mask his disbelief. "You're saying it flew through the air? How high?"

The elderly man seemed rational enough, until he answered, "At least six feet in the air. I remember looking upwards as I drove under it."

The silence that followed was so powerful, one could have heard crickets chirruping from the next suburb.

"You drove under it?" The officer wrote this down in his notebook, scratching a few times as the ink didn't flow properly from his pen. "That sounds," he paused. "Pretty close. What happened then?"

Marty pointed at where Rachael's car had come from and started answering, not noticing the officer subtly moving his eyes to the ambulance bearer who nodded. While Marty spoke, the bearer excused himself and started checking Marty's blood pressure as well. Everyone listening could see how convinced Marty felt while relating the story again. Rachael remained silent, listening and waiting, as she also noticed the expressions on the ambulance driver, bearer and police officer. They found his story too wild and the physical evidence, two undamaged cars, seemed to speak differently.

The officer turned to Rachael. "How are you feeling, Mrs...?"

"Denton," she replied. "I'm fine. As I mentioned before, I had a sneezing fit from my hay fever I guess I lost control of my foot on the brake, but as far as the car flying?" Rachael shrugged.

Marty's attitude changed, when he heard her words, and he started shouting. "What?! How could you miss it? You flew over -"

Rachael shook her head. "Things moved so fast but I am sure I would have noticed my car flying - what did you say again? - six or so feet above the ground!"

Rachael hated lying but she felt it necessary; she felt the flying car had something to do with the message on her phone, from an unknown number but claiming to be her husband, and her husband's voice on the phone. Marty was doing a great job of appearing crazy by relating the story and she saw no need to join him. The burly cop, whose name she could not remember, looked at her, studying her expression and thinking to himself then looked at the old man who simply did not know when to be quiet. Rachael maintained control of her expressions, doing her best to not appear as though she was controlling them either, although she wanted to laugh so much.

The policeman looked inside the VW Golf at Rebecca, and Rachael felt her heart beat faster. *Please, don't say anything,* Rachael wished to herself.

"Hey there," he said to her, poking his head through the window. "How are you doing, little one?"

Rebecca looked back at the policeman, shyly. "I'm good. Are we going to jail?"

The policeman laughed, "No, honey, no one's going to jail," and turned around to the ambulance bearers. "Apart from the wild story, is everyone okay?"

The ambulance driver shrugged. "As well as they can be. I'd probably recommend a hospital visit for possible shock but they seem otherwise fine."

Rachael breathed a sigh of relief to herself. A hospital trip was closer to her original day's plans anyway.

Marty continued his tale about the flying car, asking why Rachael wouldn't corroborate her story as she was there. The policeman looked like he was about to explode with laughter at the story, stepping between them and thinking what a funny story this would be to tell the others at the station.

***

What a crappy way to start a Friday morning!

Cogan's original plan of visiting the morgue to talk to the police medical examiner, Dr Kroot, was a fizzle, thanks to a pile-up on the Statton motorway. She hadn't heard much about it yet but she had a feeling it was also related somehow to the other accidents she was investigating. As she drove her unmarked police car through the back streets, hoping to make up for some lost time from the motorway's obstruction, she wondered if their victims had bullet wounds or not. When the call went out, she contacted one of the constables, Grant Lennon, to collect as much information and pass it on to her while she attended the morgue for more information. Grant seemed happy enough to do it for Cogan, she thought, possibly because she had seen him checking her out a few times in the gym when he didn't think she was looking.

Cogan turned off the car's ignition and stepped out into the sunlight, her foot just missing a puddle from the night's rain, before locking the car and walking towards the building's entrance. The receptionist, Penny, with large librarian glasses framing her young brunette features, looked up and smiled at her in greeting.

"He's in there," Penny indicated towards a door Cogan recognised as the "operating room's" entrance. "He's been working on each of the three from yesterday but two more have come in."

Cogan thanked her, adding, "You may have more through soon. There's been another pile-up on the motorway."

Penny rolled her eyes, "Oh, great! What's happening here lately?"

Cogan pushed entered the first doors before putting a gown over her clothes and pushing her way through the next doors to the autopsy room. Although she heard Frank Sinatra's smooth voice coming from inside, as Kroot often played music (either classical music, Italian opera, or whatever else took Kroot's fancy), her mouth dropped at the sight.

Dr Kroot was singing along to Sinatra's "Come Fly With Me", serenading a fresh cadaver with his hands on the female body's shoulders; his face was close to its face as though he were about to kiss it, still unaware of Cogan's presence as he sang into a pair of bloody forceps like a microphone. His thinning brown hair hung partly over his spectacled eyes, covered by another pair of goggles over them, as he belted out a louder part of the song to the ceiling. Cogan knew Dr Kroot's eccentricities, but she still felt surprised every time she saw him acting out something new and weird from his mind, and she watched on. Dr Kroot, also affectionately known as the "mad doctor from South Africa", continued serenading the dead woman's body. He bent over her, singing in her ear before prodding into the corpse's right temple with the forceps.

Cogan cleared her throat and Dr Kroot looked up. "Am I interrupting?"

The doctor acknowledged Cogan's presence with a slight hand motion before he resumed his work, finally extracting a metallic object from the wound. It clinked in a kidney dish as he dropped it in as he delivered the final lyrics of Sinatra's song; he opened his arms out wide as he accepted the applause from the recorded concert.

Kroot placed his forceps aside, removed his goggles and pulled his cloth mask aside to reveal a wide smile. "Detective Sergeant Cogan! How did I know you were coming today?"

Cogan made an ironic smile, pointing at the cadaver on the table. "Did I leave you enough messages?"

Kroot made a smoker's laugh, the rough sound catching in his throat as he found himself about to cough; he loved her sarcastic humour when she let it show. "Yes, you did that, but as always you expect me to explain them to you, right?"

Cogan shrugged, looking closer at the wound and trying to ignore the smell of aging meat. "Pleasant, isn't it?" Kroot cracked, walking away with the kidney dish in hand. He placed it next to a lunch box, from which he picked up a large cream muffin; he casually bit into the muffin with relish. Kroot noticed Cogan watching him and said, "Would you like some?"

Cogan felt a little green, shaking her head in refusal. "What have you managed to find on these new victims?"

Kroot grinned, holding a finger up as he was trying to swallow before answering. "I'm glad these people came in," he responded. "They make a change from people with broken necks, although I found the ones with mashed brains, despite any entry marks, very fascinating."

"What?" Cogan asked.

"It was strange," Kroot told her, pausing to picture it as he described it. "It was as though someone stuck a spoon or something into their head, usually through the frontal lobe, and mashed the brains about the place. Have you ever heard of such a thing?" He licked some cream from his finger and pointed to the kidney dish. "This is something more tangible for me, not as exciting, but it's a relief to find something mundane. It's a bullet. See?"

He grabbed another instrument, picking up the bullet with it to show her. It still had some bodily fluids sitting on its surface but it was definitely a bullet.

"That looks like it came from a rifle," she said, recognising the shape of it.

"Yes, it is from a rifle," he answered, "and I am betting it's been shot from a long distance. This lovely lady here (he motioned to the corpse on the examination table) is from last night, and I have a feeling it is the same type of bullet as those from yesterday."

"I never saw the ones from yesterday's victims," she told him. "Has anything come back from ballistics?"

Dr Kroot's eyes opened wider and his mouth opened

slightly. "Ah! I haven't checked my email yet. Let me see."

Turning quickly, humming the Sinatra song still, he strode towards his nearby laptop to punch a few keys. The screen, previously showing a screen-saver from Star Wars, changed and he scrolled through his emails. "Ah! Here we are," he exclaimed.

Cogan stood behind him, trying to see the screen and felt mild surprise at Dr Kroot's next words.

"You're not going to believe this!" Kroot ejaculated, excitedly. "It looks like the bullet may have been fired from an SR-98." He paused to think. "Isn't that -"

"It's an Australian military weapon," she confirmed, stroking her chin and letting her gaze penetrate the screen.

"Oh?" Dr Kroot enquired. "How do you know about that?"

Cogan stood up from looking at the screen, casting her gaze towards the woman's body on the examination table. "I knew someone who used one when I worked in the Army years ago," her voice faded a little as she answered, eyes glazing a little as her words trailed.

Ten round magazine. It's got a folding butt on it, lets it fire at a target 800 metres away, even more than that. I can shoot the balls off a flea at 900 metres with this baby.

Kroot's voice broke through her trip down memory lane, a path that took her past a sore part of the past; Cogan blinked, turning to face him.

"What?"

"I said I didn't know you were in the Army. How long ago?"

Cogan shrugged. "A lifetime ago, in the past, where it belongs."

***

Ramsey stepped from his bedroom, dressed in his immaculate black suit with royal blue shirt from Roger David, and readjusted his purple tie. It was Friday, the day when he attended a venue for high tea with the Lady Mayoress' Club. They often asked him to attend as a speaker, and to deliver his psychic readings for them. Although he never charged for that particular event, he found them useful for networking purposes and obtaining other paid jobs. The Lady Mayoress' Club met monthly and, although he felt a higher priority to the case, he had to attend this just the same; he enjoyed it anyway.

Walking down the hallway towards the kitchen, he noticed Tyrone's bedroom door was opened. Turning his gaze, he noticed the teenager laying on his bed, reading a textbook. Tyrone, although still away from school on bereavement, had buried himself in school work in the wake of his sister's death. It was only the second day since the funeral, and their last contact with Debra's spirit, but nothing had changed much for the boy who still missed his sister.

Ramsey checked his watch, still plenty of time, and knocked on Tyrone's door; the boy lifted his eyes and looked at his guardian.

"Hitting the books a bit hard?" Ramsey asked, casually, indicating the physics book in Tyrone's hand.

Tyrone's eyes appeared puffy with a tinge of pink in the whites. "I'm fine, Uncle Craig," he answered, just a bit impatiently, before looking back at the text.

Ramsey took a breath, stepped inside the room, approaching but keeping his distance so he wouldn't crowd the boy. "It's new for me too."

Tyrone shrugged, pretending to read but obviously

not taking anything in. Ramsey took the hint; Tyrone didn't want to talk about it, at least not right now.

"I'm getting a bite to eat before heading off to my booking," Ramsey started, taking a quarter turn towards the door. "Do you want me to get you anything?"

Tyrone shrugged. "No, thanks. I'll be out there later." He sounded a little brighter, maybe a little forced, but he was trying to be brave at least.

"Brilliant!" Ramsey mouthed, preparing for a fist-pump with the teenager but it didn't happen. Pausing for an uneasy beat, Ramsey turned and walked out the door. "I'm boiling some water if you want a drink," he said, walking out the door. "We can talk tonight."

Tyrone listened to his guardian's footsteps and, when the sound of a kettle being filled with water told him Ramsey was in the kitchen, he let his breath out in a sigh. Looking behind the bedroom door, he saw the apparition watching him. The dark shape moved towards him, stopping three feet away. The teenager looked it in the "eye".

"I know what you're saying but how do I know it will work?" he asked.

"Your uncle Craig Ramsey," the voice responded, with a sarcastic tone on 'uncle', "he may mean well but he doesn't have half of what it takes to get this job done, if you want to avenge your sister."

Tyrone looked at the PC tablet he had hidden inside the physics textbook, indicating its screen. "Maybe, but this?"

"It's the only way, my friend," the dark shape responded. "What do you say?"

Tyrone curled his bottom lip, letting it scrape against

his chin for a few moments, before answering. "Let me think on it. I don't want to hurt uncle Craig."

"It won't matter in the end," the voice responded sharply. "You will avenge Debra, I will help you, and you will be able to see her whenever you want."

***

Detective Cogan needed time to think, just for a moment, when she returned from Dr Kroot's.

Did she know what an SR-98 was? Yes, she did, and she had seen what they could do to someone in the hands of an expert sniper, which is why the Australian Army used them. The corpse she saw on the table in Dr Kroot's examination room served as a visual reminder of that.

Times had not changed much through history. In the old days of the Five Hundred War, the English longbow archers suffered torture at the hands of the French because of how deadly their long range weapons could be on the battlefield, decimating troops before they could even get close. They outranked the French crossbows, firing up to ten arrows in the time it took to load one crossbow bolt, which also had less power and range. Modern snipers were the equivalent, being able to pick off enemies quickly from an even further distance, and they suffered just as badly when caught by the enemy. A memory flooded through her head; flashes of pain, foreign voices, another voice, this one with a face, much friendlier, running through the desert, and hiding; she brushed it away, feeling the hot sting in her eye. It is best kept in the past.

SR-98's, while available on the internet to those who know how to find them, were not that commonly used. The shooter possessed a military background, and Cogan knew of an Army base just outside Statton.

Cogan wiped her eyes, took a settling breath, and picked up her 'phone.

***

His hands moved methodically in the darkened room, knowing their way around the weapon he held. His dexterous fingers manipulated each piece, undoing it, oiling, cleaning and reassembling. The television set provided the only illumination in the blackened room. The sound was turned right down; he didn't need to hear it; the picture provided all the words he needed to know.

Sally Green's image appeared on the screen, presenting a news story that looked like it was at a motorway. Definitely some carnage there.

He paused, the reassembled rifle felt just right in his hands, and he lifted the weapon to aim it at the television. He lowered the weapon again to watch the journalist, watched her lips as she spoke and then aimed again. There was a time, quarter of a century ago, he would have liked kissing those lips. Times change as one grows older and the "older woman crush" ages as well, but Sally still looked good.

His thoughts quickly moved to the news story itself. More crashes and deaths on the roads? Whenever there's a traffic jam, you could be assured that at least one dumb-arse prick has caused it. When there's an accident, it still only took one of them. Temporary Australians, he called them. The problem with Temporary Australians is they tend to take the innocent with them as well.

He pulled the trigger; no bang, just a dry click like a fool's death rattle.

That had to stop.

That's why he had to kill some more fools today.

Chapter 12

The women surrounded Ramsey as he delivered his reading to Mrs Taylor, the deputy mayor's wife, who hung on his every word; they did too, listening for anything they might recognise or pick up to gossip about in their circles later. Ramsey, however, was always careful whilst reading aloud for them because he knew why they liked his readings. No matter what he saw, he delivered it as positively as he could so his client felt empowered. He understood the drama and the intrigue, how to deliver the story to them, and he also knew that the future can be changed through human will.

He held Mrs Taylor's right hand in his, his face-up palm holding her face-down palm, while his other hand hovered above hers. Ramsey didn't need to use the other hand, his psychometric ability relied on touch, but it created good theatre just the same. They all loved it.

"I see a beautiful garden," he intoned, gazing off into nothingness as he described his visions. "It looks resplendent and vibrant. Your husband is not the green finger, you are."

Mrs Taylor swallowed, her pupils large as she nodded.

Ramsey continued, "I don't know all the flowers, but some names are coming to me as I can see carnations, some pink pansies - they are your favourite - and I also see, what are they? Ah! Def - Delph -"

"Delphiniums," Mrs Taylor offered.

"Yes!" Ramsey exclaimed, "but that is not all. There's a pathway through them, not stone but a lawn path, that leads towards a larger topiary like I have never seen before."

He looked at Mrs Taylor, noticing how her eyes drunk him in and changed his tone slightly, stepping back from the anticipation. "It's arranged in a fan-shape, I can see how round it, oh! Wait, there's a head on it. Is it? Yes, it's in the shape of a peacock, and I can see a plaque there."

"Yes, and?" Mrs Taylor asked, swallowing again and thrusting her upper body forward a little. Ramsey could feel it and he could also hear the hushed whispers of two of the other women who listened in. Emily's voice in his ear also confirmed it.

"Stop encouraging her," she hissed in his ear. "She's going to pop out of her dress soon."

Ramsey suppressed a grin and looked back at Mrs Taylor. "Amanda," he started. "I see the flower arrangement you sponsored winning at the Statton Botanical Gardens Flower Show."

"Oh! You are such a lucky charm!" she answered, and Ramsey found himself stepping back as she stepped forward.

"Give my regards to the Deputy Mayor," he smiled, keeping his distance.

"Do me! Do me!" a couple of other women responded, thrusting their hands out for him, and he had to hold back from laughing.

"Do me! Do me!" Emily imitated sarcastically. "They sound like a bunch of hussies!"

Ramsey couldn't help smiling at Emily's joke, and laughed, picking the next volunteer. He held her hand in his and was about to speak when a vision, dark and suffocating, enveloped him.

He breathed, relaxing, asking permission from the

vision to see everything so he could understand better. A moment later, he found himself sitting in the driver's seat of a car he didn't recognise. His right hand was on the wheel, the other was in Mrs Taylor's lap. No, it wasn't just her lap, it was on her bare thigh, moving underneath her red skirt. He looked towards her face, seeing it contorted in an ecstatic expression, pleasurable moans escaping her mouth. Ramsey tried to stop but he couldn't; he was in a vision, not a dream. He happened to look towards the window, noticing it was dark outside, just the street and shop lights outside. It looked like he was on one of the main streets of Statton, in the city's centre. His gaze caught his reflection in the darkened window, only it wasn't his face that looked back; it wasn't the deputy Mayor's either.

A ringing sound snapped his attention towards the iPhone docked on the console's charger. He reached for it, looking at its screen, reading the caller's name, Jenny, seeing the photo displayed; it wasn't Mrs Taylor's face.

His hand lifted the phone to his ear. "Hi, babe!" It wasn't his voice answering, but it sounded familiar.

"Honey," a voice responded from the phone's speaker. "Where are you?"

He paused. Ramsey's thoughts were not the same as the thoughts coming from "him" in the vision. "I've been working back, babe. Time got away from me."

"Is that bitch working you hard?" The voice sounded angry, yet sympathetic with him.

He looked at Mrs Taylor, felt her hand in his lap, fingers manipulating him down there. "Yeah, she has been. I'm the other side of town at the moment. I'll be home in about -"

BAM! He saw it a moment before it hit, glass smashing, searing pain that lasted barely a moment. The pole that speared through the windscreen crushed his head through the driver's seat. The car tipped, the world whirled about.

Ramsey woke from the vision, his volunteer searching his eyes in wonder. "What do you see?" she asked.

Ramsey looked at her, his physical vision coming back to replace the psychic vision. His eyes still adjusting, he caught eye contact and recognised her. "Your name's Jenny?"

The beautiful brunette looked back at him, starting to shake a little with worry, and nodded quickly. She knew that it wasn't the best.

He squeezed her hand, reassuringly, learning at the same time that she had two young children and a husband. "Your husband's name is Jamie?"

Her voice cracked. "Yes! How did you -?"

"You should know by now," he answered, forcing a humorous smile as he tried to settle his heartbeat. What a vision!

"Jamie has been working back late a lot lately, hasn't he?" - she nodded - "And you want him to stop it?"

She looked towards Mrs Taylor and Ramsey noticed her expression; she knew Mrs Taylor's reputation as an immoral man-eater and how she preyed on married men. "Yes, I don't want him to miss out on the children, watching them grow. They love their Dad a lot."

Ramsey excused himself from the group, ushering Jenny away to the side with him. He pulled out a chair from a nearby table, asking her to sit next to him, and took her hand again; this time it was for reassurance. He looked her in the eye.

"Jenny," he spoke clearly, "I believe you know what I know, right?"

She paused and he squeezed her hand gently; Jenny nodded, a tear formed in her eyes. "It's been going on for some time. I know what's been going on and I have confronted that bitch." Looking at him, Jenny's eyes glistened; he handed her a handkerchief and she laughed. "I didn't know that men still carried these."

Ramsey shrugged, his head moving side-to-side. "I wasn't sure why I brought it with me until now either." She laughed at that and he continued. "Jenny, what I have to say is not all good, but sometimes you have to go through hard times to grow stronger, and I know you will. Can you do me a favour?"

A little relief flooded through her; he continued. "Please understand that I don't like giving bad news, and that's because I am careful to not give you a self-fulfilling prophecy. What I know is that you will experience loss, but I want you to remain strong." Ramsey paused, picking up more vibrations from her as he spoke. "Your children will grow up to be strong and good, and you will get to watch them all get through college, marry and have children. And you will never be alone."

She bit her lip, thinking. "He's going to leave me, isn't he?"

Ramsey held both of her hands between his, looking her in the eye. He didn't like predicting death and he didn't like delivering bad news either, particularly when at a party, which should be a happy occasion. Ramsey debated in his mind. Should he tell her Jamie was going to die? No, he couldn't do that. Should he tell her to not call her husband tonight, in the hope of preserving her life? Ramsey generally believed the future is not set; there were times when he had been able to change the future by changing just one little thing. This time, however, he knew there was no way around it. He had also seen an alternative future; in that one, Jenny called him sooner and Jamie started to drive home, still answering the phone when his lover rang him, and dying in another accident. A third future also presented itself to him and, in that one, both Jenny and Jamie died. Either way, Jamie was going to die.

"Yes, and not in the way you expect, but it will be soon." Ramsey patted her hand, letting her know the reading was over. "Just stay strong, okay?"

Jenny managed a smile. She didn't know everything that Ramsey meant but she understood there would be some hard times soon, and that she had to stay strong for the kids.

***

The rest of the Lady Mayoress' Club event went smoothly, much to Ramsey's relief as he wanted to keep his contributions a positive experience for everyone. It must have worked; the other attendants still lined up for readings with him, and only a few of them wanted their reading to be private, asking him for a card to book him later. As he read each lady, he noticed a few gave him visions similar to Jenny's, visions of a horrible death by road accident. Although Ramsey still felt the aftershock of Jenny's reading, this prepared him so he could give a better response by warning them to "don't answer Gary's call while you are driving, it's not that important" or something similar.

Emily, who had been watching throughout the party

and saw the incident with Jenny, asked Ramsey about it on the drive home.

"This spirit is going to keep on killing people, Emily," he responded. "I saw it and I know one of the people he will attack tonight."

Emily looked shocked. "Do you mean he's going to kill one of those ladies? Is it that horrible tarty Mrs Taylor?"

Ramsey turned a corner, probably a little sharply but Emily didn't notice, being a phantom. He laughed. "Not exactly. She is there when it happens though."

"Ooh," she responded in disgust. "I hope that changes! Who is with her? Not that slutty Sarah?"

Ramsey looked at Emily in disbelief. "Emily! I've never known you to be so judgemental before."

Emily snorted, a hint of a smile appearing on her face with a twinkle in her eyes. "Women never change in history, Craig, dear," she answered. "There are always those who want to sample everything they can, even if it's not theirs." Her eyes lowered a little and Ramsey wondered if she meant something from her past.

"Anyway, I picked it up from Jenny's reading that something will happen -"

"Oh no!" Emily cried. "I like Jenny, the poor thing! You have to help her."

Ramsey smiled. "She will be fine," he responded. "The thing is, I think I know what attracts this spirit to kill his victims."

Ramsey started explaining what he noticed from the visions. Every single victim was in a car and using their mobile phone while driving. The spirit never attacked the passengers using phones, only the drivers who let the phone distract them.

Emily clapped her hands with the revelation. "Wonderful! How come no one has noticed it before and said something?"

Ramsey laughed aloud. "They have! For the past five years, at least, the message has been in the media. The police even lay charges and heavy fines on those caught talking on their mobile phones while driving."

Emily's eyebrow raised in disbelief. "And no one listens?"

Ramsey paused, pressing the accelerator when the light changed to green. "Yeah, some do. A few may stop using their phones altogether, a lot of hands-free devices are marketed - just like the blue-tooth I have for my phone - but there are still the temporary Australians who continue to try to use them. They know they're doing wrong and so they try to hide it by using the phone in their laps, for example. Either way, it still distracts them from the road."

"Temporary Australians?"

"Yeah," Ramsey answered. "Once they're dead, they belong elsewhere."

"And It is such a shame they take innocent lives with them," Emily responded, her voice lowered as her tone saddened.

Ramsey nodded, realising that he had been talking about Debra, Tyrone's sister; she had been using a mobile phone when the spirit attacked, killing her. Oh! Tyrone! He glanced at the car's clock, seeing the time.

"I'm meant to be talking to Tyrone tonight," Ramsey exclaimed, realising he had nearly forgotten, "but I have to try catching that spirit tonight and stop him."

"Why don't you talk to the lad when we get home?"

Emily suggested. "He seemed quiet this morning when you spoke with him."

Ramsey nodded, agreeing. He felt worried about Tyrone. Ramsey still felt sad at the mention of Debra, the mere thought of her summoned tears, and he knew Tyrone would be feeling it even worse. Emily read Ramsey's expression, placed a hand on his, sending a warm comforting stream of feeling through him. "Talk with him, Ramsey. Spend some time with him."

***

Tyrone was out when Emily and Ramsey arrived home. Ramsey found a note on the kitchen bench from Tyrone, saying that he was visiting a friend's place. Ramsey's eyebrows furrowed a little when he read it; Tyrone didn't tell him of any such plans before. Perhaps it was for the best if the teenager felt more comfortable with other school friends than with him right now. The note didn't say how long he would be away though.

He showed the note to Emily, an experienced mother herself in a past life. She agreed; it wasn't like Tyrone to not say how long he would be away for but he needed some time.

Ramsey thought about it a moment, picked up his mobile phone, tapping a message into it for Tyrone. **Hey, Ty. I'm sorry I missed you. Enjoy yourself. Which friend are you visiting?**

Placing the phone on the bench, he turned towards the fridge, retrieving some fruit and ice to make a smoothie. Tyrone's reply beeped through the phone as Ramsey sliced the fruit. With a clean little finger, Ramsey swiped the phone and it revealed the message.

Hi Unc, with Malcolm and some others. Bye. T

Ramsey nodded, a thoughtful expression on his face, and continued making the smoothie. Ramsey knew Malcolm, a good kid, and his parents. Tyrone would be fine and they'd call him if anything happened.

"Emily," he said, taking a sip from his orange and pineapple smoothie. "Looks like I won't get to talk with Tyrone tonight. How do you feel about doing a stake-out tonight?"

***

It was the late afternoon when Ramsey entered the solitude of his meditation chamber, a small room in his house he had specially altered for the purpose. Although he often meditated in the backyard, facing the rising morning sun, the meditation room proved more useful in the cold wet weather. Ramsey had earlier written down everything he could remember from the vision with Jenny. Jamie's car clock indicated it was 7:08pm when the spirit was due to attack, so Ramsey started relaxing on the futon at 6:00pm.

Ever since he first met Emily, many years ago, Ramsey had devoted himself to learning astral travel. His first astral experiences occurred when he used to be asleep, or just drifting off. He would think he was walking, bouncing as though in low gravity, sometimes he would feel like he was swimming through air and pushing himself through, followed by the gut-wrenching sensation of falling through space before waking with a bump. These days, Ramsey could accomplish much smoother landings, thanks to years of practice at entering the state and leaving it.

Laying down on the soft mattress, Ramsey steadied his breathing and centred himself. He focused upon each breath, letting it come and go rhythmically, as he concentrated upon relaxing each part of his body. Before long, he felt the internal shift as his astral self released itself from the physical body. Ramsey smiled internally, feeling himself rise gently, floating upward as though levitating. He opened his eyes, feeling calm and relaxed. Using his will, he manoeuvred his astral self into a standing position and looked back at "physical Ramsey"; the physical body lay there, breathing steadily, controlling itself so that he could move freely.

He looked beside him saw Emily standing there. She appeared more physical to him now, shining slightly, but not appearing as a transparent spirit to him as she did otherwise.

"Let's move," he said, grinning. "See you at the intersection, where Debra crashed."

He visualised the scene, thought of himself there, and felt a melting sensation across himself before he appeared at the intersection. Emily appeared next to him shortly after.

"So, here we are," Emily said as they looked around.

While in an astral self, things looked different and yet the same, to Ramsey. While in a physical state, Ramsey saw the astral and spirit things as immaterial, semi-transparent, similar to a hologram; now it was the polar opposite. Astral beings and objects appeared solid, enough for him to touch and feel, while the physical universe was not immaterial although he could influence it as well.

"We're early," Emily observed, motioning to the City Hall's clock that showed 6:38pm.

"Good," Ramsey replied, looking about at the surroundings. The physical world's sounds appeared muted and, for want of a less ironic term, ghostly. Some people walked about on the streets and Ramsey studied them, seeing most of them were spirits. The spirit world never really stopped operating, the ghosts of the dead continuing the things they used to do in their living days. Thankfully most of them passed on to the "White Light" as it could get quite crowded otherwise. "It gives me a chance to look for the hooded spirit. Maybe he hangs out, waiting for people who are using their mobile phones."

"Do you remember where the vision showed the murder?" Emily asked.

Ramsey did; visions from psychometry seemed clearer while in astral form. "Over there," he pointed across the street. "The car was heading out of the city down that direction."

"Perhaps some others," Emily pointed at the solid-appearing phantoms walking by, "have seen him?"

They moved in different directions, asking different phantom people if they had seen a hooded spirit around. A few apparitions ignored them but most confirmed that they hadn't seen any since the morning. They had seen him quite a few times before, being locals.

"Oi!"

Ramsey turned to face the same labourer spirit, to whom he had spoken the previous week, approaching him.

"Are you looking for that Reaper guy?" he half-shouted.

Ramsey nodded. "Have you seen him?"

"Not lately meself, but is that him there?" the spirit pointed towards the traffic.

Ramsey turned about, seeing a hooded figure floating quickly towards an old turquoise Corolla. He whistled loudly, summoning Emily who turned and looked towards where Ramsey pointed. The hooded figure must be starting sooner, with Jamie being the second victim of the evening. He had to stop him, just the same.

Concentrating his will, Ramsey found himself flying quickly after the Corolla. He focused, trying to see the hooded assassin more clearly, gain a better visual in case he lost him. Emily caught up beside him.

"It looks like we're in time," she shouted, above the traffic noise undulating about them.

"Let's do it!" Ramsey called back. He sped up, diving through the back window and appeared in the Corolla's back-seat.

The hooded figure hadn't noticed him and, better still, the driver had not sensed him either. Emily sat beside Ramsey, staying quiet as well.

Now they were close enough to see the hooded spirit's features much better, discerning him to be a young man possibly in his early thirties; his scarred and unshaven face appeared animated and bright as he spoke to the female driver. Ramsey eyed the spirit's hands and knuckles, noting them to also hold scars as though skinned in a fight; were they hints of violence? The driver was young; her blonde hair appeared dirty although it had been brushed into order, and Ramsey noted through the rear-view mirror's reflection that tears streamed down her face.

The spirit placed a hand upon her shoulder and she reacted as though she could feel it; otherwise she kept her attention upon the road. "Babe," he whispered, in a loving voice, "I'm sorry for being an asshole the past few weeks. With the baby due (Emily noted the growing bump on the driver's stomach) I freaked." He paused a moment to touch the baby bump, caressing it lightly and lovingly. "I think it's going to be a girl. I don't know how I know, I just do, and I know she's going to be beautiful just like her Mum."

As the spirit sniffed, Emily nudged Ramsey who looked back at her. Nodding, they decided to leave the scene and stopped still, letting the car carry the hooded figure and its driver away while they stood in the middle of the street. They ignored the other cars and trucks passing through them as they walked to the road's edge.

"There's no way that gorgeous man could be the murderer," she told Ramsey with certainty. A tear ran down her face. "Did you hear the way he spoke with her? It's the way I talked to my son after I died. That poor man only wanted to have last words with his wife."

Ramsey felt disheartened by the miss. He was hoping to have been able to catch the spirit responsible for the killings before it came to the incident in his vision. "Look around for pipes, Emily," he responded, focused on finding the spirit first. "The killer used a pipe, roughly about a foot in diameter."

"Oh, you can be like a pit-bull terrier," she told him, "only worse."

"What?" Ramsey responded, slightly distracted.

"Only a pit-bull lets go," Emily grumbled. She saw something and pointed upwards. "What about a flagpole?"

Ramsey tracked her pointing finger, looking upwards to the top of a nearby government building with its Australian flag still flapping in the darkness. He recalled the vision, nodding. "That could be it."

He started floating up towards the top of the building when he noticed a dark shape hurtle past, in the corner of his eye. Stopping in mid-flight, he twisted and manoeuvred himself back in pursuit. "There he is, Emily!" He looked ahead of the hooded figure, saw the target; it was a single driver, a mobile phone held to his head while he talked.

He didn't stop to think; Ramsey willed himself inside the car's back-seat, expecting the assassin to be there. Emily appeared at the car's side, level with the back doors. Ramsey acted first, lashing his astral palm at the driver's arm. The driver cried out in pained shock, dropping the phone. The spirit assassin screamed in anger, having been poised to strike from the front passenger's seat. He turned to face Ramsey, eyes glowing in rage. Ramsey's fist rammed through the car seat, hitting the assassin in the mouth. Although the spirit was as immaterial as himself, Ramsey felt its face seem to melt around his own hand. It grabbed his wrist and elbow, locking the joint and floating up out of the car with him; its foot lashed out, kicking him in the stomach.

Ramsey groaned; the blow hurt, as much as a physical punch would hurt his physical body. Reversing the lock, he twisted and delivered a flurry of punches to the spirit's face. Dazed, it fled backwards in the air, not removing its gaze from Ramsey. "Who are you?"

"You killed my daughter!" Ramsey shouted back.

The spirit assassin faltered slightly, appearing surprised. "We all have our losses," it responded, rocketing towards Ramsey to hit him full force in the face.

Ramsey spun back, trying to reduce the impact in an attempt to not be sent back to his physical body, which would end the fight prematurely. Lifting his hands, he blocked more astral punches from the spirit assassin before twisting to the side, catching his astral opponent's arm and throwing him to the ground. Ramsey knew the ground could not physically stop the ghost. The fighting was purely a battle of the minds and beliefs. If his opponent believed the ground would hurt him, it would.

The heavy impact reached Ramsey's ears, followed by the spirit's winded guard. Ramsey landed on top of the spirit, pinning it to the ground as he delivered a series of fast heavy punches to his opponent's face. Pain wracked his wrist as the spirit blocked a blow, catching him and wrestling him to the ground. The spirit twisted on top and delivered a palm strike to his jaw. He felt that!

Another blow landed to his face, followed by another. A car drove straight through their immaterial bodies, disorienting both of them but separating them as well. The spirit rose in the air, facing Ramsey who was still on the ground and regaining his thoughts. His spirit opponent seemed to be particularly well-practised in astral combat.

"When did you train with Spirit Force?" Ramsey called to it, but he was answered with fist-sized pieces of bitumen spraying him from the edge of the road. The bitumen passed harmlessly through him but smashed nearby store windows, setting off ringing alarms that echoed through the street-lit night.

Ramsey floated upward towards the spirit but it fled towards a nearby roof. More pieces of stone hailed towards him. Catching them, he psychically rearranged them into a large cannonball-sized rock. Looking upward, preparing to send the large missile back, he stopped in surprise.

"Shit."

He hadn't noticed the spirit used Ramsey's distraction

to its own advantage.

Ramsey was too slow.

The first flagpole flew through him, its flag flapping wildly in its flight.

Glass shattered; something crunched. Another crunch followed. Then another as the third flagpole connected with the ground.

A horn blared, followed by a crumpling impact.

Ramsey turned, feeling the sick twisting knot in his psyche, as he realised he was late; too late.

Shock filled his astral self as he beheld the impaled car's windscreen, the flag flapping in the breeze and the end of the pole stuck firmly through a man's head and car seat. The driver's hand was at his head, dropping to its side, and a mobile phone fell from his limp fingers. Mrs Taylor, her dress hitched up on her lap, exposing her moist bare privates, and her hand still in the dead man's pants, screamed loudly. The car had collided with another parked car, its bonnet popped open with steam spraying into the air.

Another sound reached his ear, something familiar. Something pulled at his astral self and he felt himself losing control.

"No!" he shouted in frustration, trying to re-centre. "Not -"

Chapter 13

Incredible! Sally Green could not believe her luck, being on the scene of three separate incidents in the one day.

It seemed an uneventful night at first, having taken the rest of the day off after the near miss on the Motorway that morning. She had managed to record the footage after the car nearly collided with her, but she knew the producers would edit the shots of the dead driver. Drew seemed calm and collected enough at the time, filming footage through his news-camera, but Sally could see his complexion paling from the shock. Even she felt shaky and lost at first, but Drew was no good for driving home. The studio bosses had sent them both home after letting them rest at work first and calling a local doctor to check on them.

However, Sally was on her way to dinner at Alphonso's Italian Restaurant for her goddaughter's engagement party when she heard the sound of glass smashing, followed by a security alarm ringing from a shop across the street. She focused her eyes, seeing the travel agent's store window in disarray but could see no one else around. Did someone throw rocks at it while passing by in their car?

Her heart jumped; the sound of metal grating and stone breaking assaulted her ears; she looked upwards towards the sound. Unfamiliar flapping sounds penetrated her, then she jumped back in time as three flagpoles crashed into the street; two of them ricocheting from the road to slide along the bitumen; a third speared into the windshield of a passing car, exploding glass. Other cars skidded to avoid the carnage, a woman screamed from inside the impaled car, and people came running from the nearby Alphonso's restaurant.

Sally instinctively reached for her mobile phone and her conscience stopped her from filming the horrific scene. Dialling 000, she barked her words at the dispatch officer. "Police, ambulance, AND fire brigade! East and Thorn Streets. Traffic accident." Sally cursed to herself as the operator asked her more details. Was it this person's first frigging day on the job or something? Her mind swung between the scene unfolding before her, the need for help, and the desire to report this for work. She noticed others also calling with their phones, calling for emergency services as well; a few other people were videoing with their phones. Cursing again, she hung up on the phone. Let them find her by GPS, if they must, she thought, and started her iPhone's video camera to capture the events.

She watched the screen, adjusting its brightness and clarity for the video, and moved the camera over the crumpled bonnet, the smashed windscreen, and the screaming Mrs Taylor who tried hiding her face from view when someone attempted to help her. It looked like Mrs Taylor's hand was still stuck in the driver's pants, his face and head squashed flat by the flagpole and the lump of concrete on its end. A dark hooded figure was in the car with the driver. Sally looked up, hoping to see who it could be, and almost dropped the phone; no one was there. She looked at the screen again. The figure was on the screen, captured by camera. Excitement gripped her, and Sally moved forward for more footage.

***

Ramsey awoke with a jolt, his heart pounding hard,

and breathing hard. What was that loud thumping? It wasn't his heart.

"Bloody hell!" he hissed with disappointment. He tried going back into astral mode but his quickened pulse refused to slow, and the thumping sound resumed, only louder.

His senses finally returned to normality. Trudging out into the carpeted hallway, he stopped to listen to the knocking. It seemed to be coming from the front door.

Ramsey felt wobbly in the legs as he walked towards the front door. Astral travelling for an hour could do that to someone and he had no idea why. At last, he reached the front door, opened it, and found Detective Sergeant Cogan standing there.

"What?" was all he could manage.

Cogan stood there, a little taken aback, gawking at Ramsey's bare upper torso. She realised her manners, picked up her jaw and answered. "I tried calling you but your mobile is off."

"Yeah, it is," he muttered, probably a little too low. His head still felt heavy and his mouth full of cotton wool; he also felt angry with himself for his failure.

"Is this a bad time?" Cogan answered, trying to keep her eyes off Ramsey's unexpectedly half-naked self. Ramsey turned around and headed back towards the kitchen, leaving Cogan wondering. "Perhaps I should come back later? You look like you've been sleeping."

Ramsey shrugged, turned around towards her. "Are you coming in or what? Shut the door after you. It's bloody freezing."

Cogan reflected on his own lack of a shirt, as she walked in and shut the door. "It is nipply, I mean nippy, tonight."

Emily suddenly materialised in front of Ramsey, talking straight away, "What happened? You disappeared so quickly. Do you know that Mrs Taylor was in -" Emily noticed Cogan a few steps away from Ramsey. "Oh! Did I come back at a bad time?"

Ramsey turned towards Cogan, speaking quickly. "Detective, please feel free to take a seat. I'm just going to get changed."

"Call me Brianna," Cogan responded, looking around at the living room and its set-up. To her, it seemed more "homey" than she expected, compared to some other men's places she had visited before. She saw no takeaway boxes littering the floor, for one.

"Oooh," Emily giggled. "It's Brianna now," she sing-songed, following after Ramsey into his bedroom, unnoticed by Cogan.

Ramsey shut the door and hissed, "Do you have to follow me while I'm getting dressed?" He dropped his tracksuit pants off and Cogan laughed.

"It's not like you have anything I've never seen before," she said, pretending to cover her eyes and sneaking a peak between her fingers. "What are you going to say when Co - I mean Brianna sees?"

Ramsey slipped quickly into some underpants and turned to look at Emily, looking her in the spirit eyes. "Her knocking at the door distracted me," he hissed so Cogan wouldn't hear him.

"Oh, yeah," Emily smirked, "I bet she did."

Ramsey felt livid and bit his tongue. Slipping on a pair of jeans and buttoning them up, he said, "Quickly. Before I walk out of here, what happened?"

Emily sobered a little, answering, "Your vision came true. Nick got shafted by the spirit assassin and, you'll never guess, but -" and she hesitated. "Why is the detective here?"

"Everything is going so fast," Ramsey responded, finding a dark blue jumper to wear. "I know about Nick dying. I saw that just as I woke up. did I miss anything else?"

His spirit companion answered easily. "I think you will want to check your phone soon. Your reporter friend caught an eyeful of something but she can tell you."

Craig Ramsey opened his bedroom door and walked back down the hallway towards the living room where he saw Cogan examining the family photos. Cogan bent to look closer, and Craig couldn't help noticing her backside and the way jeans fit so well. Emily was standing beside Ramsey and snickered when she noticed where his eyes went. Ramsey's visitor looked up, and turned to face him.

"The three of you looked like quite a family," she mentioned. "I couldn't help noticing the photos. How is Tyrone doing?"

"Ooh," Emily cracked, "she's asking about the kids. That's a good sign, Craig."

Ramsey ignored Emily the best he could by walking over towards Brianna and looking at the photo. It showed a selfie taken at Dreamworld on the Gold Coast six months earlier, during the summer. Ramsey's mind flashed back to the time, remembering better times and couldn't help smiling at it. "We had a good time then. Debra was on break from Uni then." Ramsey suddenly remembered Brianna's question. "Tyrone's still grieving. I tried talking to him today but he seems to be bottling it up, doesn't want to talk about her to me. They were always close and he's a sensitive kid."

Brianna put a comforting hand on Ramsey's elbow. "Where is he now?"

Ramsey stopped to think for a moment, realising that he had forgotten. "He was supposed to be here tonight but he said something about staying with a friend tonight."

Brianna's expression appeared concerned. "You don't know where he is?"

Ramsey laughed. "I normally know where they are, if that's what you're implying. We've always had a good bond."

"He's a good parent," Emily chimed in, although Brianna could not hear her. "He'd make a great father."

Brianna smiled, "It's okay. I'm sure you'd make a great father," and she appeared embarrassed. "I mean, you obviously make sure to spend time with him." What made her say that?

Ramsey noticed a black backpack beside the sofa in the living room. He knew it wasn't Tyrone's bag. "Is this a personal visit or business?"

Brianna's expression changed slightly, she hesitated as she looked at the bag, and replied, "I wanted to tell you about what I found during my investigation today and -"

He looked her in the eyes and she noticed her pulse become a little unsteady, something about the way he looked made it seem he was looking in her head. "Are you trying to read my thoughts?" she asked, a little uncomfortably.

Ramsey smiled, looking away a moment. "I don't read minds. Your thoughts are mostly safe."

"Mostly?" she responded. She changed track. "I saw

you on YouTube ("Oh, she's been checking you out, Craig. I think she loves you," Emily giggled) and I saw part of your stage performances. It title was Mind Reading. What was that?"

"The short answer for you, Detec- Brianna, is that I am psychometric," he replied. "I know things by touching them. That's how I knew things about you from your watch. I've got something to tell you too. Your phone is about to ring soon as there's been another killing just before you knocked on my door."

"What?" she responded, looking at her phone, which started ringing the moment Ramsey said it. "How did you know?" she asked, answering it. "Hello, Detective Cogan."

Ramsey moved around Brianna, heading towards the kitchen where he looked about for something to eat. He heard Brianna talking on the phone to some Sergeant, grinning to himself as he found some bacon he had removed from the freezer earlier for the night's dinner.

Brianna hung up her phone and approached the counter opposite to Ramsey, holding her phone up to indicate it. "How did you know about that?"

Ramsey poured some rice into a cooker with some water, turned it on, and looked at Brianna as he placed a wok on the gas stove. "Do you mean the phone ringing or that Mrs Taylor was in the car with the victim?"

"Don't show off," Emily chided Ramsey, waving a finger in the air at him. "That's not gentlemanly."

Brianna recovered from her surprise. "How did you - ?

"I hope you don't mind my cooking dinner. I'm famished." Ramsey smiled, cracking four eggs in a bowl and beating them with a fork. "As for how I know, I was there when it happened."

Ramsey told her about his astral travelling without mentioning Emily's involvement, as he didn't want to upset Brianna. Experience told him people often freak out when they learned spirits watched them a lot of the time. Brianna, who appeared to be a sceptic to the core, was only just taking the time to listen to him now. He wasn't sure yet if it was because her Inspector Myles suggested, or forced her, to work with Ramsey. Emily was quick to act put out that Ramsey failed to mention her, but Ramsey acknowledged her with a disarming smile. At last, he reached the part of the story where he had been fighting the spirit and a distraction forced him to awaken.

"That seems to fill in how you know about Mrs Taylor and the other victim," Brianna mused.

"Nick," Ramsey corrected her, chopping up a Chinese style omelette into squares, before putting the now-cooked rice in the wok to fry. "The man's name was Nick."

"What are you cooking?" Cogan asked, sniffing the air. "It smells good."

"Special fried rice," Ramsey replied.

"It looks like a lot there," Brianna commented.

"That's because I figure you're staying for dinner while we discuss the case," Ramsey grinned, "and I am famished after this evening's action. What have you found today?"

Brianna grinned. "You're not going to believe me but I want you to read something for me." Moving towards the lounge area, where her backpack was, she unzipped it and removed two items; both of the items were in plastic evidence bags. She came back to the kitchen counter with them. "Are you able to check these out with your voodoo stuff?"

Ramsey paused, looked at the bags, and saw that one of them contained a white handkerchief with a blue border on it; the other held a handkerchief as well but it was completely brown. "Picking up men's hankies, are we?" he grinned. "Do you want me to tell you which one is the better suitor?"

Brianna gave a har-de-har-har in response. "No, I found them both as part of my investigations."

Ramsey cocked an eyebrow, not completely believing her; Brianna hadn't shaken hands with him, and she kept her distance as though avoiding touching him. She was testing him!

Leaving the wooden spoon in the wok with the fried rice, he pointed at the cooking food. "Watch this for me, and I'll have a look. Be careful with the food as some of it is yours."

They swapped places, Brianna still being careful to avoid touching Ramsey. Ramsey opened the first plastic bag, removing the brown handkerchief, being careful to pick it up by the corners.

"Are these clean?" he asked, cheekily.

Brianna shrugged, letting one side of her mouth rise in a cheeky smile. "You tell me."

Ramsey snorted, amused, and relaxed. "The person this belongs to is dead. Some time back, it seems, so he's not a victim. This handkerchief has remained folded up for some time and you have only unfolded it today, shaking it up. You are testing me against the other one which is the one you really want me to read." His voice trailed off as he found himself in a vision; he felt a crushing pain in his chest, saw flashes of faces that he recognised as Brianna and her other family members, and then it went black. Ramsey felt a lump rise in his throat and a tear at the corner of his eye, and waited a moment before handing the handkerchief back to Brianna. "I'm sorry," he said, "So sorry about your adoptive father."

Brianna took the brown handkerchief back, with an apologetic look in her eyes. "No," she told him. "I'm sorry. I still felt that I had to test you."

Ramsey looked her in the eyes and she returned the look, and they both knew what each other were thinking. Emily, who had been watching the whole time, was about to say something cheeky but changed her mind. At last, Ramsey turned to look at the stove, which Brianna had forgotten about. "How is the rice looking?"

Brianna realised with a surprise and took it off the heat, checking the food out. It smelled good, and she felt her stomach rumbling as a reminder that she hadn't eaten more than a few bites throughout the day. "Mm mm I'm getting hungry."

"Well then," Ramsey said, charging his voice and mood up again. "I'll check this other handkerchief out after we've eaten. Astral fighting and psychometry make me hungry."

Chapter 14

Sally stepped out of her car, slammed its door behind her, and hurried towards the door between her garage and the house. The garage doors groaned when she flicked the switch. She swore; her fingers fumbled with the keys before at last opening the door, and she hurried inside her home. Flicking on some of the lights, she made a beeline to her PC, turning it on. While it booted, Sally hooked her iPhone up to its USB connection and tapped her foot as she waited for the computer to finish its initialisation sequence.

The computer finished booting, displaying a desktop with a background photo of herself and her three godchildren, the closest she had to children of her own. Sally clicked the mouse button, bringing up the video file from her iPhone. She watched it, listening to the dark voice of the hooded creature; its eyes seemed to glow into the camera as it spoke. Its deep angry sound filled her with dread. Sally's hand shook as she sat there, thinking. Should she send this to the station? No one would believe her although she took great pains to include as much other footage in the clip as she could. The authorities more than likely would disbelieve her too, despite her good relationship with them.

But there was one person who would believe her.

Sally copied the video clip to her PC, waiting in heightened anticipation as the green bar crept across the screen at a sloth's pace. Five minutes of video amounted to a huge file and that takes a long time to transfer via USB. It finished transferring; Sally disconnected the iPhone from the PC and looked up Craig Ramsey's phone number on her contacts list.

Did she still have it?

No!

Where was it?

Her heart beat so fast she had to take a deep breath, clear her mind and think. Her eyes rested on her computer screen and she tapped away in Google Chrome. She felt like a cigarette but had none; the old feelings felt like returning after ten years of abstinence. Search results flicked up on her computer's screen, and she found Craig Ramsey's website link.

His picture appeared on her screen, standing tall in an immaculate dark suit and his brown eyes engaging the camera's gaze. She used to feel mesmerised by the photo, sometimes still did, but she had to contact him. He had a link on the website, allowing people to send pictures of their palms or a personal object and he sometimes gave complimentary readings from those. It didn't take videos. How else could she send it to him? After searching through her Outlook's contact list, she finally found Ramsey's email and phone details. She clicked his email address, typed a quick message, hit Send, and dialled his number at the same time. Being ambidextrous could be handy sometimes.

He didn't answer his phone, and it diverted to voice mail after the sixth ring, but that didn't matter.

"Craig Ramsey, Sally Green here," she said into the voice message. "If you haven't checked your email, check it now. I haven't approached my studio with it yet."

Sally sat back, finding a Wild Turkey bottle in her desk drawer, and took a strong gulp from it before screwing the top back on. "Only you will understand it."

***

Brianna couldn't help feeling anxious during the meal Craig Ramsey had cooked that evening. Although he had prepared the meal well, and she thought it tasted great, Brianna couldn't help thinking about the second package awaiting his attention on the kitchen counter. She still felt sceptical about his abilities, but Ramsey appeared more convincing than any magician or psychic she watched before. His knowledge of her deceased father astounded her, but she had to be sure. Could he have known about those details through public records? The second handkerchief would tell everything she needed to know.

"What did you get up to today with your investigations?" Ramsey asked, appearing to ignore the second package as they began their meal, but Brianna changed the subject.

"We can talk about that later," she reflected. "I don't like talking about work while eating."

Ramsey tipped his head in understanding. "Fair enough. I can be the same."

"You seem to know so much about me," Brianna mentioned after swallowing a mouthful of wine. "What about yourself? How did you start out as a psychic?"

Ramsey's expression changed. He looked towards Emily for a moment; The spirit stood to Brianna's side, so he didn't appear suspicious by looking at her that time. A thoughtful expression crossed his face as he finished chewing and swallowed. "That depends on which part of my life you mean," he responded. "It's not a clear-cut answer."

"Why not?"

Ramsey grinned. "I assume that you researched me already. You have mentioned seeing me on YouTube, so I take it you have gone deep. How deep do you want me to go?"

"Go as deep as you like," Brianna responded. "I can take it."

Emily laughed in the background at the sexual connotation, and Ramsey choked on some rice. Brianna pretended to not understand by letting a puzzled expression cross her face but couldn't hide the cheeky glint of her eye.

"Well, we'll soon see about that," Ramsey replied after taking a sip of his wine. "I've always had a certain level of psychic ability but I don't think there's anything special about it. I believe that everyone is psychic."

"We can't all read minds or bend spoons," Brianna countered. "So how can you say we are all psychic?"

"I can't bend spoons either." Ramsey admitted it, holding a finger up as he had to pause; something stuck in his throat, and he cleared it before continuing. "Well, at least, only if I have some bloody hard ice cream for dessert," he added with a chuckle and then thought more. "I think I was a child when I first knew something was different about me. Whenever people started to say something, I always knew the rest of the sentences. These incidents, although not under my control, happened often enough that I knew I could do something that most didn't."

"But people have flashes like that all the time," Brianna replied. "There's nothing special about it as we can explain a lot of things away with body language, intuition and -"

"Yes! What is intuition exactly?" he asked. "Tell me. How do you define it?"

Brianna thought for a moment, wondering how to describe it. She knew what it was but couldn't put it into words. "Its-um - it's knowing things."

"Do you mean in the way a mother knows her child is in danger?" Ramsey ventured. "Or, to pick an example for you, how you seem to know the enemy is about to attack or ambush you?"

Brianna felt on the spot, feeling he picked that because he knew of her military background. "That's different," she responded, "because it's instinct and experience."

Ramsey nodded. "Okay, so you believe it's something to do with the five standard senses schools teach us when we're children, right?"

Brianna thought for a moment, nodding in agreement. "Yeah, of course."

Ramsey pointed to the second plastic bag containing the handkerchief he had yet to read. Pushing his empty bowl to the side, he reached across and held the bag up. "According to science, we have five senses: touch, sight, hearing, smell and taste. I believe that those are only the tip of the iceberg and I have my experience to back me up. For example, I can tell things about people by holding their personal objects. Sometimes I can tell by walking into a room."

"Do you mean like walking into a house and you feel it's haunted?" Brianna responded. Ramsey nodded and Brianna replied, "That's an over-active imagination, a result of an innate fear of the dark, or unfamiliar places or being jumpy."

"Or," Ramsey retorted, "it could be the real thing."

"Okay," Brianna answered. "You believe in what you do, and I still sit on the fence. How did you know you could read people by touch?"

Ramsey smiled, looking towards Emily, feeling himself go into reverie. Lifting the wineglass to his mouth, he took a sip. "I was twelve years old, just beginning puberty. A school bully attacked me. He liked to pick on me because I enjoyed performing magic tricks with cards and coins. My favourite trick was making coins disappear one by one from someone's hands while they held them in their fist. There was one girl I enjoyed doing that for; her name was Susan, and I thought she was beautiful. One day, she asked me for a loan of some money for tuck shop. I thought my wet dreams had all come true at once, so I told her I didn't have it. And then, when she walked away, I called back to her, said there was something in her hair. She turned around to face me, I removed a dollar coin from her hair."

"You little charmer," Brianna murmured, resting her chin on her hand as she listened. "What happened then?"

"Nothing, at least, for two days. Then she came back with a couple of her other girl friends and asked me to do it again. That's when I showed her the other trick I told you with seven coins. I made them disappear, one after the other from her hand. She looked so rapt and I can still remember her eyes sparkling. By the time the last coin remained in her hand, she was squealing with excitement."

"Are you sure we're talking about coins and magic tricks here?" Brianna laughed and then stopped when Ramsey shot a rebuking look at her.

"Yes, of course. The next thing I knew was a pain in my head and then blackness. I woke up, but I wasn't in my body at the time."

"Oh!" Brianna said with empathy. "You were king hit?"

"It's a coward's punch," Ramsey responded. "I wasn't looking, and a king has more honour than a coward who attacks from behind. But, yes, that's what it was. I watched the teacher arrive to push the other students away as they crowded around to look at me on the ground. I even watched them check my pulse, give me CPR."

"You stopped breathing?" Brianna asked in shock and then remembered something else. "And you watched this happen? How?"

"I stopped living," Ramsey responded. "No breathing and no heartbeat. It apparently took two teachers half an hour of applying CPR in turns, until the ambulance arrived. They de-fibbed me, I'm not sure why as I am sure I should have been dead. The ambulance driver who revived me told my aunt he did not understand why he even tried. He just 'had a feeling'."

Brianna started to put her hand out towards him and stopped, just a few inches away. "You were lucky he tried."

Ramsey sniffed and smiled. "Yes. While I was watching everything, I saw other people there too. Other children. Some of them had clothes from back in our parents and grandparents days."

"Who were they?"

"The same people you pass in the streets and never see," Ramsey responded. "Spirits. Just like the one who killed Debra and who has been killing those other people in the car crashes."

He paused a moment, letting that part of the story sink in. Brianna's hand retracted a little.

"That bothers you?" Ramsey asked.

"I don't know what to believe," Brianna answered. "You never told me how you watched this happen if you stopped living."

"It was an out-of-body experience. My astral body, or my soul, left my physical body. You could say I was a ghost, but there's more," Ramsey answered. "After I woke up, I later found that I could touch things and know about people. That's when I became fascinated with the paranormal and found the ability is called 'psychometry'."

Brianna was silent for some time, thinking, and then asked, "What about how you read people's minds?"

He smiled. "I am not completely telepathic," he answered. "If I can read someone's thoughts, it's through body language, which you may have guessed, and creative use of psychometry. When I touch people, I sometimes know what they are thinking. But not always."

Ramsey picked up the plastic bag again, waving it a little. "Now, before it gets too late, let's see this handkerchief."

Opening it up, he took the cloth from it and held it in his hands. Flashes started coming to his mind, faint at first but then growing in intensity, until Ramsey found himself in another vision.

***

Major Oates already knew what it was about, and he

151

wasn't happy about it either. When he received the call from his old army buddy, Superintendent Myles, and heard one of his detectives was coming in, he knew that one of his boys was acting up. He pretended not to know anything about it when Myles spoke to him. If it had been about anything else, he would have made Detective Cogan wait longer for this meeting. But he agreed to have it so soon because he wanted to know what the police knew, so he could determine what action to take. If they knew about Project Gemini, he would have to take things even deeper.

His first surprise was when Detective Cogan arrived. Wow! What a babe, but a smart one. He would have to play it cool with her. His next surprise was how fluent she was in Army-speak. She served in Afghanistan and East Timor. He didn't recognise her from his time in Afghanistan, but he blocked a lot of that out, and her name seemed familiar.

After shaking hands and exchanging pleasantries, Detective Cogan cut straight to the chase.

"I am here more as a formality," she told him in a tone that he knew she intended to disarm him. "There have been shooting deaths in Statton, which appear to be from an alleged sniper."

Oates' eyes opened wide in surprise. "Oh? What kind of help do you need?" He kept the best poker face he could as he waited for her answer.

Cogan glanced towards the window, she could hear sounds of voices outside, and then back at the Major. "The bullet is from an SR-98," she told him. "Whoever did it has had military training and I know that you used to be one of the best trainers in the Army."

He felt flattered by that, even though he felt she was making a ploy. "Thank you," he answered. "I like to think I still am. Did I train you?"

She shook her head. "No. You trained Tom Richter."

Oates recognised the name. "Tom! Yes, I remember him. It's such a shame what happened to him in Afghanistan. A good man. Did you serve with him?"

He tried deflecting her with the response.

Cogan started to reply, but her nose seemed to tickle and she tried to hold back a sneeze. It didn't work and she let off an explosive sound, sniffing again, and holding a hand over her face. Her other hand searched in her jacket and she released a disappointed sound. "Do you happen to have a tissue?"

He didn't have a tissue, so he retrieved the next best thing: his handkerchief. Detective Cogan took it from him, thanking him, and wiped her nose, made a blowing noise in it and rolled it up. She started to hand it back but Major Oates held his hands up, palms towards her.

"No, thanks," he told her, not wanting to take the soiled cloth back. "You can keep it."

"Thank you," Cogan replied, placing the handkerchief in her jacket's inside pocket. "I understand you still have the training program on at the base." She worded it as a statement, but let it sound like a question.

Major Oates hesitated, realising how close he came to falling for the bait, and calculated his response. "I don't train snipers any more myself but, yes, we still have the program going here. What do you need?"

"Have any of your trainees or graduates from the base been missing or on leave this week?"

A nice direct answer and, Major Oates figured, a

direct hit, but he wasn't going to let her know that. "I will have to check on that for you, Detective Cogan. If I can have your card, I will check and let you know. But how do you know they came from this base?"

Cogan shrugged. "I don't know at this point but I can't leave a stone unturned, as you know."

Major Oates nodded. "Of course."

***

Craig Ramsey dropped the handkerchief back into the plastic bag, pressing its seal shut. He looked at Brianna, reading the expression on his face, and a smile flickered on his face. "Well?"

Brianna tried to keep her poker face, but she found it difficult to hide the amazement that she was otherwise unprepared to accept. She remained silent, not wanting to admit she couldn't explain how Ramsey knew so much about the meeting; neither did she want to admit that she might have been wrong about him.

"So the answer is that Major Oates told you nothing," Ramsey said, not needing to read her mind or to use psychometry to know. "What I'm curious about is, was that sneeze real or faked for the sake of taking his handkerchief?"

Brianna laughed. "That's for me to know and you to work out, if you dare."

"I'm only seeing this because it's the Major's point-of-view I am receiving. There is more though," Ramsey said, with a twinkling glint of his eye. "Do you want the names that Major Oates isn't going to tell you?"

Brianna answered, "You can tell me the names, but we won't know until we look them up on the computer." She removed a notepad, from the backpack, and a pen.

"Project Gemini was prominent in the Major's mind," Ramsey responded, his expression showing he recognised the name elsewhere, as he picked the bowls up and took them to the sink to rinse them. "And he knew the name of Joseph Denton. Does that mean anything to you?"

Brianna shook her head. "I don't know of Project Gemini at all, but Joseph's name is familiar from my time in Afghanistan." Her tone shifted again, almost excitedly, as she started to see more value in Ramsey's prognostications. "What about Joseph?"

"Joseph has been on leave," Ramsey answered, coming back to the bench. "By the way, do you want dessert?"

"Maybe later," she answered, shaking her head. "What about Joseph?"

"I gained the impression from the handkerchief that Joseph is on the Major's mind. He went on leave just about a month ago, the nineteenth of May, I think, after a relative's traffic accident here in Statton. A young boy died, and Joseph took time from the Army for bereavement. He hasn't returned and -"

"And Joseph is a top marksman!" Brianna added. "That's how I know his name."

Craig replied, "Well?"

"I might be starting to believe in your voodoo stuff," Brianna replied, with a conceding smile, "but not completely. Something else that matches is the accidents in general all started in late May. It could be coincidence but it could be worth checking out."

"It's a good thing that you managed to score that handkerchief," Ramsey told her. "Thanks for bringing it around as it's given us one good lead, maybe two of them. I like the ploy you used to get it."

Brianna smiled. "You're trying to bait me to find out about my sneeze?"

Ramsey couldn't hold back his grin, knowing Brianna was onto his trick. "What do you think?"

Brianna held her hand out of him, palm facing him, and her eyes locked on his. "Do me," she said.

Ramsey laughed at her words. "I assume you want me to read you... right?"

She smiled, realising her words and blushed, before replying. "You tell me."

Chapter 15

It was Saturday, 25th June 2016. The rosy coloured sun rising in a lazy attitude above the mountain range did little to combat the hard chilling wind keeping many from leaving their bed; everyone, that is, except for Joseph Denton. Nightmares had plagued him through the night, preventing him from enjoying a good sleep, so he decided to take a drive to Ashton, one of Statton's inner suburbs. His eyes felt tired, red and stinging, but he ignored it; neither his body's pains or the wind's bone-chilling registered with him. Only the residual images and sounds from his nightmares came to him.

He drove the dirty light-blue van off the road and along a dirt track, disappearing into the tunnel of darkness formed by the thick foliage of surrounding trees. His only companions were the sound of his tyres crunching on gravel and the quiet van's purring engine. At last, he arrived at a chain-link mesh gate blocking the path. Leaving the headlights on, Joseph turned the engine off and stepped out of the van. He reached towards the passenger seat, grabbing a canvas bag and slung it over his shoulder before shutting the van's door. His confident feet negotiated him off the path down a slight decline that followed the fence line until he felt the foliage hid him enough from the path.

At last, he reached a point that he felt it was safe to stop; he could make out the van's headlights about twenty metres away. Joseph dropped the bag to the ground, opened it, and retrieved a set of wire cutters. He cut a section of the fence's links, creating an opening big enough for him, and walked through it and towards the concrete structure. Finding a thick bush near the reservoir's base, he hid his closed canvas bag under it and checked it was out of sight.

A strange sensation slithered through his mind, like the other times, and he paused. Joseph felt dizzy, off-centre, and a strange voice or thought passed through his mind. *They never listen. Why don't they take notice?* Although he didn't know what the voice was, it seemed familiar as though it were a part of him. He knew then that another accident had occurred, even seemed to know that it was the other side of Statton. Some other brainless bastard had bought the farm and died on the roads. Joseph knew because these episodes started a week before he went to find the sniper's rifle; every time he heard the voice or felt its thoughts slice through his mind, someone died. He even knew *why* they died. Why didn't the authorities know, or even do something about it? It was all up to him. He had to help the other guy control these vermin.

Sometimes he felt as though the voice spoke to him. It seemed as if it knew him and what happened; it understood him. It even seemed to love him, as though it were family, but it also sent him on missions.

It wasn't always like that, however. Years ago in Afghanistan, he was one of the top snipers at the time. Nicknamed "Blow-Jo", he hit first time, every time. Some of his Army mates said he could shoot the testicles from a flea from a kilometre away, without harming the dog. That was before the incident that made everything go arse-up.

His mission was to provide support for one of the engineer teams, while they were rebuilding bridges for the supply trucks. He watched through his sights for the enemy as they crept like snakes through the desert dunes.

The enemy never knew where he was, but they knew about him, and they were crafty. To them, he was "The Jackal", and they wanted his head; it didn't matter if the body came with it. So, he became his namesake, picking his targets off. Then came the came the day when they ambushed him instead. They were waiting, they had to be to catch him off-guard. The rocky alcove where he hid exploded around him. Three minutes of cutting chaos felt like three hours as bullets ricocheted around him, and a bazooka shell shattered the rock above him. The shock deafened him, leaving a horrible empty lack of sound before transforming a minute later to a hideous single note that played forever. Then he heard the staccato of the machine guns stuttering, bullets pinging about him like metal gnats, and he felt the shrapnel's shocking bite on the side of his chest. Somehow, he managed to escape, dodging behind more rocks before gunfire from different directions pinned him to the spot. When the rocket fire and explosions closed in upon him, Joseph thought he was going to die, that a bullet with his name would soon claim him. The enemy voices faded as they retreated; he heard an engine, the beating of a helicopter's rotors as they churned the sand around him into a sharp rising cloud. He still didn't know how the enemy knew he was there, but he was glad his own people were able to rescue him. Unfortunately, that didn't stop the dreams, the voices, the recurring nightmares and flashbacks.

His feet felt both light and heavy, alternating between the two, and his head swam for a moment. Putting his hand on a nearby tree, he steadied himself. The voice in his head, The Other One, was getting ready to attack. He needed to get his act together for the big one.

Brianna Cogan woke with a start. Something felt different, unfamiliar, and her heart pounded. This wasn't her bed.

Her eyes focused, seeing posters on one of the walls. She recognised one of them as Rhianna, another looked like an old Tupac poster, and a few others she didn't know. Where was she?

Images flashed back to her; she thought they were from a dream. Craig Ramsey kissing her; she flirted with him; his hands felt warm on her hands; looking through a sniper's scope; sandy terrain.

A warm delicious scent wafted through the air, teasing her nostrils; bacon, eggs and coffee. The smells cleared her head and her stomach murmured. She was still wearing her clothes except her jacket which draped over a chair near a desk in the corner. She moved the thick doona cover back and started shivering in shock. Damn! What was the temperature this morning?

Craig Ramsey's voice came to her; he was speaking to someone in conversation. Brianna listened and heard no one else. He must have been on the phone to someone. She heard Tyrone's name mentioned.

Although she still wore her socks, her feet felt like they were freezing in the winter air. Brianna found her shoes by the bed, slipping them on before grabbing her jacket and opening the bedroom door. Still wriggling a little inside her jacket to warm up more, she followed the smells towards the kitchen.

Craig stopped talking as Brianna entered the kitchen. Turning to face her, he said, "Good morning! Did you sleep well?"

"Who were you talking to?" she asked.

Craig looked to the side, as though at someone else, then back at her with a guilty look. He answered in an almost perfect impersonation of Don Adams' character, Maxwell Smart. "Would you believe that I can talk to the dead?"

Brianna hesitated, not knowing what to think. Yes, she believed that Craig could read things about people by holding personal objects, and she knew that he claimed to be able to see spirits. But speaking with them? She noted a twinkle in his eye. "Do they talk back?"

Craig smiled, handing her a cup of hot coffee. "Strong black, with one sugar, right?"

She took the coffee in her hand, its heat almost burning her fingers through the hot mug. Grimacing as she gingerly moved around to the mug's handle, she said, "How did you know how I take my coffee?"

Her host looked back at her for a moment, with a knowing smile that held a hint of a questioning look, before attending to the food on the pan. "Nothing happened last night," he told her, answering Brianna's unspoken question. "I let you sleep in Debra's room. It was better than letting you drive home after you had so much wine."

Craig dished the breakfast, bacon, eggs, mushrooms and tomato, onto plates. Brianna noticed he had already set a table for them, with glasses of juice next to the cutlery. The drawn curtains allowed a view of the back yard's Japanese garden with the kwoon behind it. Sunlight streamed from outside, warming the table and its seats, but Brianna noticed the wind was blowing outside. it was a good thing they weren't out there, but it otherwise looked lovely.

"Dig in," he Craig told her, setting the plates on the table. "How did you sleep?"

"With both eyes shut," she answered, a cheeky grin crossing her face to match a twinkling eye. "Pretty well. I didn't realise where I was when I woke. My own bed is nowhere near as comfortable." She started wolfing the breakfast down, a habit she picked up while serving in the Army. Feeling Craig's eyes on her, a wave of embarrassment swept over her, and she stopped to apologise.

"It's all good," Craig responded, with a smile. "I'm glad you enjoy it."

"You're going to make someone a good husband one day," she answered, savouring some more of the breakfast. Craig remained quiet, eating his own food, and appeared to be suppressing a smile. Brianna realised what she had said and blushed, feeling the heat spread across her cheeks. "I mean you're a bachelor who cooks well, and you seem to keep the house well. Is there something that you're hiding?"

Craig stopped eating; his fork, with a piece of bacon skewered on its tines, hung in the air where he held it. He paused, as though listening to something (he always seems to be listening to something else, Brianna thought to herself), and replied, "What are you trying to say, Detective Cogan?" His tone seemed serious, but Brianna caught the coyness behind it.

"I'm saying that there are a lot of men out there who don't show all the -"

"Are you saying I could be a good catch?" he asked, just the tiniest hint of a smile showing at the corner of his eyes.

"No," she answered, a slight blush coming to her face as she tried to think of a comeback.

"Oh!" he interjected. "Do you mean I must be gay?" His eyes looked serious as he gazed back at her.

She paused, not sure what to say now. Could he -

"I'm not gay," he responded. "I've lived as a single man, as well as a "single father", for a long time and there-" Craig's voice trailed off; he lost himself in thought, remembering something.

Brianna was about to apologise, but Ramsey changed the subject. "There's something I wanted to tell you about after breakfast too. You would never believe what."

She released a breath of relief, glad to remove the tension. Ramsey seemed to be holding some things back about himself, she thought to herself. He didn't mind listening to other people's problems and learning their secrets, but letting other people into his world seemed to be another matter altogether. Brianna made a mental note and answered, "What wouldn't I believe?"

Craig grinned, waving his knife like a mother waggling a finger. "After you finish your breakfast."

A few minutes later, they finished their filling meal and Ramsey stood up. "Never mind the dishes," he replied, as Brianna started to collect them. "You're my guest and I have something for you."

Ramsey led Brianna back to the hallway. Cogan couldn't help noticing the bedrooms were in the same direction, and she bit her tongue as they walked past towards another room at the end. The room was medium-sized with a large glass window overlooking the city and its river that formed a wide dirty blue ribbon through the middle. A walk-in wardrobe opened on one wall, and Brianna saw suits hanging inside its darkened space. The opposite wall sported photos of Craig in performance (one of them showed him posing with US President Obama and Prime Minister Tony Abbott) and a show poster advertising one of Craig's past performances in the late 1990s.

"The photo is from when G20 came to Brisbane a couple years ago," Craig explained, noticing Brianna studying it. "But that's not what I wanted to show you."

Brianna had been one of the police officers on duty during that time, but she hadn't been that close to either of the world leaders. she felt jealous but said nothing, as she watched Craig tap one of the keys on his laptop that sat near the window. "It looks like a great place to work," she commented, looking at the view outside.

Craig looked outside a moment, before turning his attention back to the screen. "I received an email last night which I think will interest you a lot. By the way, you might want to check your mobile phone too. I heard it ringing before you got up."

Brianna felt her jacket pocket and retrieved her phone. Five missed calls displayed on it from work. Damn!

"Before you do call them back," Craig responded. "Check this out."

Brianna watched the screen, her eyes widening at the carnage. It was almost as bad as what she saw in Afghanistan, only it seemed worse because she could tell this was in her city. The screen showed a car, its windscreen smashed with a pole speared through it. "That's what I was telling you about last night," Craig explained and then hushed so she could listen.

The car's front passenger seat contained a woman in her late forties or early fifties. Brianna couldn't be sure of the passenger's age, and the driver had the end of the pole through his head. Blood and gore splattered everything, including the screaming passenger, but Brianna saw something else. A dark shadow, wearing a hood, hunched over the driver. Was he helping? No, he seemed to be pressing something on the victim's shoulder. At first, she could only hear the passenger's screams, and then she heard another familiar voice speak.

"Who is that talking?" Brianna asked.

"Sally Green, the news presenter," Ramsey responded, hushing her. "Listen."

The black-hooded figure turned, faced the camera and its eyes flashed red as it looked into the lens. Brianna could see it focus first on the camera and then off-camera towards the person holding the phone.

"You can see me?" its raspy voice boomed.

"Y-yes," Sally's surprised voice responded. "But only on the camera."

It approached the camera lens, moving through the car's body as though wading through water until it was less than a foot away, and then its voice boomed. "This is a warning! Another one! I will keep killing these stupid selfish bastards, and you won't stop me. Someone tried to stop me but I am unstoppable and nothing you mortals can do will make me."

Brianna felt the chills down her spine and she shivered as though someone crossed her grave. The voice was cold, but it didn't sound evil either. It sounded determined, cold, and calculating, as though it had a plan in motion.

"Who are you?" Sally's voice asked.

The hooded figure kicked backwards at the crumpled mess of a car and it moved. Brianna jumped in surprise from the sound. Although it could move through solids, it was capable of manipulating them as well.

"My name doesn't matter," the creature's voice answered. "Names are words on air, and so many words are meaningless these days, falling upon ignorant ears! But my message is clear for you. Heed the warnings, or I will kill more."

"What do you want people to do?" Sally's voice asked with the slightest quiver beneath her professional news reporter's experience.

The camera image faded, disintegrated, and the voice responded, but its message was not clear. The video ended there.

Neither Brianna or Craig said anything at first, for a few seconds, until Craig finally spoke. "That's all the video, it seems. I'd say the strange stuff at the end was interference from the spirit."

Brianna sat on a second chair at the desk, her legs feeling weak from shock as her beliefs were taking a battering. "Sally Green sent this to you?"

Craig nodded. "She hasn't taken this to the television station yet. Any other journalist would have, but she's got brains."

Brianna wondered why a journalist would show the video to Craig first. He picked up the thought, replying, "Sally was one of my first media contacts when I first started out as a mentalist, and she has experienced a lot of *weird shit.*" That left the detective wondering more about Craig's contact with the female journalist, even though

Craig didn't seem like one into cougars.

The silent pause broke, shattered by both Craig's and Brianna's mobile phones ringing at the same time. Craig reached for his phone which sat charging on the desk, and Brianna walked out to the kitchen to answer her own.

Sergeant Hohenhaus' voice came through her phone when she answered. "Cogan?"

"Yes," she answered, noting the Sergeant sounded flustered.

"Don't you answer your phone?" his voice responded. "We've been trying to ring you, and you weren't home-"

"I've been out for the night," Cogan responded with a sharp tone, not appreciating that they thought they should be checking up on her. "It is my weekend off."

The officer's voice softened to an apologetic tone. "Um yeah, okay. The Inspector told me to call you. We've got more bedlam going on and we need all hands on deck."

Brianna took the details down with the notepad and pen from her inner jacket pocket. "Got it. I'll be there soon."

She was about to let Craig know she was about to leave, when he bustled past her with a leather jacket slipped on. Brianna wondered how long she had been on the phone if Craig was already dressed.

"Got to go," he said with a hint of business in his voice. He handed Brianna her backpack. "The proverbial shit could be about to hit the fan. Have you got everything?"

"Yes," she answered. "What's happened?"

"Sally Green wasn't the only one taking video,"

Ramsey said, slugging down what remained of his green tea from the breakfast table. "We've both got work to do."

***

Blow Joe knew almost before he heard the sounds of sirens floating across the river that people on the other side of town had died. The voice in his head sounded satisfied, maybe a little jubilant. Take *that, bitches*.

Joseph had parked the van off at the other end of the park and was running back to the reservoir when the voice shouted its jubilant message through his head. Blow Joe tried answering it back from his own mind, but the other voice went silent. Did it know he was answering it? Perhaps, it didn't trust him enough, thinking he could betray it and sabotage its important mission? He tried to talk back to it again.

"I hope you are watching what I do," he said, using his mind-voice as he jogged closer to the fence line. "How many did you pick off?"

There was still no reply, but he had a guess it was could be three people. It used to kill one at a time but, of late, it increased its killing. Friday's spree was phenomenal.

He found the bag under the bush, slung it over his shoulder and climbed up the ladder of the reservoir. The concrete wall's top walkway was perfect for him to balance his rifle, which he unpacked and assembled with practised hands.

Less than five minutes later, he was looking through the telescopic sights. In the distance, he could just see the blinking lights of the emergency vehicles: one ambulance and three police cars. He remembered there was another police station nearby. Swivelling his rifle around, he refocused and looked at the station. An officer was walking to his car, having a conversation with someone on his phone. The scope made him seem as though he were ten feet from Joe, who watched them with an eagle eye. Blow Joe's target opened the driver's door, sat inside, and closed the door again. The car started to move backwards. Blood exploded from the officer's head, splashing the windscreen from the inside. The dead man's head fell forward, pressing the car's horn. A few moments later officers came running out to the car, a few of them with hands on their weapons, looking for a target of their own.

He swivelled the rifle sights in another direction, seeing a young woman, who couldn't have been more than twenty-one. She appeared to be on her way somewhere in her car, a zippy little red Ford Fiesta, and busy in some conversation; her hand up to her head. The rifle didn't roar as he pulled the trigger, thanks to its fitted suppressor, which muffled the report. The young brunette's neck exploded; how did he miss; it must have been the cross winds. He didn't calculate it well enough to achieve a clean kill. He watched her writhing in pain as she lost control of the car, and he aimed again. The second bullet finished her.

He looked around towards the police station again. Things looked hectic there. Perhaps he should move.

Without another thought, he disassembled his rifle in record time, stashed it in his bag, and slid down the ladder to the ground below.

By the time the police officers realised the shooter was further away than they thought, Blow Joe was running through the bushland towards his awaiting getaway vehicle. Jumping inside, he stashed the bag in front of the front passenger seat, started the engine and drove away. It was a smooth, clean getaway without leaving many clues.

Sirens wailed as police cars approached from behind. His heart hammered a little, but he otherwise felt as cool as a cucumber, as he allowed them to speed past him. They didn't even bother looking at him, and why would they when they were heading towards the path that led to the reservoir. He was driving in the same direction, which is the opposite of what they would have expected. That was his plan to shake them off. He was otherwise unhindered as he continued driving past the scene, taking a casual look at the two police vehicles heading down the gravel path towards the reservoir's entrance. They might find footprints, maybe even where he cut the fence, and chances are they might find some traces of mud, but there was nothing else that could link straight to him. He never carried identification, and the wind was blowing a gale still; any DNA he left would most likely blow away.

However, Joe also knew about the other things, like the registration on the van. He had removed the plates from another person's car and placed on his vehicle. That way, if anyone happened to notice his van matched the description of a stolen vehicle, they wouldn't match a casual check. The risk still existed if they noticed the stolen plates belonged to a different kind of car, a silver Falcon instead of the grey van, so he kept an eye out just in case.

At last, he reached a quiet street in another neighbourhood. There was his other vehicle, his own dirty navy blue utility, just where he left it in the driveway of a house he knew to be empty. He pulled up the van, stepped out, and wiped everything down to remove any prints from it before getting into his own utility. His bag containing the rifle sat in the back, hidden under some tarpaulins.

It was time to catch up with his sister-in-law and the kids. The original plan had been to take them fishing at the Causeway, but that was before the wind. Perhaps they might want to go out and see a movie.

He continued driving, leaving his mission behind him for the time being to enjoy the other half of his life.

Chapter 16

Detective Cogan sometimes wondered if Dr Kroot stayed up all night to think of ways to entertain her. As she stepped into the medical examiner's autopsy room on Monday 27th June, her eyes and ears experienced the stunned disbelief; she didn't know how to respond.

He must have taken out all the stops to decorate the autopsy room. Dr Kroot sat in a deckchair, lazing back under a bright light that shone upon him. His loud Hawaiian shirt, decorated in colours that would have hurt a blind man, was unbuttoned and open - despite the winter chill from the weekend's cold snap. His long-legged Hookstock beach pants were rolled up, exposing his skinny hairy legs to the knees, and his feet sat in a tub of water. He held a tall glass of something that looked like a cocktail with a tiny umbrella in his left hand as he lay back under the bright light. A Beach Boys song, which Cogan thought was Surfin' USA, played in the background and behind him stood an inflatable set of coconut trees with a mock surfboard. His deckchair was one of three set up in a line; he sat in the middle chair; the chair to his right was occupied by what Brianna thought was another woman dressed in a skimpy bikini.

"Detective!" he called out upon seeing her, and opened his arms wide in greeting from the chair. "You're just in time for the party, babe!"

He stood and ran over to her, his arms still opened wide to hug her. As he reached her, he paused as though unsure how to hug her. Cogan made no effort to return it, feeling equally awkward and amused by the atmosphere. She looked at the woman in the other deckchair and noticed the person's figure was very still.

"Ummmm," she hesitated, unsure of what to say. "Who is that?"

Dr Kroot followed the direction of Cogan's gaze, towards the deckchair, then looked back at her. "Oh, her! I don't know her name. I asked her but she hasn't answered yet." He leaned closer to whisper, "She's playing hard to get but I'm playing it just as cool back at her." He winked.

Cogan moved past Kroot to look closer. "Please, tell me that's not one of the dead bodies."

Kroot shrugged. "I certainly hope not, as she seems so perfect. Never opens her mouth, at least not to talk."

That was when Cogan realised the woman in the deckchair was really a sex doll; one of the more expensive types that look like a real person and apparently feel real too. The medical examiner took another swallow from the glass, crunched quickly on an ice cube, and motioned towards the examining table. "You will never believe what I found from three of the victims your people delivered to me on the weekend."

Taking her hand in one, he dragged her along. "Come on! You hafta see this!" he cried, as though He had reverting to childhood and wanted to show his mother something. "Look at this!"

When they reached the table, he turned towards the doll in the deckchair. "Just have some more Sex On The Beach, honey," he called to her. "I'll be right back soon for some Sand In Your Shorts."

Cogan could normally take his madcap exercises with a straight face, but she couldn't help the laughter that shook her chest then. Kroot looked at her with surprise. "Is everything okay?"

She stifled her laughter. "What's different with this body?"

The background song changed to the Beach Boys song, "Don't Worry, Baby"; Kroot placed his drink to the side, near his gored-up instruments, and pulled the sheet down from the body's face to reveal a man's head with a round hole in the temple.

"It's the same sniper, right?" Cogan started, starting to feel bored and knowing the outcome.

She was wrong. Kroot shook his head. "Nope-a-roonie, no ceegar for you, chicky," he crooned with a strange accent. Picking up the forceps, he reached into the kidney dish on the nearby trolley and picked up a cylindrical shaped object covered in blood; the object slipped from the forceps, landing in Kroot's glass. Reaching in to the glass, he picked it up and fished it out again to show her.

It definitely wasn't a bullet. Instead of being made of metal, it appeared to be made of some kind of stone with a colour similar to a turquoise. "It's not stone either," he told her. "I've got to run it off to one of the other labs to have it checked."

Detective Cogan looked closer at it, noting its definite strangeness, and saw something from the corner of her eye. She turned towards Kroot who had taken the final swallows from his drink; he crunched on the final ice cube, swallowed and licked his lips.

"It's not the same sniper," he answered, ignoring Cogan's face as it went a shade greener. "In fact, this one has something that the other gunshot victims don't have! Do you wanna guess?"

Cogan forced an initial wave of bile back down her

throat, and looked back towards the body. Kroot started to say something but the detective held her hand up to silence him; she wanted to find it herself. Her eyes passed over the corpse's wax statue-like features and then she smiled in recognition. There was a tattoo, number 134, ingrained on the back of the victim's shoulder.

"This tattoo," Cogan spoke, indicating it with the end of her little finger. "What can you tell me about it?"

Kroot looked closer at it, thought for a moment, and stood up again. "It's not a tattoo."

"What?" Cogan couldn't believe it.

"It's not a tattoo," Kroot repeated. "At least, not in the sense of the one I got on the night I married the midget in drag - I really should stop making decisions while drunk. When I noticed so many of them, I took a sample and had the ink checked. It's not ink. It's a burn."

"But it's in the skin," Cogan interjected, "it can't be a burn."

Kroot moved back towards his deckchair and plonked himself back down. "It's not burned from any sun rays or lasers," he explained, picking up a sun tanning reflector board and placing it around his face. "It's been burned from inside the body, kind of like a microwave. I've never seen anything like it before and the lab boys confirmed it's just burnt meat. Now, are you going to join the party or not, Detective Cogan?"

She shook her head in refusal and lifted the sheet back over the corpse's face. "What about the other bodies from the weekend?"

Kroot turned his head back towards the detective, his eyes hidden by his 1960's style sunglasses. "They didn't tell me anything different to what the lab boys said either. The police officers they brought in on Saturday had been shot by the same rifle we talked about last week. Good luck in catching that son-of-a-bitch. He's a good shot. Haven't seen anything like that since I left Johannesburg."

***

Tak and Ray were on the third lap of the oval, practising for their school's sports day. The meet itself was less than two weeks away and their Phys Ed teacher, who happened to also be one of the teachers hosting their sports house, had been running them through a gruelling practice session. He'd given them the drill of running three times around the oval, a distance of 400 metres each lap; sprinting the first lap; jogging the second; and sprinting the final lap. After a short rest, they were to do the same again another three times. They were now on their third of four sets; sweat layered their skin, cooling them in the cold morning air from which their sports singlets and shorts offered little protection, and they did their best to match their breathing rhythm to their pace of the jog.

Tak coughed loudly, finding himself unable to breathe properly, and felt like he had drifted into a cloud of something. Ray looked back, wondering what had happened to his running partner.

"What was that about?" he asked.

Tak suppressed the urge to vomit. "I'm not sure, dude. It felt like I ran into a cloud of something rotten."

Colonel Ryan watched them, scowled a little and muttered. "It's a premium Cuban cigar, you little shit."

They didn't hear him, but Ray felt the yellow glob of spit hit his left shin at the top of his sock. He looked down, pulled a face and let out a sound of disgust.

Picking on the kids again, Colonel Ryan?

The phantom colonel turned around, clamping the phantasmic cigar between his teeth, and exhaled another cloud of smoke; this one was visible to the two runners, and they bolted. Craig Ramsey stood outside the school's fence that divided the oval from the cemetery. Colonel Ryan snorted, floating back towards the cemetery. "When I was a kid, I could have run rings around those two easily. These days, now they don't smoke as much, they're turning into pussies."

"So now you blow smoke rings in their face to make them 'man up', right?" Ramsey answered wryly.

Ryan snorted again, good-humouredly this time, and shook Ramsey's hand with his astral limb. "What's so important you had to see me this morning?"

Craig Ramsey looked around, seeing a nearby tree where less spirits congregated. He motioned to the colonel who followed him into its shade, telling the phantom he had something of potential interest for him.

Colonel Ryan asked if Ramsey had found him a ghostly woman who was willing to give Ryan some pleasurable sexual favours. Before Ramsey could respond, the colonel smirked. "That's damn decent of you, Mr Ramsey."

Craig Ramsey thought to himself, privately so that Ryan didn't catch it, that it was a good thing Emily Fraser didn't come along this time either. "I believe I have something that could benefit us both," he explained, refusing to acknowledge Ryan's comment. He reached into his pocket, retrieving his phone, and found one of the video files of the spirit assassin's Friday evening speech.

The colonel floated around to get a better look of the video playing on the phone's screen. This video played the similar scene only from a different angle. Ramsey had visited Sally Green after watching her original video on the Saturday morning. By the time she discussed the rest of the events to him, he learned that other people on the scene had recorded the same thing on their phones as well.

They watched as the black-hooded figure turned and faced Sally Green to look through her camera's lens. From this second perspective, the viewers could see the definite outline of the spirit assassin's profile.

"You can see me?" its raspy voice boomed.

"Y-yes," Sally's surprised voice responded. "But only on the camera."

It approached Sally's camera lens even closer, moving through the car's body, until it was less than a foot away from Sally, and then its voice boomed. "This is a warning! Another one! I will keep killing these stupid selfish bastards, and you won't stop me. Someone tried to stop me but I am unstoppable and nothing you mortals can do will make me."

(Colonel Ryan snorted at this point, blowing more smoke as he studied the figure.)

"Who are you?" Sally's voice asked.

The hooded figure kicked backward at the crumpled mess of a car and it moved. (Colonel Ryan snorted in mild amusement again. "Pipsqueak ****," he murmured around his cigar. He's all show.")

"My name doesn't matter," the spirit assassin's voice answered. "Names are just words on air, and so many words are meaningless these days, falling upon ignorant ears! But my message is clear for you. Heed the warnings or I will keep killing you."

("Melodramatic," Ryan insisted. "He seems like one

of those poofy theatre kinds who like to prance and dance on stage like cheerleaders, doesn't he?")

Sally's voice asked what the spirit assassin wanted.

At this point, Sally Green's recording had stopped, however this different video of the same event continued. The spirit assassin's voice boomed through the speakers, which vibrated from the volume, "The police and the authorities have not figured it out. I am killing people who use their mobile phones while driving." The hooded figure's hand swept behind him, indicating the corpse in the driver's seat.

("Yep, there's the theatrical gesture," Ryan chortled, coughing a little on his cigar smoke although it wasn't truly affecting him.)

A slight shimmering appeared around the corpse as the spirit assassin continued speaking. "This idiot was one of them, fingering this woman's genitals just before talking on the phone to his wife while he drove!"

Although Craig had seen this through YouTube the day before, he still couldn't help feeling sorry for Jenny, the victim's wife. It wasn't for him to judge the victim's cheating streak, but he felt it was a terrible way for the man's wife to find out about his cheating. He was still her husband, the father of their children, and his mother's son. Colonel Ryan, on the other hand, still let out a snorting grunt; Craig wasn't sure if that was because the victim's karma had bitten him on the backside, or something else.

The spirit assassin's voice and image continued on the screen.

"All of you people, even you filming this with your camera, deserve to die if you are using your mobile phones while driving," the spirit boomed.

They heard the surprised voice of the man filming the spirit. "W-what?"

"W-what to you too!" The spirit moved closer to the person filming, forgetting to look in the lens as it faced the human. "You have all been warned! All of you! You not only risk your own lives, which you seem to value far less than the piece of shit phones you will be replacing in a year or two anyway, but you also risk the lives of those who are doing the right thing! The innocents!"

Some static came through the video, and it corrected itself so the playback continued.

"You all deserve it!" The spirit's voice boomed through Craig's phone even louder, and he was aware that the two students on the oval looked up again as they made another circuit. "You've received messages before. Here's another one! Since the police can't catch you, I will catch you-AND - I - will - kill - you - when I do!"

The spirit assassin reached towards the camera's lens and the image crackled away to silent blackness. The video ended.

"There are other videos like that from the same time, including one by a news reporter who was there too, but this is the best one," Craig told Colonel Ryan.

Colonel Ryan removed the cigar from his mouth, blew a large cloud of putrid smoke that smelled like death into the cold air, and replied, "I still don't know this guy." He paused for a moment and Craig could see him thinking. "I may know someone who can track him though. I'll meet you back at my office."

With that, he disappeared. Feeling tired this morning from the cold temperature, Craig followed the path back to Ryan's office and met the Colonel there.

The Colonel had another ghost with him by the time Craig arrived. The second spirit had a wiry frame, apart from a pot-belly that poked from underneath his black Pink Floyd t-shirt and spilled just over the belt buckle of his torn jeans. His beaten up Nike shoes looked like they had seen better days at least a year before the spirit died. "Meet Chaz," Colonel Ryan grunted around his thick cigar. "He's our tech boy."

"Spirit Force has hackers?" Craig's eyebrows lifted in surprise, as he reached forward to shake hands with the ghostly IT guy. "I had no idea."

"Of course we do," Colonel Ryan laughed, standing back for Craig to get a better view of the laptop, which looked as ghostly as its user. "They don't all live forever. Hell, even Chaz here died at a computer keyboard, didn't you?"

"Hey, dude," Chaz said, reaching out a pearly-white hand. As Craig did likewise, Chaz moved his outstretched hand so that they ended up fist-bumping instead. "I remember seeing you on YouTube years ago. Until I died, I didn't think you were real, man."

"Unreal," Craig answered, managing a grin.

Chaz peered at Craig's other hand, seeing the mobile phone it held; he pointed at it. "The Colonel says you have something there for me."

Craig handed his phone to the hacker who looked it over with studious eyes. "Holy shit! An iPhone 6S. I read about them online but this is the first I've seen," Chaz exclaimed, turning it in his hands before inserting a USB cable into it and connecting it to the laptop.

Files flickered up on the screen, mostly photos and video files, and Craig marvelled at how quickly it responded on the spirit's computer. Chaz wasn't using iTunes or Microsoft either. The hacker quickly flicked through the icons until Craig pointed at the screen.

"Those two videos there," he indicated with his finger. "This is the one I showed the Colonel."

"Rightio," Chaz mumbled, clicking on the file and scrolling through the video file until he found a few worthwhile frames. He double-clicked on the frames so that they appeared on the screen beside each other, clicked another icon to the side of the screen and sat back as a green line moved over each picture; a banner appeared across the screen briefly, captioned, "Scanning", before disappearing from the display.

The whole process happened so quickly that Craig felt breathless by the time a three-dimensional composite image of the spirit assassin appeared on the screen; the rendering rotated on the screen. Craig felt impressed. Chaz tapped furiously at his keyboard and a multitude of photos flicked by on the screen until, at last, an alert appeared on the screen.

SEARCH COMPLETE - NO MATCHES FOUND

"Are you kidding me?" Colonel Ryan sounded exasperated. "How up-to-date are the files, Chaz?"

The hacker replied matter-of-factly, scratching his neck nervously. "They are constantly updated every day. This guy must be newly-deceased."

"Crap!" Colonel Ryan exploded. "This guy has been dead for at least a month. He's the bastard behind half of the crap we're going through now." He paced away, a plume of smoke drifting behind him, and then turned back abruptly. "You've checked the databases for the other cemeteries in the city?"

"I've scanned the whole world," the hacker replied. "He's simply not there."

Colonel Ryan took a long deep breath, held it for a moment, and let it out slowly. When he felt more relaxed, he patted Chaz on the shoulder. "Thanks, soldier," he said. "You've tried but we can do more. Send a copy of this turd's picture out to the other units." Ryan paused a moment; an idea came to him. "Send it out to all the bases around the world. Tell them to keep an eye out for him, and someone, somewhere, has to have seen him before. I know he's here in Statton but I don't want to take any chances. I want to know the moment he's seen, and I want the bastard tracked."

Craig sighed, feeling the hope drain from him again.

"It's okay," Colonel Ryan told Craig, handing his phone back to him. "I will send word to you the moment I know anything. For you, and for Debra."

***

That afternoon, Craig Ramsay was watching a DVD movie in his living room when his mobile phone beeped. He picked it up, read the message, and a smile curled one end of his mouth. He returned the phone to the side table.

Emily's voice spoke from the chair at the end of the sofa he was sitting on. "Oooh," she crooned. "I know what that smile means!"

Craig's smile grew slightly bigger as he tried to suppress laughter; he couldn't stop the light blush. "I don't know what you mean," he replied.

"She's coming here, isn't she?" Emily answered.

"No, she's not," Craig responded, and realised he answered too fast. "And it's not a date."

Emily raised a knowing eyebrow and counted down from ten in her thoughts. As she reached three, Craig stood up, turned off the DVD, ("Hey, I was watching that," Emily told him, indignantly, but with a smile on her face) and went to the bathroom. A moment later, Emily heard the shower start and laughed to herself.

"I suppose I should help him," she said to herself, moving across to Craig's mobile phone. She waved her hand over the phone, unlocking it, and saw the message popping up. He let out a "Ha!" as she read it. "No, she's not coming here. He's going there!"

Less than ten minutes later, Craig breezed through to the living room after his shower, fully dressed. He grabbed his mobile phone from the sofa's end, slipped it in his leather jacket's pocket, and saw Emily looking him with a cheeky look on her face.

"What?" he asked innocently.

"That's the quickest I've seen you shower and dress in a long time, Mister! Going somewhere?" Emily asked, cheekily, as she looked him up and down. "You're looking neat but you seem too casual."

"It's *not* a date!" Craig insisted, heading to the door. "I'm meeting her at Nemo's Restaurant."

He didn't notice that Emily's look betrayed she already knew his destination.

That's a fast food restaurant, Emily thought to herself and then called out after him. "I didn't know they did candlelit dinners there!"

"They don't," he called out, shutting the door behind him. "Don't wait up."

Emily hesitated, thinking. Not a date? Don't wait up? Who did he think he was kidding? A cheeky look crossed her face again before she stood from the sofa, straightened her ghostly clothes out, turned invisible, and headed out through the door after him. He didn't invite him along but that didn't mean she couldn't have some fun watching.

Just as she passed through the door, she saw a familiar face; he looked different, completely different, but he she still knew who he was, and she stopped in surprise.

"What are you doing here?" she asked in surprise. "What happened?"

Chapter 17

Craig was only telling half of the story to Emily when he told her he was going to Nemo's Restaurant to see Brianna Cogan. It's not that he planned it that way. When they arrived, other people already packed the venue to the point they both knew it would be impossible to discuss things. So, they found another little Turkish restaurant down by Statton's river, which seemed quieter and allowed for a semi-private conversation, where they could fill each other in on what they found. Craig sensed Brianna seemed uncertain about talking with spirits, so he hurried through his story. As sceptical as she claimed to be, Ramsey believed she felt apprehensive about them just the same. At last, he came to where he mentioned that the spirit assassin wasn't on Colonel Ryan's network, or on their database of known rogue spirits.

Brianna chuckled at that, taking a bite of some lamb. She chewed a bit before speaking. "So, that's your way of saying the spirits don't exist?"

She jumped with a startled cry, looking around and not seeing what Ramsey could see; a little girl spirit stood next to Brianna, wearing a pink dress that looked like she must have passed away in the 1960's; she clasped a lollipop in her hand and licked it while smiling back at Ramsey. She had smacked Brianna in the back with her hand.

"What's up?" Craig smirked as he separated another skewer.

"It felt like-Never mind," she replied, rubbing her back where the little girl's spirit had slapped her. "What are you laughing about?"

"Nothing, it's all good," he replied, about to bite into

some Turkish pide. "Tell me about what you found today."

Brianna stopped eating for a moment, wiped her mouth on a napkin, and reached into her jacket pocket to remove a plastic bag with the odd-shaped turquoise-coloured object, or at least another particle that Dr. Kroot let her have. "It mightn't be the sort of thing to be taking out at the dinner table, since we're eating," she told him, "but it's some kind of bullet. I think we have a third killer unless the living guy has been changing his ammunition."

Craig didn't even reach for the plastic bag but continued eating just the same. "You can put it away," he told her. "It's not any ammunition you would have seen, and I doubt it'll come up with anything for forensics either."

Brianna looked at it again, feeling curious as she did. "I think it's shrinking."

"And it'll continue shrinking." Craig smiled a knowing look and spoke around the food in his mouth. "Your sniper didn't use it; the flesh-and-blood one, I mean. It's a piece of ectoplasm. Forensics won't be able to work with it because there will be nothing of it left by the morning, anyway."

"Ectoplasm?" Brianna spoke the word like it was something she had not heard of in a long time. "Do you mean the slime off Ghostbusters? But it's solid."

"Yeah, that's right," Craig replied, nodding. "It can take different forms. Usually it's a gelatinous mess that seems to flow, but spirits sometimes create it in solid form as well. For a new-comer to the spirit-world, this one seems to know what he's doing, and I feel he has some kind of connection to -"

Something made a sound, a ringing sound. Brianna

felt for her pocket and removed her mobile phone. "Excuse me," she said as she answered it, standing up to walk away towards a quieter area.

Craig continued eating his Turkish food, enjoying the taste, and listening to Brianna's side of the conversation that floated in his direction. He couldn't pick up everything but heard some words that sounded like names. One of them was Denton which he recalled from his Friday night vision from the Major's handkerchief. A couple of minutes later, Brianna came back to the table and sat down.

"Work?" he said, as Brianna made herself comfortable.

She nodded. "It was someone I know from work," she explained. "I had him check the computers to see what he could find for me."

Something in her response didn't ring true to Craig. "He wasn't really from work, was he?"

Brianna's expression flashed for a moment, and she replied, sharply. "No, but it was work-related."

"Down, Syndrome," he replied, with a strong, calming voice. "I mean I knew he wasn't from work. He's a hacker, right?"

Brianna's brow crinkled in a frown. "Are you reading my thoughts? I don't you knowing my private -"

"Settle, Gretel," he replied, steadying her with a cheerful but assertive tone. "Your body language told me, that's all. Now, take a breath, relax, and tell me what your friend found out."

Brianna stopped, considered Craig's words, and glowered at him. "My body language?" Craig nodded, a friendly smile on his face, although he did wonder about her sudden change in mood; Brianna thought for a moment about it and relaxed.

"Let's start again," Craig offered with a calm voice. "Is it related to our case?"

Brianna took a sip of water, and said, "After Friday night when you voodoo-ed the Major's hanky, I thought I'd ask a guy I know to do some checking for me." She saw Craig flinch and his mood darkened a touch, and she responded, "No, he's not with the police, but I find him useful every now-and-then."

Craig took a sip of water as well, to wash his mouth, and replaced the glass, a little to the side.

"I asked him to look for anything related to Project Gemini, which you mentioned the other night," Brianna continued, noting Craig's eyebrows raise in deeper interest as he listened. "You would never believe what Project Gemini is."

She paused a moment and Craig shrugged. His expression appeared blank, but she thought she saw something else flicker across his eyes. "Something to do with twins or stars?"

Brianna shook her head, lightening up a little. "Close, spooky boy," she answered. "My contact told me it's like the projects the old USSR and the United States used to have with psychics."

Craig nodded, feeling an uncomfortable recognition as he remembered reading about Stargate Project; it was a United States Government-funded program formed in 1978 to study psychics for military application. A few memories raided his consciousness, and he found himself back ten years earlier in a similar project for the Australian Government that began as a private study with another organisation. Brianna noticed his million-miles-away look.

"Oh, my God," she said. "You were on something similar? Really?"

"They never stop," he responded with a cold voice, as he shut out the memories. He brought things back to the present. "Before telling me more," he told her, "can you pass me your phone please?"

Brianna was about to ask why, but then she saw the serious look on his face, and she felt it was best to comply. He didn't take the phone, just touched it a moment and his eyes fluttered. Brianna was about to ask him if he was seeing a vision when he took his hand away. Craig held a finger to his pursed lips, pointing at her phone, and picked up his own phone in his other hand. He turned his own phone off, miming for her to do the same. He still had the no-messing-around look on his face, so she did it too.

"Someone has bugged your phone," he told her.

"Bugged? By whom?" Brianna asked, feeling this seemed far-fetched although it was still exciting.

"Have a guess," he said, standing up. "Let's go."

Craig strode towards the restaurant's front counter. No one was there, so he rang the bell, waited ten seconds and rang it again. A waitress hurried over, apologising for not coming sooner; Craig looked over his shoulder, straight at a table near where he and Brianna ate. He paid with cash, telling the waitress to keep the twenty dollars change as a tip, and ducked out the door without another word. Brianna hurried to keep up with him.

"Keep up with me," he hissed to her, and hurried down the street.

Brianna noticed a man and a woman leaving the restaurant behind them, hearing their shoes on the footpath. Their footsteps seemed relaxed, but it wasn't the usual casual walking pace people take after enjoying a pleasant meal. Then she felt Craig's strong hand grab her wrist, pulling her with him into a shop's doorway. His back was to the shop window, the shop's door on his left; her back was to the other shop window. It happened so fast that she didn't realise at first until she felt his mouth on hers, and their lips moving with each other. He held her close to him, the warmth of their bodies mixing, the excitement causing her heart to beat faster, awakening a primal hunger inside them both. Meanwhile his ears listened to the footsteps, their hesitation, and another sense of something close to panic; their followers didn't know what to do. Craig started to pull from the kiss; Brianna sensed it too; he didn't want to, but he had to. The footsteps passed by. Their lips parted, their respective breaths warm against the other's face.

"Did you just do that for the kiss?" Brianna whispered, catching her breath.

Craig shushed her with his own whisper. "Those people were following us. We confused them."

Brianna had enjoyed the kiss, and a part of her felt let down, but the soldier part of her remained keen. "Who are they?"

Craig shook his head. "Not sure, but I suspect that your visit to Major Oates has something to do with it. I noticed the same couple were at Nemo's Restaurant too. It's too much of a coincidence that they're here at a Turkish place, don't you think?"

Brianna nodded. "They did follow us straight out too." She glanced past Craig's shoulder. "They've stopped up ahead, not kissing or anything, just looking lost."

"Are they looking back here?" Craig asked, and

Brianna confirmed that they were.

"Unless they're trying to pick us up for group sex, I don't believe it's coincidence," he responded, shocking Brianna with his humour. "Let's walk down towards the river."

Craig held Brianna's hand, leading her from the jeweller shop's doorway, and back the way they had come. They passed the Turkish restaurant again before taking a turn through the centre's restaurant strip that led towards the parklands by the river. The river breeze chilled them, despite their warm clothing, but they both ignored it; their senses were on alert, listening above the lapping of the river's waves on the muddy bank below their path. Craig Ramsey's ears listened, hearing the sound he thought would come. Footsteps. Being a Monday night, there were very few people down by the riverbank, which made it easier for him to listen.

Craig squeezed Brianna's hand gently. She looked up towards him, but he didn't look back at her as he whispered just loud enough for her to hear him. "Get ready just past this pathway light ahead. Wait until we are just starting to walk in the dark again."

They passed the light pole beside the path, into its bright illuminating halo, then into the darkness. Craig's hand relaxed its grip on Brianna's; hers relaxed as well.

"On three," he whispered.

Brianna didn't wait for the count but spun on her left foot to face their shadows. Craig spun at the same time. Taken by surprise, their two followers stopped in their tracks.

The male follower had a stun gun in his hand; he lifted it faster than an eyeblink; sparks flew from the unit as he attempted to hit Craig with it. Craig was already twisting to the side, grabbing the man's wrist and elbow in his hands. Using his grip to control the man's forward motion to his advantage, Craig pulled him off-balance while aiming a hard kick to the man's centre. The breath exploded from the man's chest and through his mouth in a groan as Craig aimed a Gum Sao strike to his attacker's elbow; the man pitched forward in a somersault, landing hard on his back upon the concrete pathway. The stun gun clattered to the side. Craig kicked downward on his attacker's shoulder blades, winding him more, before looking to help Brianna.

The detective didn't need help. She had used her Krav Maga techniques to down her female opponent and now stood there with her foot pinning the unknown woman to the ground by her throat.

Craig Ramsey picked up the stun gun from the ground, looked at it in disgust, and threw it away so it landed with a splash in the river. Lifting the groggy male attacker to his feet, Craig forced him into a nearby park bench where he slapped the man into consciousness. Craig bellowed into the man's face, "Who are you, and why are you following us?"

The man, whose face had a sharp chin, said nothing, looking defiantly back at Craig. His ruffled greasy black hair fell in his face, not quite covering his eyes that glinted from the nearby light. Craig looked around and saw a couple of nearby spirits, which were otherwise invisible to the others. They were watching the scene with interest.

"I assume you know who I am," Craig growled, signalling for the nearby spirits. "Your name is Seamus, right?"

The greasy-haired man tried to remain inert but his eyes flickered with something. Even Brianna could see that the man knew Craig, and it wasn't from his stage shows. The greasy guy, or Seamus, tried to stand but Craig's open palm strike knocked him back to the seat. He spat at Craig, the spittle falling short and dribbling down his own chin.

Craig leaned in closer, signalling to the nearby spirits - two young men - and they grabbed Seamus' arms through the park bench's backrest. Seamus looked surprised, struggling against the unseen hands that held him fast. Brianna watched, not knowing what was happening, and thought that Craig had another power he hadn't told her about. Could he control things with his thoughts?

"Why are you following us?" Craig repeated.

Seamus failed to respond in time.

"Tell me now or you're going to be making love to the fish," Craig said, allowing the dark tone to cover his voice.

Seamus snorted in defiance. Craig paused for a beat then signalled to his spirit helpers; they picked Seamus up by his arms, hauling him towards the river. With a leap, they jumped over the guardrail, carrying him through the air until they landed in the river with him. He screamed in a mixture of horror at the unseen hands and discomfort from the icy river water.

"Bring the girl closer," Craig said, walking to the guardrail to stand watching Seamus splash about in the water. The spirits were dunking him in and out of the water like a teabag. Although he fought back, he couldn't see them nor could he resist their supernatural strength. "Bloody scary, isn't it, Seamus?"

"What are you doing?" Brianna asked. "We don't need

to kill him."

Craig turned towards Brianna, looked her in the eye with a dark look. "Don't we? He was prepared to do the same to us, weren't you?" He turned to the girl who Brianna was restraining. "Watch your boyfriend closely."

Craig pointed in Seamus' direction and lifted his hand higher. The spirits got the idea, lifting Seamus out of the river water and back towards the pathway where he shivered in the night air. He looked back towards the girl who he could see better now from the path light. She looked young, about twenty-to-twenty-five; this could have been her first assignment. Craig flicked his hand back towards the river, and the spirits through Seamus high into the air, somersaulting until he landed in the cold water again with a screaming splash.

"I can keep doing this until he dies from fright, exposure or shock," Craig told the girl. "Who told you to follow us?"

The girl swallowed, watching Seamus rise again into the air above the river water. She didn't understand what was happening and stammered in fear.

"What?" Craig said.

"Major Oates!" She blurted the words out as Seamus took another dunking in the river. Seamus screamed at her to be quiet.

A hard look came over Brianna's face, and Craig realised she was starting to see the picture now.

"Are you with Project Gemini?" Craig asked. Seamus coughed up water with a deep retching sound before he descended with another splash.

"Y-yes," the girl replied, nodding. She tried struggling against Brianna's hold, hoping to escape, but Brianna held her fast in a headlock.

"Just a warning for you, little girl," Craig responded. "Don't think that my friend here is going to be gentle just because she's a cop. You would have killed her without blinking because you're a mindless little drone incapable of thinking about what you are doing. Do you think she's going to be easy on you?"

The girl stopped struggling and listened. Seamus was still screaming as his unseen captors dunked him in and out of the water. Craig signalled to the spirits and they lifted Seamus back to the pathway where he stood, bent over, and shivered while coughing up water.

"I have a message for both of you to take back to Major Pain-in-the-arse," Craig hissed. "No more following us, or bugging us. He and the Project are to stay away from us unless he is willing to be part of the solution which I doubt. And if I see either of you again, you will know hell on earth, understood?"

Seamus nodded in understanding, his temple throbbing as he clenched and unclenched his jaw.

Craig waved his hand and both Seamus and the girl flew through the air until they landed halfway across the river. The spirits returned soon after and Craig grinned. *Thank the Colonel for me,* he told them telepathically. *I appreciate the assist.*

The spirits, both of whom served as office cadets for Spirit Force, saluted to Craig Ramsey before vanishing.

"How the hell did you do that?" Brianna asked, feeling the adrenalin still pumping through her. She had felt conflicted, watching the proceedings, and wanted to intervene upon Craig. But, even as a police officer, she had no way of backing up her story, especially if she reported seeing people fly through the air. She didn't realise at first that he was playing the good-cop-bad-cop routine until he mentioned her to the girl.

"With your help, of course," he responded, stretching his wrists and patting his clothes down. "I hadn't planned on things happening that way. I only wanted to get away from anyone listening to what you had to tell me about Project Gemini."

Brianna snorted, straightening her own jacket. "I reckon you know a lot more about it than I can tell you."

Craig smiled, taking a deep breath before letting it escape from his lungs. He didn't realise how much tension he had until then. "The first I heard of it was when you had me read Major Oates' handkerchief. I didn't know the ins and outs of it all. I've had some time to think and I believe it is something like another project the military persuaded me to work on years ago."

"My hacker friend told me they work with twins," Brianna divulged, realising that Craig was now walking them back to her waiting car. "Something to do with their ability to perceive thoughts and know what each other is thinking. I think that would be up your alley, right?"

Craig thought for a moment and he felt a light bulb light in his head. "Do you remember we talked about Joseph Denton?"

Brianna's eyebrow cocked as her eyes widened. "The marksman from the Army? It's funny you should ask about him too."

They stopped at her car. Craig placed his hand upon the car's hood, almost absent-mindedly, but she knew otherwise.

Craig smiled. He felt he knew the answer, but he

wanted to be sure. "Why?"

"Joseph Denton has a twin brother. According to my hacker friend, both of them served the Army, and they both were involved with Project Gemini. The twin brother scored better on psychic tests. Something called remote viewing, whatever that is."

Craig nodded. "Remote viewing is the ability to see things from a distance. It was a big part of Stargate Project back in the 1970's," he explained. "If you've seen that movie about men staring at goats, you would know about the project although it never mentioned it in blatant terms. They planned to use remote viewers to gain intelligence on countries, enemy sites, and that sort of thing without actually sending a live person there. Cameras, satellites, and drones can be detected; so can the stealth fighters to a degree; and it's cheaper to use a clairvoyant. Your car's safe of bugs and devices, by the way."

Brianna, although having guessed that he was "psyching" her car, still felt surprised but continued the conversation; she clicked the button on her car's remote, unlocking it.

"Are clairvoyants reliable enough?" Brianna asked, opening the passenger side door. "Apart from you, I've never seen one above dodgy status. They're always vague, speaking in riddles and fishing for clues while acting all knowing when they get a hit. Half the time their clients are telling them everything already."

Craig laughed. "That's called cold reading," he explained, "and, yes, there are clairvoyants, true clairvoyants, who operate out there. I know some of them, but I also know a lot of fakes, and a good deal of them are people with a low self-esteem; they mean well but need serious psychological help themselves. It takes all kinds. Anyway, if you read online, the story is that Stargate Project shut down in the 1990's. That's just a cover as the government doesn't want to be openly involved still."

"Then how are the Army involved, if that's not the government?"

"Private funding," Craig explained. "What happened with Joseph's twin?"

"My hacker friend has no more information on that yet, but he's still looking."

Craig nodded, biting his bottom lip. "Is he a conspiracy theory nut, by any chance?"

Brianna laughed. "Yes, he is. That's why he knows how and where to look these things up. How did you know?"

"I could say it's a lucky guess," he grinned, "but I am hoping he is. I'm concerned that he may be under surveillance himself."

"I'm pretty sure he is," Brianna replied, pressing Craig into the car's front passenger seat. "He's even on the paranoid side when he talks to me."

"Maybe he's seen the Krav Maga moves you've pulled on others," Craig responded. "My car's over there, by the way. Where are we going in your car?"

"My place," Brianna replied in a matter-of-fact tone. "We haven't had dessert yet."

Chapter 18

Joseph had been awake since 4am. The voices and images flooding his nightmares still clutched his mind, squeezing him with painful memories that woke him from his restless slumber. Even after leaving his warm bed to brave the winter morning's cold and blustering wind before sunrise with a ten-kilometre run did little to relieve the anxiety. It kept building in him, and then came the other voice, the one that seemed to know him although it didn't seem conscious of him. Now, as he drove another truck through the darkness, following his headlight beams along the forest road towards the highway, he could feel the memories squeezing him again. Why wouldn't they stop?

He screamed, long and hard into the dark cabin, and his scream seemed to shake a little of the anxiety's grip. It now seemed to hang on with one tentacle-like finger, so he screamed hard and loud again.

His mission was important, and he had to fulfil it today. The Other Guy planned it for himself, and he couldn't sit by without contributing.

This would have to be a quick job, quick and dirty, with no time for great plans like the other day. He had to rely on memory. The traffic was growing; people were driving to work already at 5:30am. Society seemed to demand that people work crazy hours as though they were unthinking machines. Once upon a time, people used to go to work to support their family. Nowadays corporations seemed to expect that people came to work because they loved the company so much they forgot their lives, families, and children - the things they wanted to support in the first place.

The car ahead of him was driving at forty kilometres instead of the posted sixty. What the hell? There was no one ahead of that car, just empty lane as vacant as a politician's head. Joseph huffed. Why couldn't the other driver speed up and meet the limit instead of holding up the traffic? He changed lanes, speeding up to the posted sixty kilometres per hour limit, and looked in at the car's driver as he passed it. The dim-witted guy was talking on the phone, acting like there was nothing wrong with it. Did he think his high visibility vest would protect him from his stupidity? Do people think the problem is only about their speeding while talking or texting on a mobile phone? Well! He would see about that!

Joseph brought his own truck in front of the other car and slammed the brakes hard. He braced for the impact, just in time, before the car slammed hard into the back of his truck with a crunching jolt. He pulled over to the side of the road, noticing that the guy behind him was doing the same. Joseph's thoughts numbed; just one thought went through his head, an objective, and he had to fulfil it. He opened the truck's door, stepped out into the cold biting air.

"What the hell were you thinking?" the other driver, a soft-faced man with dark hair cropped close to his head (perhaps to disguise developing male pattern baldness) approached. He had the type of fake smile that belongs to someone in corporate management, maybe some kind of "solutions manager" for a bank or similar place. Another silver-spooned nappy-rash yuppy who thought he was above everyone else he shat on to get his promotions. What Joseph thought to be a high-visibility vest was a high-visibility running outfit, made of a clinging material that did little more than show a thin frame.

Joseph didn't answer, pretending not to hear, and didn't respond as he approached the driver with a purposeful gait; his hands relaxed, and his heartbeat felt steady. The driver sensed something, but too late; he slowed his approach; a wary look crossed his face. Joseph struck like lightning, using the web of skin between his extended thumb and forefinger, hitting the man in the throat. The driver dropped to the ground, choking as his crushed larynx bled and filled his airways, his eyes opened wide with the horrible realisation of his impending demise.

Joseph picked the man up, draping the dying man's right arm over his shoulder and holding him there as he walked him back to his car. The driver's door was still open and Joseph dropped the guy inside, sitting him up behind his wheel. No one stopped to look, not that it mattered as Joseph was certain no one would have his description; his coat's collar was up and he wore an old woollen beanie on his head. He'd found the clothes at the Salvo's store and he would give them to a homeless guy later, anyway. The stranger's dead blue eyes stared through the car's windscreen towards Joseph's truck as Joseph got back in and drove away.

***

"Wakey, wakey, hands off snakey."

Craig opened his eyes with a start, unsure where he was. The room's closed curtains prevented blocked outside light, and everything was silent except for a familiar voice in his ear. He could just make out the woman's face in front of him. He turned, attempting to roll onto his back, realising it wasn't his bed; this bed felt uncomfortable.

"Come on, Craig," the woman's voice spoke again, and then he recognised it. Brianna.

"What happened?" he asked, his eyes adjusting in the darkness. "Did we?"

Brianna laughed, walking across the room to open the curtains and let the light flood in. "Did we what?"

Craig blinked in the light and realised he was at Brianna's flat. They had stayed up the night, sharing chocolate rum and raisin ice-cream from a bucket while watching a re-run of some terrible 1980's horror that starred William Katt. Another one started after that; Craig couldn't remember its name but he remembered a farmhouse surrounded by murderous scarecrows. At some point, they had snuggled underneath a blanket, as it had been a cold night. Craig had half-expected sex to happen that night when Brianna lay back in his arms, and there had been plenty of words filled with innuendo already. But they both contented themselves with sharing each other's heat and more deep kisses. They were both tired but their minds raced. Brianna was the first to fall asleep. Craig had carried her to her room and, although he wanted to snuggle with her, to hold her close in bed as they slept, he slept instead on the trundle bed that pulled out from her sofa. Emily would either be so disappointed with him for not making moves, or she would coo over how much of a gentleman he could be. He was just going to keep Emily guessing although she was close with her assumptions.

Craig lifted the doona away from himself, finding his shoes so he could put them on his feet. He looked at his watch. "We're up early. I thought it was your day off today."

"I have the morning off," Brianna grinned, her eye

twinkling. "But it's not that early. It's only six-thirty."

Brianna moved towards the kitchen and was about to tell Craig that she lied about having the day off just to have him stay but changed her mind. Brianna wasn't sure if Craig had picked up on her thoughts, knowing she would have enjoyed sex with him, but she was also glad they didn't. Apart from a handful of men, including officers she knew at the station, she had only been with one other man. It had been a serious relationship, serious enough that they talked about marriage, but it had ended all too soon. Snuggling with Craig under the blanket, feeling his warm hard body, even noticing the slight hint of an erection poking against her, awakened feelings and thoughts that she had hidden deep since Tom died. Tom was also slow in moving forward, similar to Craig, and she found that charming. She enjoyed the chase, but she still wondered how much of her thoughts Craig could pick up. Was he slow in moving forward or could he read her when his hands touched hers as he held her from behind?

"Great," Craig told her. "Go grab your jacket and your phone. We need to uninstall the bugging from it."

"I swapped the sim into an old phone I still have," she responded, using her peripheral vision to watch his reaction as she looked in the fridge. Craig could be hard to read but Brianna saw a slight flicker on his face. Was it disappointment? She stood, screwed her face up, and shut the fridge door. "Nothing in there," she huffed. "Maybe breakfast out is a good idea."

A half hour later, they were enjoying breakfast on Mount Staid, overlooking the sprawling city, its suburbs and the river that passed through the centre like a python that had just eaten. The wind was whipping by outside, blowing the trees and tables about, so they chose to sit inside where it was warm. Their conversation turned towards Brianna's interests, including her skills in Krav Maga, which had intrigued him the previous night. But, Brianna's mobile phone rang, interrupting their breakfast conversation; there had been another shooting.

"Now?" Craig replied. He had been enjoying the conversation too, something that Brianna felt good about inside. "You haven't finished your eggs yet."

However, she still had to go. Crime scenes don't change, and she could use flex time, anyway. So, they both bolted their breakfast down and Brianna gave Craig a lift, dropping him off near the secure parking spot where his car waited. He waved back when she tooted the horn as she drove off towards the scene on the expressway on the other side of the river.

The traffic was thick, jammed, and congested. People were sitting in their cars, waiting with varying degrees of patience; most of them looked resigned to yet another delay, and others looked ready to burst as they swore in their car's enclosed air-conditioning. As Brianna watched the traffic, scanning for a possible shortcut, she realised the shooting incident could have caused the delay in the first place. It was at times like this that she wished her car had a siren, so she could start it up and at least crawl past the cars packing the lanes.

Twenty minutes later, she managed to steer her car towards a legitimate parking spot and stepped out of it. She figured she could be there in less than ten minutes by walking. So she hurried along towards some stairs that took her to the pedestrian way by the expressway.

"Did you walk all the way?" Sergeant Hohenhaus

called to her when he saw her approaching.

The detective took in the scene. She had only seen photos and video footage of the carnage from the week before on the motorway. This could have ranked a close second if not a tie. A helicopter hovered above, but she didn't look up. She knew it was more likely to be the traffic watch for one of the local radio stations. Some of the other emergency vehicles were present, treating some survivors from the massive pile-up of vehicles.

"I hate to ask exactly what happened," she muttered. "Has anything been pieced together yet?"

"Five fatalities shot by the sniper," Hohenhaus told her, in a hushed voice. "And we've already had one of the media people nosing around. Sally Green, I think."

The name meant something to Brianna. Where did she hear it? Oh, yes, back at Craig's place. She had shot some video of the spirit assassin. "At least we know how they died," she said, holding back an urge to lose her egg-and-bacon breakfast from before.

A team of forensics officers took swabs and photos of a nearby shooting victim. The poor person, whoever it was, was missing the top of their head. Brianna walked around the car, to get a better look at the windscreen. Some glass crunched under her shoes. A female forensics officer, her eyes blazing with the passion of her job, approached.

"Detective Cogan?"

"Yes," Brianna replied, trying to remember her name. "Delta Smith, right?"

The forensics officer nodded. She was still young, fresh out of university, and seemed to love her job. Brianna had heard that Smith was part of the Goth community, so this work would have been right up her alley. "Looks like the sniper guy again," she said, holding up a crushed bullet in a plastic bag. "Standard SR-98 bullet again. We found this one in the guard rail over there."

"It's got some blood on it," Brianna observed, turning the bag over in her hand.

"Yeah," Smith nodded. "It went straight through the lady two cars back from this one. Passed through her, then the car window, and hit the guardrail."

"Any others?" Brianna asked.

Smith hesitated, her eyes looked upwards and her lips moved without verbalising the words as she made calculations. "We managed to check the entry and exits on the others. I would have to check them on the office's computer," she responded, pausing to think more. "At a guess, I'd say they came from one of those two buildings across the river."

Brianna looked in the direction that Smith's finger indicated. She noticed three buildings there, almost all warehouses. "One of those is the abandoned biscuit factory," Brianna said. "It could be a good vantage point for a sniper, given the range of an SR-98 rifle. Would that be about right?"

Smith looked, thought for a moment and nodded. "I believe so, but I can't be sure yet."

"Have you told the others yet?" Brianna asked, turning back towards the direction she had left her car.

Smith shook her head. "No, not yet."

"I'm going that way now," Brianna responded. "Tell Sergeant Hohenhaus that I will meet him there. If he can't make it, I need others there too, with another forensics team."

The police had already started traffic control, attempting to divert it through a couple of other detours, but it was a gradual process. So, although the traffic was now better than a car park, it was still moving at a sloth's pace by the time Brianna reached her Nissan Skyline 370GT. She opened the driver's door, sat inside, and opened her phone's GPS to find a back street route towards the sniper's likely vantage point. Getting there was a gradual process, and she only needed to cross the main traffic flow once, waiting for traffic to move out of the way enough, so she could continue onward. Most people, in their daily commuter habit, were on the main road; few drivers thought to take the back streets, which helped make it easy for her to find her way there.

A stray random thought drifted into her mind; driving past the restaurant strip reminded her of the previous night's dinner, the fight, and the snuggling afterward. She caught it in time, reminding herself that she was working, and realised that Craig Ramsey still seemed to know more about her than she did about him. Brianna decided she would have to do something about that.

The phone rang, snapping her thoughts back to the present. Looking down, she picked it up to answer.

"Hello," she answered, with an almost loving voice.

"Well, hello to you too."

It was her hacker friend.

"Oh, sorry, I thought you were someone else," she replied, feeling a blush spread. She composed herself in time. "What have you got for me, Wez?"

"I found out more about -"

Brianna dropped the phone. She felt the sharp

dagger-like pain in her shoulder. It numbed her. A fleeting thought crossed her mind. Someone had shot her.

A shock ripped through her again, disconnecting her. She felt like she was-

Chapter 19

When Brianna dropped him off, Craig walked straight through to the secure parking complex and made his way to his Jaguar. Emily stood at his car, waiting and tapping her foot.

"Mister Ramsey!" Emily's tone sounded like a mother who had been waiting up all night. Craig thought it's because she was a mother in a past life. "Where have you been?"

Craig opened his mouth to answer.

"Never mind," she snapped. "You just had me worrying all night. I thought you were only going to Nemo's Restaurant, not out with some woman you have hardly known for a fortnight."

Craig smiled, pressed the button on his car's remote, and opened the driver's door to sit inside. Emily floated in beside him, looking upset. Craig thought she seemed a little testier than usual and, knowing that ghost women don't have the same issues as living women, he had to wonder what it was. "This isn't just about me being out late, is it?"

"It's nothing unusual," she responded. "I know it's a sign of the times. People are so much more selfish these days. It's all me, me, me."

Craig felt anger rise in him and felt like blasting back at Emily, believing that she was being selfish herself. But he stopped. Maybe he was being selfish. Then he remembered. "Wait a second. What do you mean selfish? I'm an adult and I also place a high priority on the kids; I mean, Tyrone," he roared.

He saw Emily's face change from anger to something

else; concern. Before Craig could ask, Emily said, "He came home last night, just after you left, but he left again this morning. He told me he was going to stay with a friend this weekend."

Craig started the car's engine, released the handbrake, and started the car forward towards the parking complex's exit. "Oh, okay," he answered. "I suppose he still wants some space from me and feels he's better with friends. He's got time off from school still for bereavement."

"You should talk to him," Emily said, sounding perturbed again. "Boys can be so sensitive and high-strung these days. I guess they were when I was alive too, but there was also more pressure on them to be men and warriors."

"I'll call him tonight," Craig promised. Emily knew he meant it so she said nothing more on the subject.

Craig drove the car out into the traffic, driving in the opposite direction to his home. The traffic seemed congested towards the bridge, so he took a different direction. He commented on the traffic to Emily, adding that there had been more shootings on the expressway.

"Ah!" Emily said, brightening a little. "And how is that lovely lass?" She winked with a cheeky grin at Craig who realised he was blushing a bit. Emily cooed when she saw that. "So did you?"

"Yes," Craig replied, letting a pause sit there for a moment. "We had some action last night."

He knew Emily would bite at that and he couldn't stop laughing when he saw the shock on her face. "Not that kind of action," he added.

So Craig told her about what happened that night with the people from Project Gemini. Emily shook her head at what she heard. Having lived in Scotland during the Jacobite era, she had a strong dislike for the English; at that time, many of them were cruel, ruthless and dominating over the Scottish. Since Australia started as a British colony, Emily saw the Australian government as another extension of the English government's treachery. For her, there were many things going on that the government hid from the people they should have been serving. Hearing of this one solidified her belief.

"They're using twins psychic connections to kill and suppress more people," she replied. "And they won't even deal with their own who are killing innocent people. The dogs! What are we going to do about it?"

Craig, used to Emily's outbursts about governments, responded in an even voice. "I've got a hunch I want to check out."

Emily noticed that Craig had driven the car into the local hospital. "What's this?" she asked. "Is everything okay?"

He grinned. "It's all good. I want to check something out. While I'm doing that, can I ask you a favour?"

***

At nine o'clock, Craig walked up the hospital's front steps and into its foyer. He hated hospitals, preferring not to go near them unless he was visiting a sick person, such as the time when he visited Tyrone a few weeks earlier. No one was at the reception desk; he figured they were out the back; so, he went by memory, following a few signs along the way until he reached the ward he wanted. A nearby sign told him visiting hours started at 10am. Deciding he didn't have that much time to wait around, and that it would be better now before more people were likely to arrive, he made his way forward, anyway. His mind raced a little, trying to think about what he would do when challenged, and an idea came to him.

He still had a folded unused napkin in his pocket from breakfast that morning. Retrieving the napkin, he folded it over itself a few times until he had a long white rectangular shape; satisfied it was the right size, he slipped it under the collar of his black shirt. He checked it in the reflection of a painting's frame on the wall and grinned at the result; it was not perfect but it would pass a casual glance.

Craig walked straight to the ward nurse's station, rested his arm casually on the desk, and leaned towards a nurse who hadn't noticed him as she concentrated on her paperwork. He cleared his throat and spoke in a gentle voice. "Excuse me, I am here to (he almost said "speak", and changed his word) see Mr Shane Denton."

The nurse, bleary-eyed from the late shift and still waiting for the new one to arrive, looked up from her paperwork. Her eyes were a soft blue, very clear, but somewhat bloodshot from the late night. She noticed the white part under his black collar. "Ah, yes, Father, of course." She stood, pointing down the hallway. "Room 6."

Craig thanked her, staying in character as a member of the clergy, walked down to the room and hesitated at the door before entering. The room seemed empty, soulless even, and he felt like crossing himself before entering. A solitary bed with a male patient sleeping on it sat in the middle; the curtains, although open, did not allow much light inside; and a machine in the corner beeped at regular intervals, displaying vital statistics. Flowers with long colourful petals that looked like exploding fireworks sat in vases on a nearby bedside cupboard. A few greeting cards stood amongst them, messages written inside with loving messages; Three drawings stood out amongst them; one of them had a stick figure man with a stick figure girl, holding hands, and a message scrawled in green crayon, "gEt wELL dAddY. i loV yOu".

Could this be the man he sought?

Craig approached the bed, looking at the patient's sleeping face, took out his mobile phone and flicked through the photos and screenshots until he found a couple of the spirit assassin from the video clip. The clip's resolution was blurred by comparison, but when Craig compared the photo against the sleeping patient, he knew.

Craig allowed a small smile to cross his mouth as his eyes took in the patient's features. The man's face had a strong chin, as though he could be a determined man, and a short dark stubble covered his cheeks and chin line. He didn't look evil or vindictive, but the machines beeping to the side indicated that the man had been monitored for some time. A bandage curled around the man's head, covering the scalp, and some light brown hair poked out from the side. Craig moved to the foot of the bed and pulled the patient's file from the folder. He flicked through it.

Shane Denton was the man's name, and he had been in a coma since mid-to-late May. Craig wondered what had happened. He felt a few random visions niggling, little tickling images crossing his consciousness, and concentrated on them.

Surgeons standing over an inert Denton, a machine helping him breathe. A piece of skull removed, his brain swelling through the hole.

A pretty young woman, looking scared and worried, holding Shane's hand as he lay silent on the bed. A little girl sitting on her mother's lap, jumping down and kissing her father's face as he slept.

The doctor talking to the young woman. "We're sorry, Mrs Denton. We have no idea how long he will be comatose. He may never wake, and we have no idea how functional he will be."

Another man who looked like Shane, but not quite identical. His twin brother?

"He's breathing on his own now."

The random images flooded through Craig's mind and he struggled to keep a track of them all. He was beginning to see something behind everything but he needed more. He reached towards Shane Denton's blanket.

It was an idyllic scene. Father and son were out with each other for a day together, playing with a Maisto Rock Crawler remote controlled car. The little boy's name was Jai; he and his twin sister Rebecca were the youngest in the family. Shane's wife Rachael was at the movies with Jai's twin sister Rebecca. His oldest son, Nicholas, was also at the movies. The time at the park seemed too short for little Jai; he felt disappointed they had to leave, but the car's battery had run out; it was time to go home. Shane and Jai began their journey home from the park still talking about kid stuff. Although Shane felt love for all of his children, he felt close to Jai. Both of the twins were intelligent for their age; one specialist claimed they also registered on the scale for Asperger syndrome, but Rebecca refused to believe it; she said they were just gifted, very particular in their interests and needs, and very intuitive.

As Shane and Jai walked home, talking about superheroes (Jai loved Green Lantern, but he also knew about the less trendy The Shadow and Doctor Fate), they didn't feel a care in the world.

The traffic sign said, "Walk"; they took their first steps to cross the street; Shane heard a crunching noise. He looked up, jumped between the car and his son, trying to protect his flesh and blood. *I give my life for you.* Pain. Darkness. Disconnection. Floating.

Shane saw his body floating below him, laying next to his son's body. Blood; a growing pool of darkness surrounding his body's head; Jai's body was so still. Jai's body seemed to double, to reproduce itself; the second Jai that emerged from the original appears pearly white but transparent. A ghost.

Brilliant light exploded in front of both Shane's and Jai's spirit bodies, and they heard a scraping sound, like a door.

"What is that?" Shane said aloud through his spirit mouth.

"It's a door, Daddy," Jai's spirit responded. "The doorway to Heaven. Come on, Daddy!"

Shane loitered, wanting to follow his son but also feeling torn as he saw his son's body below. People were surrounding them, including the driver of the car that had hit them. He noticed another driver step out from the car behind that one again; she was a young woman in her early twenties and resembled a slutty bitch like that American with the dog in her handbag. She had a mobile phone in her hand, talking into it. It sounded like the conversation was a long one, one that had started before her car collided with the one in front of her. Had the skinny slut been talking on the phone while driving?

The woman lifted her large round sunglasses off her eyes, perching them in her bleached blonde hair, and started to mouth off at the driver of the car in front of her. The other driver, the one from the car pushed into the father and son, took no notice; he was still panicking, feeling responsible for killing them.

"Someone call an ambulance," the man cried, his Italian accent blurred through panic and concern. He turned around, saw the slutty bitch with the phone still to her ear as she mouthed off at him. He bellowed at her. "You! You caused this! You hit my car and killed the child! You and your fucking talking and texting on phone while *driving!"*

Anger. Growing inside him. Not just anger; this was Anger with a capital A for Angry. Shane felt as angry as the Italian man who he now recognised as his next-door neighbour, a man who would not hurt a fly, a man who loved to plant roses and talk about his childhood in Sicily.

Shane heard the scraping echoing sound and looked up in time to see the door disappear. Jai! Jai is gone!

Anger grew stronger again and Shane felt like exploding. He turned around to see the slutty mobile phone bitch, heard her trying to place the blame back on Luigi. What a lying bitch! He did not stop suddenly in front of her. She had not been paying attention, but had been more interested in talking to her other slutty friends on the phone instead.

More images flew by in the psychometric visions Craig picked up. He felt his heart pounding, almost palpitating, and he sat down on a nearby chair, breathing hard. He coughed a moment and let the rest of the images and memories piece themselves together in his mind. At last, he felt the crushing feeling leave his stomach, and the cramps faded. Sadness flooded through his being and hot tears came to his eyes, the salt water burning them.

He understood the anger and grief felt by Shane. When he walked into the hospital, he still felt like he wanted to kill the man responsible for murdering his adopted daughter, the closest he had come to a real daughter in his life. Understanding Shane Denton's other experiences put a new light on things.

Craig remembered the next vision after the accident.

Shane could not believe it. He wished he could hug Rachael's words to comfort her after the judge gave the verdict to the young slutty driver Tori Stamford. Not guilty? How could the judge have allowed that? Who paid him off? Or still, who performed fellatio on him?

*Shane wished again that he could hug Rachael, but he couldn't even hold her hand. Damn this business of being dead. That slut, Tori Stamford, took his life and the life of his Jai. She tore a family apart and had the audacity to tweet about it on Twitter with a message saying, **"I love the judge - not guilty. Justice."***

Justice? That little bitch who probably had enough STDs to scare the World Health Organisation thinks she knows justice?

Shane's other memories as a spirit still came through his body, including each of the killings; he had managed to kill Tori Patterson after some time, but he still felt the need to kill anyone using a mobile phone while driving. The obsession would last for an eternity as long as he was dead.

Craig removed his hand from Shane's blanket and thought for a moment, clenching his fists and dropping his head in his hands. A part of him still wanted to kill Shane for killing Debra, not so much everyone else, but another part of him recognised the distraught and angry parent. Violence was not the answer. If he killed Shane now, Shane's spirit (or astral body) would still be out there. If Shane were to wake, nothing would stop him astral travelling and killing people while he felt so angry at the world. Further to that, the law would not recognise him as a murderer, because no one could prove he was using his astral self to kill the living. The judge would laugh it out in court.

Craig sighed. What could he do?

Chapter 20

Brianna's fingers felt fuzzy, not feeling the steering wheel in her hands, and her head numbed as though it would roll off her shoulders. Even her vision flicked about, as though someone had flipped the vertical hold switch on her eyes. It seemed as if her own thoughts were not controlling her body; she explained to herself that this was shock from the gunshot to her left shoulder, which felt like a battering ram had punched it. She wanted to cry from the pain that invaded her shoulder, spreading across her upper body, but then it seemed to disconnect from her as well. She felt like she was floating, not in control of her anything.

Brianna watched as her left hand switched the mobile phone off. Then she heard a zinging sound; a hole opened in her leg; blood spurted in a geyser. She screamed, a shocking composition of pain and fright. Her left hand threw the phone to the side and clasped hard on her wound to staunch the flow of blood. She craned her head to look for the sniper.

You won't need that phone, dear, a voice spoke in her mind - a Scottish voice. *Those things only cause trouble. And you won't see the sniper from here.*

Brianna's hands were not acting of her volition. As her left hand left the wounded leg, Brianna noticed the bleeding had slowed. With both hands gripping the steering wheel, she plunged her foot on the accelerator. The car whipped forward, and the force pressed her back into her seat. A whooshing sound came to her ears as she passed the car in front, her car's engine roaring with attitude.

Something thumped into the car's roof, penetrating through the ceiling, and the car stereo seemed to explode from impact. The song stopped. Brianna realised she hadn't even been listening to the song that played until it stopped.

So many people act on habit and lose track of what is around them, the Scottish woman's voice said in her mind. Something about the voice in her head sounded familiar to Brianna. Whose voice was it?

My name is Emily, the voice told her, as her hands quickly steered the car into the driveway of an office building. The car's engine stopped. *We used to know each other, dear. I am sure we will know each other again soon.*

Another bullet pinged, penetrating the windscreen, only things seemed to slow down. The spray of glass particles from the windscreen hung in the air like a halo of tiny crystals that reflected sunlight. The bullet glinted too as it made its slow-motion path towards her chest.

We can do without that!

The turquoise-coloured bullet changed course as though deflected; her left hand flopped at the same time. It was an ectoplasmic bullet, not a real one, and it dropped with a dull tap onto the dashboard. Brianna thought it looked like an invisible hand had plucked it from the air and dropped it there.

It is an invisible hand, the voice assured her. *Consider me your guardian angel for this trip, but we are much more, dear.*

Brianna's left hand recovered from flopping, as though something regained control of it. *I'm sorry, Brianna, but I am in charge for this little adventure.*

* * *

In the hospital room, Craig was looking hard at

Shane Denton's still body, processing the information in his mind. One simple squeeze; that was all it would take to crush the comatose man's larynx. He could then walk out, knowing that he would be killing no one else through his astral body. He wanted to do that so much. He took a deep breath, keeping his eyes on his deadly enemy's physical body, and set his jaw before leaning forward towards Denton's ear.

He cleared his throat before speaking with clear enunciation so his words could not be mistaken or misconstrued.

* * *

A shower of ectoplasmic bullets came towards the car. Brianna watched them appear as though from nowhere. As sudden as they appeared, they stopped then hovered outside the car window a moment before dropping to the ground. A surreal feeling passed over her, and she wondered if she was dreaming. She looked at her shoulder, feeling daggers of pain twisting in the nerves, and saw blood pouring out. That hurt too much to be a dream. Brianna wasn't sure if it was her own thought or her invisible friend who lifted her hand to place it over the wound.

That's you, Emily's voice said inside her head, keeping her from passing out. *I do have some control, but you need to get out of the car. I can't hold back every one of those bullets.*

"Where is he?" Brianna asked aloud, feeling it best to verbalise.

I can't see him from here, love, the voice told her, in an almost motherly fashion. *I can see the others, but the bad one is probably above us.*

Others? Panic set into Brianna's mind, and she

pushed it away. If there were others, she needed her wits about her. Brianna crawled out towards the passenger's side, opened the car door, and pushed it out. It hurt her shoulder to move, but the adrenalin coursing through her must have had painkilling abilities. She unbuckled her seatbelt, and lifted her legs.

THUMP THUMP

Brianna's heart tripped; her eyes jumped towards the sound. They hadn't hit her.

That was lucky. Emily's voice sounded like a shout in her mind.

Brianna focused, pushing her legs against the driver's door to catapult herself past the front passenger's seat, so that her left hand touched the footpath. She wiggled again, flinching as more bullets hit the car; the windshield shattered; she found herself on the ground now. Her shoulder still hurt to move but she could do nothing about that. She shut the passenger door.

You must not tarry, dear. He's a spirit. He can move wherever he wants. Nothing will stop him coming around the top of us.

Brianna felt a trapped feeling overcome her, remembering something from her time in Afghanistan. Back then, she dealt with living people; this time it was someone with nothing to lose, not even their life.

A clattering sound, with a sound like heavy stones on a tin roof, punctuated the air. Brianna dropped, more out of instinct than from Emily's help. She squatted down again, and remembered her pistol. How could she forget it? The shots continued from above as she reached towards her hip holster.

What exactly are you going to do with a pistol against a spirit? Emily's voice asked her. Although her words sounded blunt, Brianna could sense that Emily saw the humour in the situation. Brianna left the pistol in its holster, leaving her head down as the bullets started coming from a different direction.

* * *

"It's up to you to decide when to live, and to appreciate the opportunity you have." Craig's voice held his determined tone as he spoke into the comatose man's ear. He paused for a moment, watching as the man's face started to shimmer; a tear formed in the corner of Shane Denton's left eye; its lid flickered a touch, but remained shut. Craig's eyes never left Denton's sleeping face, watching him closely for almost a minute before he exhaled a breath he didn't realise he had been holding.

Silence fell over the area; it was as shocking as the hail of ectoplasmic bullets had been.

"Is he moving now?" Brianna whispered, feeling uncertain and shaky; her heart was beating like a trip-hammer.

I don't know, dear. Emily's voice seemed cautious too. Brianna sensed that her invisible friend and ally was looking about as well, and wondering about their attacker's actions. *I can't see him around. He could be -*

A sound shattered the silence close behind them; Emily's voice shrieked in Brianna's mind; Brianna cried out in surprise too. It was Brianna's mobile phone ringing. Brianna let out the breath she had been holding, with a laugh, and then stopped.

Was the spirit assassin still around? Would he hear her laughing?

It's Craig calling you, Emily reported, her voice filling

Brianna's mind with warmth. Brianna noticed how familiar Emily's tone sounded when she mentioned Craig's name. How did she know Craig?

Brianna felt dizzy, woozy, wanting to throw up as she collapsed and fell hard to the ground. She tried to get up but exhaustion filled her body, so it could not respond. Blood pooled around her. She couldn't stop it. Her limbs felt weak, heavy and useless.

"Emily?" she called, barely stopping her head hitting the bitumen. "What's happening? Am I dying?"

There was no answer, just silence's report. Brianna's body even felt emptier with Emily's silence. She felt alone, darkness filling her eyes. She could just hear the engine of a car as it approached, a fading sound as she passed out.

***

Craig felt exhausted, mentally and emotionally, as he stood from his chair and walked out of Shane Denton's hospital room. He stretched his back, pulling his shoulders back and puffing his chest out, feeling the kinks come out. A nurse walked in, her eyes surveying the scene as she did so, and approached the foot of the coma patient's bed. She offered a small smile to Craig, nodding her head when she saw his clerical collar, and read the chart.

"I heard you talking to Mr Denton," she told him. "How long have you known him?"

Craig smiled, doing his best to adopt a priest-like manner. "I witnessed his wedding," Craig responded. One of the psychometric impressions he had received earlier had actually been of Shane's marriage to Rebecca. Although he wasn't there on the day, he *had* watched it.

The nurse smiled, eyes shifting towards Denton's face. "Tears," she observed. "He must know you're here."

"Really?" Craig excused himself, letting the nurse go about her work. "His family will be glad to hear that."

He felt an excitement welling inside him as he hurried down the hall, avoiding two orderlies who were pushing an empty wheeled-stretcher from a lift. Craig side-stepped them to get in the lift and rode it down to the ground floor.

Hurrying down the hall, without drawing undue attention, he stepped into the lift and rode it to the ground level. Once outside, he took out his phone again to dial Brianna's number. She had not answered last time and he hoped everything was all right. Craig wondered if he might have been getting too attached to Brianna as he waited for her to answer her phone, or was he justified in feeling concern. The phone went to message-bank again. This time he didn't leave a message. *Brianna is probably busy,* Craig decided, and hung up. *After all, she is working on catching a sniper.*

His Jaguar seemed to shine in the morning sun as he approached it. Unlocking it, he sat down in it and started the engine before fastening his seatbelt. It was time to go home. Perhaps he would catch up with Tyrone and have that "father-son chat" to catch up.

Tyrone wasn't home when he arrived. He picked up the phone, telling its voice-activated assistant to call Tyrone. Craig waited until Tyrone's voice message greeting played. Feeling a slight niggle of worry, he left a message for his adopted son. "Hey Ty, how are you feeling today? Do you want to talk?"

This was the first time in months that Craig could remember feeling at a loss in finding something to do. He felt happy with his accomplishment that morning and there was no one to share it with; not even Emily was around, since he had sent her on her -

"I'm back," Emily reported, walking through the wall from outside as if never existed. "You will be happy to know that your girlfriend is nice and safe."

Craig noticed Emily's worn inner expression although she sounded bright. "I was just wondering where you were," he answered. "You would not belie-"

"Oh!" Emily exclaimed, her hands thrust on her hips. "You sound so happy. Didn't you just hear what I told you? Your girlfriend, Brianna, was nearly killed this morning. I assume you cared as you tried to ring her twice."

Craig's jaw slackened and his eye opened wide. "Died?" He remembered that he had tried calling her and she hadn't answered. "I take it that she's alive?"

"Of course, she's alive," Emily retorted. "You did send me out to keep an eye on her like some jealous boyfriend, didn't you? Although she -"

Craig held a hand up, raising his voice to interrupt. "Where is she now?"

For the second time that morning, Craig headed back to the hospital and hurried towards the A and E entrance. He slowed himself down as he approached the desk, breathing hard from worry, and asked where he could find Detective Cogan. After a brief conversation, he convinced the receptionist that he was Cogan's relative. It is amazing how saying you are someone's partner can mean so many things. Although Craig was Brianna's partner with their case, the receptionist assumed he was Brianna's partner in other ways. He didn't object. They may not have let him in otherwise.

Following the receptionist's directions, he soon found himself walking past some beds, each separated by a dark green curtain wall, until he came to the detective's cubicle.

Craig gasped at the sight. Emily had already filled him in on the way to the hospital about what happened earlier. But seeing Brianna's bandaged shoulder, her arm in a sling, and her bandaged leg, was worse than hearing it. Brianna's head was resting upon a pillow and her eyes closed as though asleep. Being careful to make no sound, Craig moved into the room, and sat in the chair by her bedside; the chair made a tiny squeak as it took his weight. He stopped still as a mountain, not daring to breathe as he didn't want to wake her. She didn't respond to the noise, so he let himself exhale gently.

"Oh, the poor dear," Emily said, bustling around to check on her bandages. "She's a tough lass still, this one."

"Emily?" Brianna's lips whispered. "Where did you go?"

Emily looked as shocked as Craig did at Brianna's perception of her. She stopped still, wondering if it could be true, and whispered a reply. "I'm right here, Brianna."

Brianna's eyes opened, still feeling heavy from fatigue and the sedative. She winced as she tried to move. Her eyes opened wide when she saw Craig sitting beside her. Her voice sounded croaky. "What are you doing here?"

Craig smiled, a concerned look still on his face. "I heard the spirit assassin came for you."

Brianna blinked her eyes, trying to recall what happened, and lay back on her pillow. Her tired eyes turned towards Craig. "Yeah. I shouldn't have used my phone while driving."

"That's what I told her," Emily told Craig. "Shouldn't

she know better?"

Brianna reacted, turning in Emily's direction. Seeing nothing, she turned back to Craig; her brow and forehead held a slight furrow. "Who told you?"

Craig was still speechless after Brianna's reaction to Emily's voice, and he didn't know what to say. He paused for half a beat. "I talk to spirits, remember?" He tried to force a grin but Brianna saw through it. "Would you like some water?"

"Who is Emily?" she asked, her voice still carrying a croak, as she looked him straight in the eye. Her eyes pierced his, reading his expressions, and Craig felt certain that Brianna had cottoned on. "Is she one of the spirits you talk to?"

Craig felt confused. Few people could see or hear Emily unless she wanted them to. Brianna hadn't shown the natural signs of sensing Emily before, not in the way that Tyrone, or Debra, could.

"I must have been dreaming," Brianna decided.

Craig shook his head. "Emily is a spirit I talk to," he admitted. "She used to live in -"

"I used to live in Scotland, many years ago," Emily explained, sitting on the side of Brianna's bed opposite to Craig. She continued speaking as Brianna turned to face her voice. "You could say I have known Craig a long time ... a very long time."

Brianna tried to move quickly, unsure what to think. It had been shocking enough to find Emily, a spirit, was controlling her body in the car earlier; But, she didn't have time to feel and express that surprise before, given ectoplasmic bullets were flying about the place. She even tried explaining to herself that it had been the adrenalin-charged moment playing tricks with her mind. When she woke just now, she thought it might have been the after-effects of shock, maybe even the sedative doing something to her. But now, Craig was in on this as well, knowing about Emily who was talking to her now still.

"Is this the drugs doing something to me?" she asked, shaking her head. "Craig, I feel like I'm hearing this Scottish woman's voice talking to me. She almost sounds like Karen Gillan from the Doctor Who show."

Craig smiled. "No, it's real," he told her. "Can't you see her?"

Brianna shook her head. "No, but I can hear her."

"You could find that changes, given time," Craig told her. "I found the same thing when I was a kid. Do you remember me telling you about that?" Brianna nodded. Craig added, "Emily was the first I could see. I couldn't hear her at first but, after thinking for a few days I was going crazy, I could hear her as well."

"Now we know for certain he's crazy," Emily quickly chimed in, and Brianna laughed.

Chapter 21

A rich shuddering orgasm exploded through Joseph's mind as he bit into the burger. Egg, barbeque sauce, fried beef patty and bacon swam through his mouth, filling him with comforting satisfaction as he mauled it about with his tongue. His teeth chomped through the food, and he swallowed it, allowing the flavours to wash through his mouth and disappear as it went down his starving gullet. He wiped his mouth with the back of his hand, licking the taste's residue from his otherwise dry lips. He felt he needed that meal after the morning's efforts.

The television brought light and life to the darkened room in his forest cabin, driving back the shadows and voices in his mind. The old voices, those of the enemy were there, but he could not hear the other one. Where had his partner's voice gone, the one who worked with him as a reliable teammate?

Joseph recalled hearing the voice earlier, declaring he would kill the bitch, the rotten pig bitch. The Other Guy thought that the detective, although a pain in the bum, was all right; someone he could count on to look after the civilians, help protect them from themselves. So Joseph felt surprised when The Other Guy declared war on her. He remembered the voice of frustration as she survived The Other Guy's bullets, and waiting to hear how it went. The Other Guy had managed to wing the policewoman, right in the shoulder ("Hey, sometimes we miss," he remembered telling him at the time), and two more in the leg and arm. Then it all went silent.

Sally Green was looking into the camera, describing the carnage on the expressway. That was his carnage. It hadn't been as easy as it had before. Saturday had been hard enough in the afternoon, and he wondered if it might have been The Other Guy's handiwork. Somehow, he had allowed the press and the public to believe he was some kind of ghost; it was probably due to how no one had managed to catch him. So, someone had created a fake video, placed it on YouTube, showing it from different angles. It looked like a ghost had been killing people, killing them because they were using their phones while driving. But, there wasn't just one video. There were at least five different videos out there, all showing the same event. Something about the spirit seemed familiar, reminded him of someone he'd lost. It had to be coincidence, right?

Whatever. The views on it had gone into six digits, way past five hundred million, and they were growing. The comments below indicated that some people felt sceptical of it, seeing it as another piece of the propaganda to get young people off their phones while driving. Of course, he knew that people would see it that way. The authorities had been posting these warnings for so long, nearly twenty years, but no one listened. Even the authorities, the police, did the same.

That's why he loved The Other Guy. He knew what it took to stop people from doing it. Tough love. That's what it needed. Despite the sceptics, there were still those who listened and heeded The Other Guy's warning. Joseph had noticed the drop in people using their phones while driving. Yes, there were still those doing it, but it had taken him longer to pick those targets.... And it made the game that much more fun.

He watched the news story with more interest. The

female detective, Cogan they called her, had survived the shots. What happened? Had his good buddy dropped the ball or had someone managed to get him? Was he hurt?

Well, whatever was happening, Joseph knew what had to be done. There were still plenty of them out there, defying the laws set up to protect them from themselves, playing with other people's lives.

Joseph had to save the Innocents. The Other Guy may have missed this time, but that's life. If you fall off the horse, you have to get back on.

He finished the burger, swallowing the rest of it and screwing up the wrapper. It landed in the bin at the other side of the room without hitting the sides.

Damn, right.

"You have to get back on that horse," he growled before chugging back on the soft drink.

Joseph stopped drinking, and stared off into space, a wistful crossing his face. What was that? He turned around, away from the television screen, letting his finger dance in the air. Something wanted to come out. It could be the idea he needed. Ah! Of course!

His friend had the right idea, whether it was by planning or accident. Tell the world! That's what he had to do, and that's what he would do.

Joseph looked in the corner where several electronic devices sat. He was close to finishing them. He just needed to test them. If they proved successful, Plan B would be ready to rumble.

***

The black cat's eyes glowed a spooky white, reflecting Joseph's car's headlights as he drove down the street towards his sister-in-law's house. It seemed hypnotised by the dazzling light until the moment when his car entered a slight dip, breaking the spell. He smiled as the eyes disappeared and he watched the feline's outline as it darted off into the darkness, probably behind one of the flowerbeds. Joseph didn't want to kill the cat anyway.

He had been working late into the night on his project and needed the sleep. Rachael had offered him the spare bedroom to use, figuring that she knew he wasn't feeding himself properly. Since her husband was in hospital, Rachael may have felt she needed someone else to look after in that time - as if her children weren't enough. Joseph didn't mind. It made him feel useful too, being a second father to the kids and they still needed that feeling of security another male family member could give. Rachael also understood his need to be a lone wolf, letting him come and go as he wished.

He turned the car into their street and felt his senses prickle. What was that?

Joseph took his foot off the accelerator, letting the car slow a little, as he watched. Did he just see two faces then? He looked at the car ahead of him, flooded by his headlights.

Hackles rose on the back of his neck and across his arms. Slowing down from fifty to thirty, he watched the other car's front seat as he passed, trying to focus his eyes. They were waiting opposite from Rachael's house and he could have sworn he saw them duck down when his car approached. He could see nothing now but he was taking no chances.

Joseph decided to drive past Rachael's place. It was too much of a coincidence if the Other Guy's voice in his mind had stopped. He didn't know if the cops had caught the Other Guy, and if he was seeing people staking out the house, then he needed to watch his back. His family didn't even know of his plans and he didn't want them involved. One of them looked like he had caramel skin too, like the Muslims in Afghanistan. What if they were after him now too? They could still have had a price on his head.

He planted his foot on the accelerator, speeding back up to fifty. Unless they caught sight of him, he would have appeared to be just any other Joe driving past. He laughed to himself at his own pun.

Then he saw it. A brake light lit up. Someone was in that car. Did they suspect him? He shouldn't have slowed down so much to watch, but they had surprised him. Too sloppy; that's what it was.

His mind raced, thinking. Joseph had planned for this, but he had allowed himself to grow complacent and not drilled himself enough for it. He calmed himself and allowed himself to speed up. The pursuing car was still some distance off, so it was worth a try. Allowing his foot to press the accelerator more, but no more than the speed limit, he approached the corner and turned it. His eyes scanned to the sides, looking for driveways, until he found an empty one.

Wouldn't you know it? There were none! At least, there weren't any he could try.

He felt his breath catch in his chest, just a little tight, but it was only adrenalin thrilling him. His eyes flicked to the mirror, watching the corner, and he could see the glow of the following car. It looked like it was coming closer. Joseph closed his eyes a moment, opening them again, as he thought. The engine's sound provided the only replying voice and he swore.

The best thing to do, he decided, was to continue driving. They hadn't flashed their lights at him yet, nor had they hit the siren; but he still felt the anticipation clawing at his belly. He drove the car towards the motorway, which still had plenty of moving traffic on it at 1am. Reaching the on-ramp, he pressed the accelerator, speeding up to keep the traffic flow. All the time, he kept an eye on the police car through the rear view mirror. It was still following. What now?

Keep going, he told himself, imagining it was The Other Guy telling him. His heart almost stopped when he saw the car speed up, changing to the lane next to him. Joseph tried to control his breathing, but his heart kept pounding like a loud drum as the other car came up level on his side. He allowed a casual glance to the side, expecting to catch a glimpse of a police officer flagging him down. A teenaged girl, about nineteen years old, sat in the front passenger's seat. He thought he recognised her, but he couldn't be sure; she could have been one of Rachael's neighbours. He sighed with relief, feeling his stomach relax. The girl had probably been giving a blow job to the driver and felt spooked when they saw his headlights approaching.

Joseph thought to himself, chewing the end of his thumb, and debated if he should take the next exit to double back to Rachael's place. This time he was lucky. What if it had been the police? A thought flashed through his mind. What if the neighbour's teenager was in a second car? He hadn't noticed if the driver with her had caramel skin, and he was certain the driver he passed back there had it. That could mean he was right; perhaps they were police officers staking out his sister-in-law's place. They just hadn't noticed or recognised him because the light hadn't shone on him. That changed things. He didn't want Rachael and her kids involved. While Shane was in a coma, it was his job to look after them. He couldn't do that in jail, could he?

No, he decided. Something didn't feel right, and he couldn't afford to take undue risks yet. There was too much at stake, and with what he had in the car's boot, he couldn't afford to stuff everything up now; not when he was so close. He had only just finished building them now. That settled it then, didn't it?

He had to move to another place.

Chapter 22

Joseph took a breath as he looked at his handiwork, a couple of black boxes attached to a car battery. He had hardly dared to breathe earlier while setting it up. If he made one little slip, people would be scraping his guts away from the bottom of the maintenance walkway and wherever else it landed. He flicked a switch he had attached to the battery. Two of the boxes lit up, emitting a soft green glow, and he smiled as he watched them. Feeling sure that they were working, and safe to leave for now, he let his breath out.

He covered the lights to make sure they weren't obvious to passers-by, and once he was sure, he climbed down from the walkway. After dropping the final two feet to the soft ground below, he dusted himself off and took a final look upwards. The lights were invisible from below, even in the semi-darkness. A person would have to be up there looking for them to notice, and even then they would have to trip over it first.

Joseph trudged away from the bridge's supports and headed towards a path leading into the city's botanical gardens. A cloud of steam billowed from Joseph's mouth as he trudged across the grass, and his shoulders shivered. He wiggled his torso about in his jacket to warm up.

Earlier, he had placed one of these devices at the Statton Entertainment Complex. Breaking into the venue's building had been an easy job. The security guards may have looked tough, but their shiny tin badges were just for show. Their uniforms failed to disguise their bulbous stomachs, which were too large from eating too much rich food and too little exercise, and hung over their groaning belts. "LA Law" is what he used to mutter every time he saw one of them walking by with their keys jangling with each step. Even while carrying the heavy load in his hands, taking two trips, he had dodged them as though they never existed. They didn't even stir from their Playboy magazines when he stifled a sneeze. *Bloody amateurs*, he thought to himself. Just a lot of bulk for show with little brains between their ears.

There were just a few more of these to plant around the town.

He opened the door on the 1979 Suzuki Carry van; this was not a stolen vehicle, but one he bought in a private sale with a fake ID for registration. Although it was old, it's engine worked well, and its owner, a retired mechanic, had serviced it well. Its engine may have been noisy but it still sounded healthy when he turned its ignition and started driving.

Joseph braked at the junction to wait for a passing semi-trailer and looked into the back of the van. A thin smile appeared on his tired face, as he looked at the remaining units, before disappearing a moment later. He turned back towards the road ahead and felt a trickle of satisfaction come across him.

"I love it when a plan comes together," he muttered, driving to his next target.

Chapter 23

It was Thursday 29th June. Things were somewhat quieter and more relaxed for Brianna as she watched the sunlight spreading into the hospital room as the sun rose in the sky. The nursing staff had moved her into a private room as soon as the doctor felt certain she was stable. It was two days since the shooting, and she was surprised to find the road deaths had dropped a significant amount in that time. Apart from the sniper killing by his SR-98 at random positions, and a few genuine accidents that didn't appear mobile phone-related, there were no other incidents. She knew this because Inspector Myles had come in to visit the previous night.

"I don't know if our friend Craig Ramsey had something to do with it," he told her with his gravelly voice, "but I'm not looking a gift horse in the mouth."

Brianna recognised the Inspector's attempts to bait her. Maybe Myles wanted her to admit her mistaken scepticism of Craig's abilities, but Brianna only smiled back at him with a knowing look.

He noticed her expression, having made a similar one some months earlier when he had first met Craig and seen his psychic abilities at work. "Of course, if it is, I would like to know what he did and how he did it... My only problem would be in knowing how to fill out the report for it." He grinned for a moment, watching Brianna's face for another reaction, before answering his question for her. "That's why I have you to do the paperwork, isn't it?"

Brianna avoided the question by feigning greater interest in her meal: a medium rare steak with mushrooms, gravy and vegetables. She had needed the break, she knew that, but had been too absorbed in work to take annual leave. Now that the gunshot wounds had forced her to take a break, she didn't like the thought of going back to work!

Inspector Myles asked Brianna again if she knew Craig's involvement had stopped most of the killings.

She shrugged, indicated she was still eating the food in her closed mouth, and made him wait before answering his question.

Craig had already told Brianna his side of the story on the Wednesday morning; he had made her wait a whole day first as he wanted her to rest. Craig Ramsey hadn't known straight away that the spirit was in fact a living man's astral body. Despite having experience in astral travelling and receiving training in astral combat from Jing Yong. After all, an astral body is another form of a spirit - often referred to as a ghost. Yes, it seemed strange that a dead man would come back from the grave to exact revenge, killing people. But, to Craig, it wasn't unheard of. He knew of another man who had died years earlier and come back to wreak vengeance as an unholy vigilante targeting paedophiles. (Brianna had found that a strange tale to swallow as well despite the stories she heard from both criminals and authorities. of paedophile rings breaking under unusual circumstances. The criminals were always blaming a ghost that burned tattoos into their skin. She thought it was an urban legend among the police and the criminals.)

Craig also observed the strange road deaths started just a month ago in May 2016. That matched when the sniper's brother, Shane, had the accident that threw him into a coma. A search of the newspapers in the library confirmed it too. But, that's not what inspired Craig to visit the hospital. It was a hunch, and a stab in the dark, to possibly track down the sniper. Craig's initial hope was to find something that could lead him to the sniper.

"And has he found anything?" Myles asked, engrossed in the progress and awestruck by Craig's abilities. He didn't care how they found the killers, only that there would be enough evidence to back it up in court. Without it, the judge would laugh the psychic evidence out of court and the negative publicity would not help.

Brianna didn't know at the time. Craig had spent most of Tuesday afternoon in the hospital with Brianna before he went home. He had only been in once on Wednesday morning, saying he was visiting someone else in the hospital too. She knew he meant Shane Denton's room. There must have been other things there he could "feel up" for clues.

Inspector Myles nodded at that. "I have officers outside Shane Denton's room now," he confirmed. "No one outside of hospital staff, his wife and kids, and Mr Ramsey can go in there. And we have an APB out for Joseph Denton too. He'll turn up sometime soon."

A knock at the door interrupted Brianna's thoughts and she looked up towards the sound. Craig entered and Brianna noted his eyelids looked almost as heavy as the dark bags under his eyes. Despite that, Craig still appeared happy and energetic; or he projected that appearance anyway. What had he been up to? "Hey there," he smiled. "How are you feeling?"

Brianna noticed Craig's suit. It looked well-pressed and fit him well, making him look even taller than his six foot two. She wondered for a brief moment how he managed to look after himself so that he always looked so damned good. Even despite today's lack of energy, he otherwise looked smart. She smiled back, aware that he had seen her perving on him. "I'm feeling great today," she said, moving her left arm. "I can't believe how mobile my shoulder is."

Indeed, she did feel a slight twinge still, but it had otherwise healed completely. There wasn't even a scar. A part of Brianna felt disappointed by that as she was getting used to relaxing for a change. Besides, scars are sometimes great to show off too. But, Brianna knew she needed to be active again.

Craig's head started to tip forward and he quickly corrected it. He looked back at Brianna and smiled, trying to cover his tiredness. "You were lucky the bullet passed through your shoulder," he explained. His eyes twinkled a bit as his smile broadened more. "I bet that surprised your poor doctor. A normal bullet would have injured you for longer."

A distant look crossed Craig's face for a moment and Brianna wondered if he was starting to drop off again. It disappeared soon when he recovered. "Inspector Myles was here yesterday afternoon," he said in a matter of fact tone.

Brianna nodded. "He's impressed that the road accidents have dropped back a lot," she replied.

Emily started to speak and Brianna, who still couldn't see spirits, jumped in surprise. "Oh, I'm sorry, dear," Emily said in slight amusement. "I forget you can't see me yet. What I was about to say is the killings were bound to drop once we calmed Shane Denton. Craig has just been looking for clues on Shane's brother, which is why he looks so tired."

Brianna had spilled some cereal on her lap when Emily surprised her, and now she was wiping it off. "What did you find?"

Craig shrugged. "It took me a while to go through the gifts and such in Shane's room," he answered. He spied a banana on Brianna's breakfast tray. "Are you going to eat that?"

Brianna shook her head, and Craig picked up the banana as he continued speaking. "Most of the things in his room gave me some glimpses on his wife and their kids. His wife, Rachael, has been doing what she can. Seems to be coping well, thanks to the help of a few friends. Their oldest son is starting to show he's the man of the house, and Mr and Mrs Denton's little girl Rebecca seems to be speaking to an imaginary friend. At least, that's what Rachael thinks. She might be right, but I think Rebecca might be a gifted child."

Brianna's eye rose in curiosity. She wasn't sure how this related to things, but she knew Craig sometimes rambled. "Gifted?"

Craig grinned. "Yes. I think it's related because the visions were so strong. I'm just not sure how. It could be Shane's astral self she spoke to, or it could be an imaginary friend. Or, it could be both. In parts of my vision, I thought she referred to her Dad."

"And did you pick up anything about Joseph?"

"Ah!" Craig's eyes lit up. He knew he was keeping Brianna in suspense and he loved it. "None of the cards or flowers were from Joseph, but I did find a cricket ball there. It gave me a lot of information, and it still is. It's just that the information has been mostly a history of the cricket ball in their lives."

"A history?"

"Yes. It's hard to explain, but the two brothers have had a game between the two of them. It's like the party game, Pass the Parcel, where they pass it to each other whenever they meet. The difference is that they pass it to each other, but they try to do it so that the receiver doesn't even know they have it. For example, Shane might hide it underneath all the things in Joseph's backpack, and it could be hours, days, or even weeks before Joseph finds it. They have been playing that game back and forth for years now."

Craig paused, looking at Brianna's coffee in its paper cup. He appeared to be about to ask for it as well, having finished the banana, but he changed his mind.

"Is that all you got from it? I thought you could get everything from it."

Craig shook his head. "Not always. Sometimes I get things that don't even seem related, and so far, I have been picking up more of their escapades as children... Except for one thing, I can confirm that Joseph is the sniper."

"Well, that's something, right?" Brianna said. "We can't use your vision to take him to court, assuming we catch him. Have you got anything tangible that could lead us to him?"

Craig's face lit up, a bright expression replacing his tiredness. "I'm glad we got to that," he told her. "I think we may actually have something."

Brianna couldn't help look up at this point. "What?"

Craig shook a finger, beaming with a cheeky grin. His eyes moved towards the final triangle of toast on Brianna's plate as he spoke. "One of the visions I picked up showed me a little cabin in a forest. It seems to be a fresh vision too. I reckon our friend Joseph has visited it a few times in the last month."

Brianna noticed where Craig's eyes looked and picked up the toast, which smelled nice from the layer of butter and strawberry jam. His eyes followed it like a hungry dog's, and Brianna laughed. "Tell me more and you get the toast."

Craig swallowed, still feeling famished, and watched the toast as Brianna moved it side to side, which made her laugh. "I not only saw it in the vision, but I believe I know how to get there too," he told her. "I was thinking about calling old Myles-ey up and letting him know about it. Do you think he'd let me tag along?"

She tossed the toast, which Craig caught easily in his hands, and stepped out of her bed to get her clothes on.

"Not without me, you're not."

Chapter 24

Sally let out a scream, but the handkerchief in her mouth muffled it. Her eyes strained in the darkness, and her body felt cramped. She felt ropes on her wrists and ankles, biting into her flesh. It sounded like she was in a car or truck, which was driving somewhere. Something had woken her, some kind of bump. Could it have been a pothole? The tyres made sounds on bitumen.

What happened?

She remembered being at a pier, the one at Bluecliffe. It was a bright sunny day, but that did little to warm against the biting winter wind. Seagulls in the blue, almost cloudless sky. Then something stung her shoulder, something with blue feathers. It felt like a punch in the arm. Everything went black. Then she was here, in the dark.

What was she doing at the pier? It was out of her way.

Oh, yes, it was the story. Sally knew she should have gone to the police but she didn't want to miss the exclusive. It would have been her next best story since she first brought Orion, the masked mystery man, to the public's attention in 1987.

'It was a simple message on her voice mail. She hadn't even heard the phone ring; she had been in the shower. If she had, Sally could have had a chance to get more information again. The caller's voice sounded distorted, as though to hide the caller's identity, but its words were distinct.

"Sally. I have a story for you." The voice sounded deep, distorted, but not so distorted she couldn't catch its cheerful expression. "I know the Statton sniper, and I know why he kills, and more. Meet me at Collins Pier, Midday. Be on time. Be alone."

It came from an anonymous number, making it difficult to call back or trace.

All the pieces started joining, connecting dots, and she wondered how long they had been driving. She should have told someone else where she was going. Who was going to know her story?

Brakes squeaked and the vehicle stopped with a jolt; Sally rolled a bit, feeling queasiness in her stomach. A car door opened, someone stepped out of the driver seat to walk around the vehicle. The steps seemed closer to her. The door opened, loud enough to wake the dead as it slid, and Sally thought she saw a glimmer of light through the blindfold she wore. Strong hands grabbed Sally, lifting her from the vehicle's hard floor before slinging her like a sack of potatoes onto a shoulder. Whoever carried her was strong and carried her with barely a grunt. She couldn't be sure but she thought her captor was a man. Sally thought to herself and decided to stay quiet, let the man think she was still unconscious. It could make escape easier if she found an opportunity. He carried her the whole time; he didn't even rest her on the ground while the lift carried them up however many floors it took. She tried counting the seconds but she still could not be sure how fast the lift was going. If asked to guess, she would say between ten and fifteen, but that was only how many floors. It didn't show how tall the building was or where it stood.

His body felt warm against hers, warm and hard with muscle, and she guessed his age to be in the thirties or forties. Strong hands held her as her captor leaned forward, placing her on a bed. He pulled the handkerchief from her mouth. Sally fought the greedy urge to suck air in, now that she could breathe more through her mouth; it had been difficult to breathe through her nose before with inflamed sinuses. It was hard not to gulp hard at the air now too.

She felt her captor's fingers check the ropes binding her wrists behind her, before he moved to loosen the bindings around her ankles.

"I know you're awake." His voice was firm and carried strength.

Sally remained quiet, her eyes still closed underneath her blindfold.

"I heard you scream when you woke up," he explained, displaying his certainty in her level of consciousness. "The gag only muffled you, but just enough to stop you screaming."

His fingers reached her face, grabbed the blindfold, and removed it, pulling it away from her hair. The interior lights blinded her, stinging like a migraine for a moment, before her eyes re-adjusted. Sally took a deep breath to scream but his voice stopped her, confident and commanding.

"Try screaming if you like. The room is soundproofed."

***

The police Special Ops unit's vehicle arrived just after Brianna and Craig pulled up in his Jaguar. The officers, each holding high-powered assault rifles and wearing body armour, piled out of the armoured vehicle. The superior officer sent two other officers to survey the terrain and check the surrounding area for tactical advantages. Craig watched Brianna as she donned some body armour too. The detective winced as she slipped the vest on.

"Are you sure you are up to this?" Craig wanted to know. He could see the pain in her eyes, as if every shoulder movement was agony, but she did it.

"I'm fine," she grunted, buckling everything up, and indicated a nearby vest. "You better put one on too."

Craig looked at the bulky piece of protection gear. "But I'm going to be back here," he protested. "That's not my job, and I don't think you're well enough for a gunfight yourself."

Brianna Cogan looked straight in Craig's eyes; determination and something darker. Craig felt a twinge of intimidation but refused to acknowledge it. "Put the damn thing on," Brianna hissed at him, "and stay out of the way. I don't want you hit by a stray bullet."

"But you're still injured," Craig responded, not changing his stance.

Emily appeared beside them. "Children! Children! Stop the bickering, the both of you."

They both turned to face Emily who looked back at them like a scolding mother. Emily turned her gaze to Craig. "Mr Ramsey," she spoke with a haughty tone. "If you would stop patronising women, you would realise that real women can handle more pain than you mere men. That's why none of you give birth."

Brianna burst out laughing, and one of the nearby Special Ops people turned to look at her with a scowl. She hushed herself, remembering they should be sneaking up on a suspect, not pre-warning him.

The two officers returned from surveying the terrain, meeting with Brianna and their own Sergeant Paulsen.

They found the cottage, but there was no vehicle about. There were tyre tracks and footprints around the scene, and it looked as if the tracks were a day or two old.

"We've missed him," Craig said, biting his thumbnail when Brianna told him the news. "What are you doing?"

Brianna replied in a pragmatic tone. "I've got a warrant. It would be stupid to waste the opportunity of searching. We just need to check for any booby traps first?"

"Booby traps?"

Brianna nodded. "Denton is a military man," she explained. "I know from experience that he would have learned survival. If he had been hiding out here, he would have planned for unexpected visitors."

Craig shrugged. "I didn't pick up the signs of any from my visions -"

"But we still need to be sure," Brianna interrupted, "unless you're so keen to go ahead of us. If so, be my guest."

Craig stopped to think and looked at Emily who returned her gaze. "Do you want to meet the Reaper again?" she quipped.

Brianna ignored Craig's embarrassed silence, turned towards the officers and asked them to check for any traps. A quarter hour later, they signalled the all clear. They could find no booby traps. But Brianna pointed out that meant there was nothing in front of the cottage. They had no idea what was inside.

"That's where I come in," Craig said, striding towards the cottage's front door. When he reached it, he slowed down and paused before taking a guarded stance. Lifting his hand, he applied a gentle touch to the wooden door. It felt sturdy and steady enough. A few visions flashed through his mind: a face, which could have been Joseph's; a view down a rifle sight; and a few black boxes. It all seemed good.

Craig lowered his hand, waited and took a breath when -

"BANG!"

Craig jumped backwards before he realised it, and groaned to himself. Emily laughed aloud at her joke, shouting from behind him when Craig was at his most tense.

Craig swore at Emily as she continued laughing. The Special Ops officers, who couldn't see or hear Emily's joke, looked on at Craig and then at each other. They didn't know what had happened, and they weren't sure what to think of this so-called special psychic investigator. Then Craig turned back towards the door, turned the handle, and walked inside. The others waiting outside held their breath for what felt like a long time. One of them expected the cottage could blow up, but a moment later, Craig poked his head out and waved towards Brianna.

"Detective," he called out. "You might want to see this."

Chapter 25

The cottage's interior looked like a madman's dream. The kitchen and bathroom were the cleanest parts. The rest of the unit showed the signs of an obsessed mind. Newspaper stories, detailing the traffic accidents and killings, covered the walls in a dark mosaic of terror and violence. Black plastic covered all the windows, except one, to keep out the natural light. The uncovered window allowed a tentative ray of light in from outside that shone onto a coffee table littered with the fast food wrappers. A lingering stench of dead animal fat and stale potato chips hung in the thick air.

"It looks like it could use a woman's touch," Emily commented, as Brianna surveyed it all.

"A picture of obsession," the detective replied. She laid a latex-covered finger upon one of the news clippings and tried to read it in the faint light. "These aren't just the stories of those he shot," she observed, passing her gaze towards another news scrap. "There's also the story here of his brother and nephew's accident. The girl responsible for it was let off by the judge for community service."

"I wonder how that worked out for her," Craig muttered as he looked at another wall. His hands were also wearing gloves, on Brianna's advice. She didn't want any evidence contaminated by his fingerprints, and that made it difficult to check on any psychometric messages. He looked at a large map of Statton's central business district and some of its surrounding suburbs, printed on four A1-sized pages taped together. The sniper, presumably Joseph Denton, had marked points on the map with drawing pins, some connected by pieces of red cotton thread. He called out to Brianna, pointing to it. "What do you reckon of this?"

Brianna stepped around a couch laden in assorted junk and stood next to Craig to look at it. She studied a few areas and pointed to one of the drawing pins. "That's the warehouse we thought the sniper used on Tuesday. I was on my way there when the other killer got me." She pointed along the red cotton rays that emanated from it in different directions. "He used it as a vantage point for a number of shootings, by the looks, or at least he planned on it."

They noticed red drawing pins marked the sniper's vantage points. There were some blue points without threads attached.

"I wonder what these are," Brianna murmured.

Craig started to remove a latex glove. "There's one way to find out." He stopped, pausing to think. "I'm not sure this is the best idea."

Brianna's eyebrow arched. "Why not?"

Craig stood back for a moment, as Brianna took more photos of the cottage's interior. "What happens when this goes through court? If the other side's lawyer sees my fingerprints, which will be there if I put my hands on this, they will try to turn it around somehow."

Brianna shook her head. "We'll have a notation on the report that indicates your prints are on it. We needed to use you for -"

"But that's just it," Craig responded. "Psychic evidence can't be entered. Yes, you believe in me. Inspector Myles does too, but it's still not something that can be proven. The defence lawyer will turn around, perhaps even saying that I contaminated the evidence, or even that I am in league with Denton and turned traitor on him. What is there to defend me?"

Brianna stopped, wearing her detective role for a moment to think about it. Craig had a point there; they didn't need to have seeds of doubt planted in the jury's minds. "But we have a warrant already that says you are here. We also have confirmation from another source that this property belongs to the Denton family. It used to be his father's cottage, given to him through his father's will. Your involvement here today is as a consultant."

Craig thought about it a moment. Everything would have been fine if he had stopped after finding Shane Denton, the spirit behind most of the killings. He'd done that now, as agreed upon with both Myles and Brianna. But helping with this part of the case was also a good thing. He couldn't cut out now.

Brianna noted Craig's hesitation. "Do we have a problem here?" Craig shook his head, but his hands stayed still instead of removing the gloves. Brianna looked at the map and then back at Craig. "If there is a problem, let me know because we do need your help."

"I just can't shake this feeling that something is up," he responded.

"Like what?"

Craig shook his head. "Probably just nerves," he told Brianna. Somehow she didn't believe him, and she started to feel a bit tense about it all too.

His latex glove came off, making a tiny snapping sound, and Craig's fingers reached out towards the maps. His slowed as he was about to -

"Craig! Brianna!" Emily's voice sounded urgent, almost panic-stricken. "Get out! Hurry!"

Craig's head whipped around towards Emily. "What - ?"

"NOW!" Emily's voice roared.

Craig's head snapped around, looking towards the door. Brianna started running with Craig just behind her.

They squeezed through the door together. It seemed like time took ages, as they had to move one at a time. Craig followed Brianna still, pushing her ahead of him.

Craig's back felt hot, as though his back was facing an open furnace, and a burning shock pushed him into Brianna. They both tumbled to the hard stony ground fifty metres from the door and they heard glass shattering. Craig held the back of Brianna's head, holding it down to shield her from the blast, protecting her head as well as his own. But there was no explosion, just the incredible heat radiating over them.

They slowly uncovered their heads, looking towards the house to see it engulfed in orange and red curtains of flame.

"It was a fire bomb!" Brianna shielded her face from the heat. "He must have booby-trapped something inside that we tripped off. Could have been in the floorboards."

The Special Ops officers who had been outside hurried over. Craig saw a dark figure on the ground nearby; it was another Special Ops officer who must have been just outside the door. Craig crawled over to him to check his vitals.

"Officer down!" he called out, noting an absence of a pulse.

Chapter 26

The remaining Special Ops officers transformed into a ball of activity. Two of them started administering CPR, a third started calling in for an ambulance, and the fourth ran for the van for something. Craig assumed there may have been some kind of first aid kit and stood back to watch. He had nothing else to do at that moment. He absent-mindedly removed his latex gloves, crumpling them together and holding them in his hand as he looked on.

His eyes clouded over, and he felt himself shift in consciousness as the sights and sounds seemed to change around him. He looked around him and he saw himself sitting in a car, parked in a shopping centre's parking area. Looking in the car's rear-view mirror, he saw the glass sliding doors. A man and a woman, pushing a child in a stroller, emerged from the open doors; the parents were talking to each other, seemed to be having an argument, and the little girl was crying her eyes out. Tears streamed down her eyes. An older woman who appeared to be in her sixties walked past them, casting a backward glance at their loud bickering as she entered the doors.

Craig didn't know what it was that made him look. His eyes flicked towards a nearby dumpster, close by to the entrance, close to another parked car.

A fireball erupted from behind the dumpster, hurtling it across the car park so that it hit the young couple from behind. The young couple, the pram, and the child smashed into the back of the car Craig was in. He felt the force crush him, squash him against the window, and tasted his insides coming through his mouth.

The vision faded and Craig found himself flat on his

back. Brianna stood over him, looking down at him, and calling his name.

"Are you okay?"

Craig blinked his eyes, turned over and vomited; Brianna jumped back in time to avoid it. It was such a strong vision; he could still taste his guts in his mouth although they weren't his real entrails. He sat up, wiping his mouth, and spitting more of the taste out.

"He's been setting bombs in the town," he announced, trying to steady his shaking legs as he stood.

"What?" Brianna asked. "How do you -"

Craig showed her a torn scrap of the map. "I must have grabbed at it as we ran out of his hut," Craig explained. "I think he's set a few others too. We need to find them first."

***

Sally felt a strong hand, gentle but firm, on her upper arm, shaking her. A voice, her kidnapper's voice, spoke. "Wake up, Ms Green. It's nearly time for you to work."

His hands lifted her to a sitting position, and she pushed him away. "I can do it myself. What's the work?"

Her captor, wearing a ski mask over his face, looked at her through the eye slits. "We're going to be on television."

"And you're going to be wearing that?" she asked.

He didn't reply, only nudged her towards a door into a living room that looked like they were inside someone's house. A brown leather lounge-suite sat against a white wall with a painting of two elephants walking away from a river; its frame looked to be the most expensive part. The opposite wall had a large flat-screen television on it, but it wasn't turned on. In front of the television sat a tripod with a camera attached to a nearby laptop. Sally saw a modem router nearby. Other furniture sat to the side; it looked as though her captor had pushed them to the side. She tried to hear some sounds, any sounds, from outside. Somewhere, in the direction of the television, she heard heavy traffic. It must have been a main street, but she didn't know which one. If only she could hear something else to give her bearings.

"Where are we?" Sally asked. "Is this your home?"

His silence was its own reply, punctuated by his hand on her arm as he pushed her onto the lounge-suite. Her legs spread a little as she landed, and she saw him catch a glimpse up her dress. But, he did nothing more than push her legs together, murmuring an apology before he snapped cuffs over both her ankles.

"It's not going to be a good look if I'm cuffed here," she told him. "What are you doing with me?"

He stopped, looked at her, and regarded her with his steely grey eyes. They stared at her for what seemed a long time, never wavering from her eyes. Sally thought the worst could be about to start happening, but his eyes started crinkling and she knew he was smiling. "You're safe, as long as you do as I tell you. Then he pointed at the camera.

"We're going to give a news report to the city," he replied, "and the whole world will be able to watch as well."

***

"Hey, Fiona! Isn't that the chick from the news?"

Fiona, the man's companion, looked up from her Kobo e-reader to look at his iPad and took a deep breath to calm her impatience. Why did Steve always have to interrupt her reading at the book's best parts? It was probably some pornographic cartoon featuring female television personalities he loved to ogle. Fiona took a glance at his screen, which showed his Facebook newsfeed, and then looked again at the video clip playing. Her eyes opened wide when she saw the headline above it.

THIS MAN WILL CHANGE YOUR LIFE #STOPMOBILEPHONEDRIVING #STATTON #BOMB

The woman snorted. "Is this another one of those personal development life coaches?"

He shook his head. "No, this guy looks like a terrorist or something. Look at his mask. And it has the hashtag #BOMB."

"Yes," the woman said, looking closer. "Can you turn it up?"

Another passenger on the train overheard the word "terrorist" and lifted her gaze. "Terrorist?" she murmured. She saw the couple looking at the iPad screen.

The word acted like a virus as, with each mention of its name, it spread throughout the train's carriage. Soon, every person in the train was either looking at their mobile device, or over another person's shoulder, to watch the live stream video. The train slowed, stopping at Northbridge station, but no one noticed. If anyone intended to disembark there, they didn't hear the driver's voice on the intercom as their attention was already captured. Its doors closed, and it drove onwards.

***

Finding the bomb at the shopping centre was easy enough. Craig's vision was accurate and the police bomb squad were quick to respond. The hardest part had been evacuating the shopping centre first, and since the

Northbridge Shopping Fair was undergoing construction to extend the centre, they also had to move those workers as well. Some people wanted to come upstairs to the car-park to drive their cars away, but the police stopped it despite the protests.

Brianna and Craig were waiting in his car a couple of blocks away. Her mobile phone, a replacement for the one destroyed during the shooting incident, sat on the dashboard. Both were quiet as Craig continued holding the torn and shredded piece of map in his hand in an attempt to gather more information from it. Some random flashes came to him but most were hard to catch; it was like watching a video on fast forward.

The silence became too much for Brianna. "What was that about at Denton's place?"

Craig ignored her a moment, his brow furrowed in concentration. At last, he released a breath he didn't realise he had been holding. "What was what about?"

"You hesitated before reading the map. Was this all about being implicated in something?"

Craig shook his head. "It doesn't matter now. I've got a piece of the map here and you have photos of the evidence from before the blast."

Emily, who had been watching and listening from the back-seat, whispered something in Brianna's ear. Brianna started to react, changed her mind about saying something, and then decided to say it anyway.

"Is this related to Debra?" Brianna asked. She had an idea about it, but Emily had confirmed it for her.

Craig stayed silent, focusing his gaze on the map still, but Brianna knew he was just sitting there. Nothing was coming to him. She was about to ask again when Craig turned to face her.

"When Debra and Tyrone's parents passed, I promised myself that I'd look after and protect them as though they were my own. I know they're not my real children, but they're the next closest I've been to having kids of my own." His expression looked grave and his eyes looked set with determination. "When I received the call from the police, telling me that Debra had died, I blamed myself. I wasn't there when she needed me. Did you know that she came and visited us the night before the funeral?"

Brianna shook her head, staying silent to allow Craig to continue.

"She looked so beautiful, Brianna, even more than when I remember her," he explained. "I'm not sad so much that she died. I know that she's going on to something better, and that she's got some more work to do on a spiritual level. You mightn't understand what I mean, and I wouldn't tell you this if you weren't able to hear Emily talk to you. Otherwise, you would think I was some kind of grieving whacko. But she told me to forgive the guy who killed her."

Brianna's hand went over Craig's in comfort. It wasn't something she would normally do, but she felt the situation warranted it this time. "And have you forgiven him?"

Craig started to reply but stopped to gather his words. "I didn't think I would be able to forgive him. That was when I thought we were dealing with the spirit of a dead man, and I didn't know it was a comatose man's tortured mind. Did you know I was ready to kill him when I first found him?"

"And what stopped you?"

"When I realised that he had lost his own flesh and blood," Craig responded.

Brianna's phone vibrated, jumping about on the car's dashboard. She picked it up, answering, "Detective Cogan," and listened to the male voice on the other end. "We're on the way." She hung up the call and put the phone in her jacket. "They've defused the bomb."

Craig started the car and was about to start driving when Brianna stopped him. "You're thinking that you would have done the same thing as Shane Denton if you were in that situation, aren't you?"

"I probably would," he admitted, pressing the accelerator and negotiating the car through a roundabout. "Who wouldn't do it?"

The traffic was still clear, thanks to the roadblocks on a wider radius, and Craig approached the shopping centre from the back road.

"That doesn't make you the same as Shane Denton," Brianna told him. "Believing someone's ideals and beliefs doesn't make you just as bad. Our character comes from following through upon them."

A few minutes later, they were at the shopping centre. A police officer, upon seeing Cogan in the passenger's seat and recognising her, let them drive to the top floor car parking area. It was an open air car park with most of the cars parked in the warm winter sun. Craig negotiated a few turns and saw the bomb squad looking at a strange assembly of gadgets on the cement ground. An officer was taking photos of them for later. Nearby another officer was ready with the fingerprint kit.

"Are you going to be right to check this with your magic hands?" Brianna asked, as Craig stopped the car's engine.

He turned to her with a grin. "Let's do it."

They stepped out of the car and approached the group gathered around the bomb. Craig felt a little jump in his stomach, never having seen a home-made bomb before.

"What the hell is that?" Brianna asked, looking at the Frankenstein-like mess.

One of the bomb disposal officers approached. "I've never seen anything like it either," he answered, "but it's an interesting set."

He started pointing at the device. "The whole thing is powered by a car battery. It keeps the mobile phone charged. (He pointed at a thin box with four antennas sticking out of it) This is a 3G mobile jammer. It's deactivated now. It looks as though when some calls the mobile phone attached to it, it activates the jammer. It also turns on this timer here, which he has attached to this C4 explosive."

Brianna looked, thinking to herself. "You've got three or four loose items here with just cables connecting them. Were they sitting like this?"

The bomb expert shook his head, pointing to a nearby milk crate with cardboard lining its edges. "He had it inside that. It would have made it easier for him to carry it when he set it up."

The fingerprint guy was dusting it and recovering prints. Craig watched, looking for something he could touch on it as soon as the powder was removed.

"But why have a jammer on it?" she wondered. "How long was the timer set for?"

"It would have allowed ten minutes," the bomb

expert answered. "I don't know why he would have done it either."

The fingerprint guy moved away and Craig moved in. Before he leaned forward to touch the defused bomb, he turned back towards Brianna and the bomb expert. "He's just like his brother," Craig explained. "His brother Shane doesn't like people using phones while driving. Joseph seems to have a similar profile. He would have wanted it as some kind of 'poetic justice' before killing them with the bomb."

"Why at a shopping centre?"

"Why not?" Craig replied before putting his hand on the battery casing.

Brianna watched Craig's eyes glaze over, and she knew flashes were going through his head. It was a good thing, she thought, because the torn map had given her all it knew. Only half a minute had passed, but it felt like a year as they watched him. At last, he stood, waving his hands as though shaking water off them.

"Well?" Brianna asked. "What did you get?"

Brianna's mobile phone rang, interrupting them. Craig signalled to Brianna, indicating she should follow him as she answered the phone. He stepped into the car, half-listening to Brianna as he turned on the engine. She stepped in the car as well, and he pressed the accelerator.

"Thanks, Inspector," Brianna responded. "I'm in the car with Craig now. We'll have a look."

Brianna hung up and looked towards Craig. "You're friends with Sally Green, aren't you?"

Craig looked towards Brianna. "What's happened?"

"Joseph Denton has kidnapped her, and she's interviewing him on the internet," Brianna replied. "It's streaming live now."

Craig looked at her. "Really? I was going to tell you to call for backup, anyway. I'm taking you straight to where Joseph has taken her."

He floored the accelerator, taking off through the back streets towards the river district.

Chapter 27

Sally felt a mixture of emotions and thoughts through her tired mind when the kidnapper first sat near her on the opposite end of the sofa. She realised this interview was a mock-up of a talk show setting, right down to the couch and seating arrangements. That part seemed funny, and she guessed this man must have always wanted attention. But she hated sitting so close to him. He had explained to her, before the interview started, that he was responsible for the shootings. This reviled her even more, to be sitting so close to someone who held other people's lives to judgement.

"The broadcast is ready to go," he told her. "Let's get started."

"What about-"

"Now!" His voice was so commanding she couldn't resist.

Sally faced the camera, her professional mask melting onto her face as she spoke into it. "Good evening," she said. "I am Sally Green, and this is- I don't have your name..."

The ski-masked man spoke up. "My name isn't important, but you can call me Blow Joe."

"Blow Joe..." Sally said the name, wondering if this man was having fun with her or not. "Is that a nickname?"

He shook his head and Sally looked back at the camera. As she spoke, she felt amazed with how calm she sounded; there was barely a quiver in voice, but she couldn't mistake the tension in her chest and stomach. "I am here this evening with Joe. Joe has kidnapped me and, if you can see my feet, he has me shackled so that I can't escape. Joe, why have you kidnapped me?"

Joe didn't know which way to face, the camera or Sally, as he tried to look both ways at once. "I have a message for everyone in Statton, and I want the world to hear it as well," he announced, his voice full of conviction. "Stop using your mobile phones while you are driving."

"That's quite a community service announcement, Joe," Sally responded, and her voice snapped to a no-funny-business tone. "That can hardly be the reason you kidnapped me. You could have done this yourself without involving me, right?"

"No," he retorted, looking her dead in the eye. "People need to know that I am serious, and I am holding each of them accountable."

"Have you been holding people accountable already?"

Joe said nothing, staying silent for a moment, and Sally pressed the question again.

"Yes, I have," he said, his determination showing. "The authorities have already tried their best, but people are unthinking and selfish sheep. They keep using their mobile phones when driving, even after seeing the news of people dying. People like my brother and his son. They still want to Twitter, and text, and talk to each other. So you leave me no choice but to kill those people before they kill any more innocents."

Sally's jaw dropped. She thought this man looked familiar. "Are you the man or ghost I filmed last week?"

This seemed to unnerve Joe for a moment. "What?" He paused another second, shook his head. "That is someone else, and I don't know what happened to him. He had the same idea too."

"What makes you think your efforts are going to have

a better effect?" Sally asked, pressing forward with her questions, making them almost accusatory.

"So many times, I have seen people driving on the streets with a phone stuck to their head," he replied. "They think they're not noticed, and some don't even care. When they kill someone, those who don't wake up to their stupid selfishness try to rationalise it with lies. They try to place the blame back on the innocents. I want people to take responsibility for their actions, so I am holding them accountable. If I see you using a mobile phone while you are driving, I will kill you."

"You mentioned someone else is killing people too," Sally said, taking another tangent. "What can you tell us about him?"

Joe flinched, his head gave a twitch, and his eyes darted to the side for a moment. She had caught him off-guard. "I don't know," he replied. "I have had contact with him but I haven't met him."

His voice trailed a moment, and he bounced back to his former confidence. "But I do know that he feels the same way as me. I remember that we managed to kill people at opposite ends of the city, almost at the same time. No one has traced him, or even reported how he has killed them, but it has been interesting to watch the authorities unsure of where to go next."

"You enjoy having the authorities in confusion?" Sally asked. "Why?"

"I don't enjoy confusing them, but they haven't been doing their jobs in stopping people from killing others with their mobile phones," Joe responded. "I am helping the police do their jobs, getting these people off the streets."

Sally nodded. "Was that you who killed a policeman, Joe?"

He nodded. "There is no room for bad apples, and he was setting a bad example. He deserved to die."

"And who or what gives you the right to decide who must live and die?" Sally asked, levelling her voice at him.

Joe shuddered a moment before straightening again. His voice harshened as he roared back at her. "Who the Hell gives them the right to kill other people through their selfishness? Who the Hell lets these people drive cars, which are really just a guided missile, with their brains already distracted?"

Sally went silent. She understood his point, but she also knew the cost of his mission.

"Why did you kidnap me, Joe?" she asked. "Was it just to tell people how you feel? Why did it have to be this way?"

A terrible glint flashed into Joe's eyes and they narrowed. His voice deepened into a growl like a lion's voice. "I want people to stop killing. I want people driving, while using their phones, charged and convicted for murder. They know what they are doing, and they need to pay the price."

"Is that it?" Sally asked, before wishing she hadn't asked the question.

"There's more," Joe nodded, bringing a mobile phone from his pocket. "Here's my next warning."

His fingers flicked through the phone's address book, and he pressed the screen. There was silence. Sally looked on at Joe as he waited.

"Wrong number?" she asked.

Joe remained silent. He seemed to be listening to

something.

***

The people in the train carriage were still watching the video link, not caring about what happened to their mobile phone data plans. If they didn't have a mobile phone or iPad to watch, they found someone else and peered over their shoulders.

"Who's he calling?" someone asked aloud.

The carriage lurched, tipping them off their feet and seats, throwing them about with the wrenching sound of metal tearing apart. Blood ran and bones burst as they flew about the carriage, and a wall of fire overtook them. The train rocked off the tracks and seemed to float in the air for a moment as the bridge underneath it gave way. The bomb had blown its support out. Screams filled the air in an off-key accompaniment to the deadly chorus playing.

***

The sound of the explosion reached Sally's ear, and she looked at Joe. "What did you do?"

Chapter 28

Craig pressed the accelerator hard, pushing the Jaguar through its paces and manoeuvring between the other cars as though they were standing still. Brianna gripped the seat hard as the engine roared and looked towards Craig. She shouted something, asking why he was going so fast, when she felt the car shake. It wasn't the car, it was the road beneath them, and then she saw something in the side mirror's reflection. A flash; something flying; cars disappearing. A huge explosion went off with the sound of cracking thunder.

Brianna turned her head back to look, and Craig braked hard to avoid hitting a car in front of him.

The two of them turned around, seeing that a section of bridge behind them had disappeared. Screams permeated the air and a plume of smoke rose upward and spread out.

"How the hell did you know to speed up?" Brianna asked.

"I thought I heard someone tell me," Craig answered with a shrug. He looked towards Emily. "Was it you?"

Emily turned from looking at the carnage through the back window and faced him. "No. I was going to ask how you knew too."

Brianna looked at her phone. "That was weird," she said. "My phone went dead first as it was playing the video. The signal's back now."

Shock filled Brianna's face as she turned to face Craig. "Was that one of his bombs?"

Craig nodded. "We need that siren of yours so we can get through this traffic."

Brianna removed the red flashing light from the backseat and reached out the window to attach it to the car's roof. It started flashing and wailing as she plugged it into the car's cigarette lighter, and Craig gunned the accelerator again to push through the mass of cars and rubberneckers looking back.

Craig swore as a few people stepped out in front, slowing down a bit as they jumped back, and honked his horn to keep them moving. "Did you see what happened on the video before the bomb went off?"

"He called someone," Brianna replied, trying to get the link back again. "Does that mean there's another one out there?"

"No, he called the bomb," Craig replied, tension filling his voice as he dodged through the traffic. "We have to disable those bombs before they go off."

"But he could do that at any time," Emily said from the back-seat. "How are you going to stop him?"

Craig's face lit up, his eyes opened wide, and a grin crossed his face. Turning to face Brianna, he said, "Can you make a phone call for me? We need to reach a friend of yours."

Chapter 29

Sally's stomach clenched, tightening, and she felt the tension spreading through her body. She fought back the urge to scream and did her best to stay calm. But burning anger still dripped from her voice. "What have you done?"

Joe seemed as though in another world as his head tilted to one side, his eyes not focusing on anything in particular. The end of his mouth curled as he heard the faint rumbling of explosions. He heard sirens passing about three blocks from their location, their wails fading as they hurried towards the explosion site. He put his phone away in his pocket, sat back on the sofa and interlocked his fingers behind his head.

"No one answered my warning, Ms Green," he responded. "I had to leave another message."

He looked away and stared in the camera's direction. It was still recording. The flat screen television above the camera showed the interview as it recorded, and he looked at it without taking in the whole situation. Sally watched, noting that he had done that not long after the first explosion as well. She had seen this sort of thing before and she tried to remember where. Joe's head and shoulders started moving back and forth in a slow but constant rhythm. Then he stopped, blinked his eyes, and looked at his watch.

"Where were you then?" Sally asked, realising the truth.

Joe turned towards her. "Right here, of course," he replied.

Sally knew he was being evasive. "No. You were thinking of something else, something from the past. Was it your brother and nephew's accident?"

He shook his head, standing up and removing the mask from his face. Sally looked at Joe's face, taking in his strong features, and noting how he seemed almost eagle-like. His eyes seemed less sharp but she should still see the intensity they held. His nose appeared determined, sharp, and his chin looked strong with just a hint of a dimple. Joe clenched and unclenched his jaw, and Sally watched it make his temples throb.

"You were in the armed forces, weren't you?" Sally asked, now recognising where she had seen this behaviour before. He didn't answer so Sally said his name.

Joe turned around. "Fourth batallion," he answered. "Operation Slipper."

"Afghanistan?" Sally asked. She paused, not knowing what else to say, and tried to steady the sound of her heart beating. "Do you still serve?"

Joe didn't answer, staying silent as he sat back down again. Sally continued watching, her mind flicking through different scenarios.

"Tell me what happened in Afghanistan," she replied. "I know you're still having flashbacks."

His hands started wringing, his eyes zoned out, but his voice remained present. "I used to be a sniper in Operation Slipper, a damn good one. The enemy had a name for me that meant 'devil's long arm'. I could pick them off before they even knew I was there."

Joe's voice trailed away, the flashback returning. His breathing changed, chopping to a panicked rhythm, and then he reached for his jeans pocket again. He pulled his phone out, looking at Sally. "Do you think I don't know what you're doing? They tried the same thing, trying to distract me with your ambushing questions!"

He stepped forward without thinking and slapped Sally's face hard, punctuating the air with the sound. She screamed, her head turning from the force, and raised her arms up to stop any more blows. Joe stopped and looked at her. Exhaling hard through his nose, he held up the other hand with the phone.

"No, Joe," Sally pleaded. "Don't do it. These are your fellow Australians you are killing."

Fellow Australians? Joe stopped, looked at her, this time with an expression like a little boy lost in confusion between two decisions.

Sally pressed forward with her words. "Some of those could be your friends."

Joe's hand started shaking, almost dropping the phone, and he hesitated.

"Or your family," Sally added.

Joe's features softened more at the mention of his family. His bottom lip quivered as he remembered Rachael... Rebecca... Jai... and Shane.

His voice was hardly a murmur. "They killed my brother and nephew."

His finger punched the third number on his phone's contact list, and he waited, listening.

"No!" Sally cried. Her eyes felt hot with impending tears and her face burned as blood rushed to it. "Not again!"

They waited.

It seemed to be forever.

Joe's face took a puzzled expression. He looked at the phone, tapping the number again, and held it to his ear. Hearing nothing, he looked at it again. No signal showed on the phone. "Fuck!" He wound up, ready to throw the phone and smash it against the wall. Then he stopped and looked at the wall, seeing another phone there.

Whatever relief Sally started to feel slipped away like water from her fingers as she watched Joe walk across the room towards the landline. He picked up the receiver, smiled when he heard the dial tone, and started punching the phone number from his mobile phone's contact list.

The sound from the phone was loud enough for Sally to hear as it emitted a high-pitched two-note chord. A smile of relief came back again when she heard the automatic voice speaking.

"We're sorry. The number you have called is either not connected or out of mobile range."

Joe ripped the landline phone from the wall in rage, then he hurled the phone at the opposite wall. It smashed with a dinging sound as its bell rang its death knell.

Chapter 30

The Jaguar's engine roared like its namesake as it rounded the corner to the otherwise quiet residential street. Craig resisted the urge to slam the brakes, lifted his foot from the accelerator, and slowed the car to a stop beside the waiting Special Ops van. Craig and Brianna stepped out of the Jaguar to approach them. The Ops Leader approached them.

"We got your message, Detective," he told Brianna. "But we couldn't respond. The mobile towers are down."

"Yes, we know about that," Brianna smiled, putting her body armour back on over her clothes.

Upon Craig's suggestion, she had called Mick, her hacker friend otherwise known as M1CK. Craig's idea was two-fold: get M1CK to track down Joseph Denton's location and disable the bombs. The only drawback was that M1CK didn't know how to track down the bombs, but he knew how to stop them exploding. It took him less than ten minutes to hack the social media site that allowed Joseph to stream video. With that information, he was able to find the IP Address of Joseph's computer and report that information back to Brianna who relayed that information to the Special Ops team. When Brianna asked M1CK what he could do about the bombs, he gave a simple answer: Leave it to me, Bree, but don't rely on your phone, and don't ask me how I do it. Of course, M1CK's best option was to hack into all three of Australia's mobile networks and disable the towers.

The Ops Leader's comment confirmed that Craig's and M1CK's plans worked. It was a lot easier than calling the companies and asking them to shut down. They couldn't afford the wait in the queue.

"With any luck, that means he can't trigger any more bombs off," Craig added, being careful not to mention their involvement with the hacker. He knew M1CK was not with the police, and he didn't want to spoil the boy's fun by informing on him. Craig actually thought he could like that kid.

"He's the top floor unit on the left," the Ops Leader commented, pointing towards a lit window. "There has been some activity, but nothing clear that we can see through the curtains. We could hear some shouting from there, and some neighbours have called the disturbance in as well."

Brianna checked her pistol's action. "I'd say he's worked out that the mobile phones aren't working. That could make him jumpy. Have you evacuated the building?"

"Done," another Special Ops officer responded, pointing down the other end of the street.

"Then let's make moves." Brianna turned towards Craig. "You hang back here until you're called."

"Yes," Emily told Craig, smiling broadly, as she followed Brianna and the Special Ops team. "You stay here like a good boy while Brianna and I head off with the lads to get this man."

"Why are you going with them?" Craig asked, trying not to sound pathetic. "You're not even one of them!"

One of the Special Ops men looked around at Craig, wondering to whom he spoke. He saw no one else but Craig who shrugged. Shaking his head, he followed the others and left Craig behind.

The next ten minutes seemed to take forever. Time slowed and Craig entertained himself by talking to a few spirits on the street who were also watching the events from the street. While he was talking to one in particular, the spirit of an Aboriginal elder whose tribe used to live in the locality, Emily appeared suddenly beside him.

"Craig!" she urged, excusing herself to the Aboriginal spirit Jiemba before turning back to the psychic. "Come on up. He's already escaped."

"Hey, Bunji," the Aboriginal called to Craig as he left. "Wait!"

But Craig didn't hear him as he was already running into the block of units and running up the internal stairs to the fourth floor. His heart threatened to knock itself out of his ribs by the time he reached the top, but he didn't notice. Craig slowed and walked through the door, noting its splintered condition thanks to a battering ram. He noted the officer standing near the splintered door.

"First time door-knocking?" Craig quipped, stepping over the rubble. He looked towards Brianna who was sitting beside a dishevelled Sally and giving her a drink of water. "Sally," he exclaimed, walking towards her. "Are you okay?"

Sally nodded between sips of water. Her hands and arms were still shaking from the shock, but she seemed otherwise fine. "I've been through worse," she told him, trying to downplay things. Craig knew of her past involvement with a mysterious man named Predator, a masked vigilante with supernatural abilities, and nodded in response. "Listen, Craig," Sally told him. "This fellow is suffering from post-traumatic stress. It's serious."

Craig acknowledged her comment with a nod. "How long ago did he leave?"

"It was about quarter of an hour before you arrived,"

she replied. "He tried making a phone call, which I believe was meant to detonate one of the bombs he's placed around the city. His phone lost connection, and the landline didn't work either. He went into a rage before leaving me here."

Craig went back towards the smashed door's remains and found the door handle. He placed his fingers upon it for a moment, and stood up again after a moment, shaking his head. "Nothing. I was hoping to have a clue."

At that moment, Jiemba the Aboriginal Elder's spirit walked up the stairs and along the hallway. He poked his head in the door, looked at the mess and shook his head. "What a mess! Hey, Bunji," he said to Craig who turned around. "Didn't you hear me calling you? You won't find him here. He left some time ago."

Brianna had heard Jiemba and Craig talking and came to see who Craig was talking to, but saw no one. "Who are you talking to?"

Jiemba looked at Brianna, eyed her up and down. "You white women shouldn't be made up for war like that, you know?" He turned back to Craig to say more but Brianna interrupted.

"Who the hell is that?"

Craig shushed her and Jiemba laughed. "Yeah, mate. Sometimes you just have to tell them that."

Jiemba's teeth flashed white as he grinned. "Listen, Bunji, the man you seek with the tortured spirit, he's heading to Karri Point. He's carrying thunder stick with him."

"Thanks, mate," Craig said and looked back towards Brianna. "Well, don't just stand there. You heard the man. Let's go!"

Emily and Brianna followed after Craig who was already running down the stairs. Jiemba hung back for a moment and stepped inside to have a look around the unit. "That's the trouble with all these white folk," he muttered to himself. "Always in a bloody hurry and they wonder why they miss so much in life. Lucky for them Jiemba could point them in the right way, eh? Damn, what a bloody mess this place is!"

Chapter 31

Brianna held on tight as Craig pushed the Jaguar through its paces, the police light flashing red and blue from its position on the car's roof. She couldn't help notice how focused he was on the drive, and his determined look. Somehow, she felt that he wanted to take out his adopted daughter's death on Joseph, even though Joseph's brother's spirit was the real culprit. She asked him who belonged to the other voice.

"That was another spirit," Emily responded when Craig failed to answer. "He's one of the Indigenous people who used to live here."

"Oh," Brianna mouthed. "I thought you were the only spirit I could hear."

"You can hear all of us if you really want to, dear," Emily told her. "The spirits are almost everywhere. You just have to open yourself to them, and maybe you will be able to see us too."

The detective was about to ask something when she saw something ahead. She placed her hand on Craig's arm, pointing with her other hand to a vehicle parked on the grassed area. "Wait a second, Craig. Stop here."

Craig swerved the car and stopped, shining the Jaguar's headlights upon the beaten up old van. Brianna unlocked her seatbelt, opened the car door and stepped out towards the Suzuki. She turned towards the psychic, but he was already there and placing his hands on the driver's door. He waited a moment and Brianna couldn't help notice the worn look the shadows from the headlights gave his eyes. She wanted to say something but now was not the time. He needed rest but there was no stopping him now.

Craig looked up, turned his head, and started running towards the brightly lit Story Bridge. "Come on!"

***

It had been a long climb to the top of the bridge. First, he had to pass the locked gate, but that was no big deal. The hammer in his bag helped him bash that away after just three hits, leaving the mangled lock as debris on the ground. Then he had to walk up the stairs. Damn, that was work. The cold winter wind blowing him and the inevitable light-headedness of the slight vertigo made him think he wanted to fall. But, he didn't. After what seemed like hours, but was only fifteen minutes, he managed to reach a position near the top of the bridge's structure. He was able to see through railings towards the road below, and the riflescope was good enough to let him see them illuminated by the bridge's lights. He just had to bide his time now and wait.

Joseph peered through his riflescope, slowly rotating the weapon as he focused on the people below. He watched one young woman with beautiful blonde hair, blue eyes and a fake tan, as she drove. Her hand moved towards her mobile phone and she looked at its display. Was that a look of disappointment on her face? He knew the mobile service wasn't working right now, and he knew he wasn't the only one affected. Yet these people still felt compelled by their addictions to play with their toys while driving. Don't they know a car is just a guided missile on wheels? Take away the driver's concentration, the missile's guidance, you have a runaway missile that can kill.

He steadied his finger on the trigger and took a breath.

Well, he decided. *If they want to be in a runaway missile, I'm going to grant it.*

Mobile signal or no signal. They were still trying to use their phones, allowing themselves to be distracted.

He noted the partially revealed breast of the blonde, aimed for the turquoise pendant in her valley, exhaled a gentle stream, and pulled the trigger.

Chapter 32

The sickening crunch of vehicles, accompanied by squealing brakes and more car collisions, shocked both Craig and Brianna. They paused slightly in their running, took another breath, and hurried faster towards the bridge. Someone screamed and a few shouts rang out through the night.

By the time they both reached the bridge, traffic had jammed in a pile-up of cars and trucks, along the southbound lanes and stopped all movement. Craig saw the hole in a windscreen and then the victim behind the wheel. Blood had spattered through the car's interior, and another curtain of red passed over Craig's eyes that sparked a furious vengeance inside him.

Spinning around, Craig's eyes searched about for any sign of the sniper. Then his gaze fell upon the smashed padlock at his feet. Brianna looked about and saw the nearby gate.

"Over there," she shouted. "He's gone up those stairs."

"Call for backup," Craig called back to her, as he ran towards them with Emily just behind him.

Brianna reached for her phone out of reflex and groaned as she realised the mobile towers weren't working, anyway. They had no way of calling for backup. There wasn't even a payphone nearby since Telstra had been shutting most of them down over the past ten or so years. They didn't see the need with the mobile network so readily available to the public; and who would think the network would fall down?

She hurried after Craig, looking ahead in the mixture

of darkness and shadows cast through the bridge's structures by its lights.

Chapter 33

A numbing, yet comfortable, blankness filled Joseph's mind. It was as though he was in the zone. His finger poised as he watched the woman in his scope. She looked as though she was talking to someone else in the car. He looked towards the front passenger's seat, saw it was empty, and then peered to see if it was someone in the back-seat. But he couldn't see anyone there either. The woman must be shouting at the traffic, he decided and wondered if perhaps she didn't know what was happening. He panned the scope, settling upon another car's occupants, and saw the next car had a family inside. No. He couldn't take that one, even if they looked like Muslims; he had no quarrel with them and they appeared harmless. Then Joseph saw just the right one; it was some young man in a flashy suit, his shaved head's dark skin reflecting one of the streetlights. He was shouting into the phone, maybe having an argument, with his other hand gesticulating as he did. His mouth, containing pearly white teeth, opened wide with every syllable he pushed out as though he were ramming the words through the phone at the other person. Joseph though he must have been a liar or at least his argument had no legs to stand on. Some people, especially preachers, seem to shout louder when their points are weak, he thought to himself. And, this man was one of them.

"Bye bye, baby boy," Joseph whispered to himself, stroking the trigger ever so slightly as he allowed himself to zone in on the target's forehead, just above the eye line.

Joseph felt the impact first. Something hit his gun, although he thought it seemed more like a kick, but he couldn't see what happened. His rifle jumped again, leaving his grasp, and he could have sworn it hung in the air for a moment before flying straight down the stairs. For a brief moment, he watched as the deadly weapon clattered and slid down the stairs before a man's leather shoe stopped it ten feet away from him. He looked upwards, taking in the man's features, and stopped when he saw the stranger's angry face staring back at him with a look of dark fury. Lightning crackled from the coast's direction, briefly illuminating the man's straight-bridged nose that seemed to resemble an eagle.

The man lifted a finger towards him, his eyebrows settling on Joseph as the target. "You. Joseph Denton," his voice boomed above the thunder that cracked and rolled about them as the first drops of rain spattered upon them. "I want you."

Joseph stepped back as another flash of lightning flared from behind the stranger whose eyes seemed to glow, but it was a trick of the light.

"I don't know even know you," Joseph shouted into the thunder that rolled around him. "Who are you?"

"You don't know the people you killed either, Joe," the stranger roared back. "But that hasn't stopped you wantonly killing them."

"But they deserved to die!" Joseph retorted, watching as the tall stranger reached his level.

"Just as Shane and Jai died?"

Joseph stood still, shaken, and recovered after a brief moment. "You leave them out of this."

Joseph lunged forward, whipping out a knife to slash towards Craig who dodged backward and to the side. The sniper recovered his footing, preventing himself falling down the stairs, and circled to face Craig who had moved behind him. Each wanted to say something but there was no time as they faced off like two wild beasts in the jungle. The cobra and the mongoose. Joseph lashed outwards with his large knife, slicing through the air; Craig sidestepped again, pushing Joseph's knife arm away to push him off-balance before delivering a triple punch to Joseph's head.

The rain puddles created a slick surface on the metal platform and their boots slipped under them. Both Craig and Joseph regained their balance easily, but there wasn't much room to manoeuvre. Joseph shook his head, holding his guard up to stop Craig's advances, and blinked away the pain in his head. He knew his opponent was not military trained, but his fighting technique was strong. Using a criss-cross pattern with the knife, he steadily moved forward towards Craig who stood his ground.

"It doesn't have to be like this, Joseph," Craig shouted into the drumming rain. "The police are coming too, and there's another detective already here."

Joseph kept moving forward towards him, inching closer with the wicked blade. Craig knew it was going to have to end soon. He stepped forward, catching and locking Joseph's knife hand as his foot planted a hard boot heel into Joseph's foot. The sniper screamed, his fingers releasing the knife which clattered off the platform and down to the river below. Craig repositioned, keeping the joint lock and thrust his elbow into his opponent's face. Joe slipped on the platform, overbalancing, and Craig pushed him; he thumped down the stairs, rolling and bumping halfway to the next platform down before he stopped himself.

The sniper reached out with one hand, grabbed a railing, and pulled himself up. Craig didn't move, just stood there, waiting on the high ground. Neither of them noticed Brianna hurrying up the stairs, about thirty metres away from Joseph. It may not have mattered even if she was closer.

Joseph's hand moved quicker than a striking taipan. No one heard the loud report as lightning struck and thunder slapped the air, rumbling around them. Something flared from Joseph's hand at the same time.

Brianna screamed, and Emily yelled something, but it was too late.

Craig spun to the left, his head jerking to the side, then fell to the ground as the bullet hit him.

Chapter 34

Brianna screamed into the thunder, but only Emily heard her. They could do nothing but watch the handgun's muzzle flash. Thunder outclassed the sound of the gunshot.

Brianna watched in horror as Craig spun on the spot. His hands flung out wildly, but he couldn't control his fall, and he landed like a rag doll on the platform above. She reached for her own handgun, and watched, as things seemed to slow down. Joseph Denton turned towards her voice, his handgun raised to fire at her, but his hand flew to the side. Brianna thought she heard Emily shout something; she sounded angrier than a swarming hive of hornets. Something thumped, clanging. She saw the small shape of Joseph's handgun drop from his hand and then his head snapped to the side. A vague shape, like a black rag or cloak, moved through the air and whirled around the sniper.

Joseph Denton's mouth screamed, and it was the bastard child of unadulterated fear, confusion and pain. His arms flailed about to block the blows but it was no use. Then his hands clawed at his throat, and his voice was little more than a choking gurgle as Brianna finally came close enough to hear. But, there was another voice as well, one that seemed familiar but she couldn't place it. A male's voice that hissed in anger.

Then Joseph rose into the air as though something were holding him up by the throat. His legs kicked at empty air, one hand grasping for something near his throat and the other trying to push at something else. Could it be a face he's trying to push back? Brianna wondered.

"Emily! Stop!" Brianna implored. "Don't kill him."

"It's not me," Emily's voice answered from beside Brianna, making her jump. "I'm right here."

"Then who -?"

Joseph screamed as he fell into the murky darkness towards the black river water below. Brianna knew it was too late for Joseph Denton, but she didn't care about him, anyway. Her feet pounded and her breath burned her throat as she ran up the stairs towards Craig's body. Had that been Craig's ghost that killed Joseph? Why couldn't she hear him?

Both Emily and Brianna sat near Craig's still body that lay in an uncomfortable heap. The detective squeezed his hand. Lightning flashed, illuminating Craig's face, and she could see the rain washing the blood away from his mouth. The same storm disguised her cries as she held Craig close, cradling his head to her chest.

The thoughts in her mind were only for her loss of Craig, but this was so like when she lost her first love while serving in the Army. Memories flooded back with painful vengeance, reminding her of their arguments when they first met, his cocky attitude, and their first kiss. Tears came to her eyes. She knew she should call for help, but her phone wasn't working; even if it were working, the rain would have waterlogged it beyond working order. Brianna settled for holding him close, rocking with him back and forth in the rain. She couldn't save him, but she could comfort him until-

Brianna heard a cough, and Craig's body stiffened. His head moved, and she felt embarrassment crawl over her. Not daring to breathe, she watched as Craig turned his head to the side and opened his eyes before looking up at her. His eyes seemed to jump from one thing to another without focusing; grogginess. How long did he have to go?

"Emily, we're going to need an ambulance," she murmured. "I know you're a spirit but can you do something?"

Craig's expression changed, and he seemed to wake up and regain lucidity. "Ambulance? We don't need one." His voice sounded strange, almost choked off.

Brianna tried to shush him. He shook his head, pushing her back a bit so he could have room to sit up.

"Rest," she said, shivering against the cold wind blowing in the rain. "You've been shot."

Craig looked amused. He held out his hand, leaned over it, and spat something into his upturned palm. He held it out to show her. She looked at the small glob of blood in his hand and gasped. She thought it was a tooth, but her eyes focused in the dim illumination from the bridge's streetlights reflecting upward, and she saw a small object. Her eyes opened wide in surprised relief.

"Holy shit!" She couldn't stop herself from saying it when she recognised it as a bullet. "How did you do that?"

Craig picked the bullet up in his fingers, held it up for her to see better, and grinned; he had a tooth sitting askew in his mouth. "With my teeth," he answered.

Brianna couldn't help laughing, and she hugged Craig close. His arms went around her too as he joined in with some chuckles as well.

"Should I do this more often?" Craig quipped, only to be punched hard, but playfully, by Brianna in response. He groaned with a laugh.

Chapter 35

Craig Ramsey woke the next day with a start to find sunlight flooding in to his room. His room? It wasn't his own bedroom. He took in the sterile details of the walls: a simple painting of a tree; a wooden carving of Jesus on a cross, and a stench of disinfectant in the air. He winced from the lump on his head and turned to see Brianna sitting in a padded chair next to the bed. Craig watched Brianna's face, the peacefulness of her closed eyes, as she breathed in gentle sleep. Emily appeared at the foot of his bed, the television on the wall showing through her translucent blue figure.

"Well, well, well, sleepyhead," Emily whispered with a smile. "How are you this morning?"

Craig blinked, trying to remember how he came to be in hospital. "What happened?"

"You passed out again," Emily explained. "You were concussed from the fall to the ground after Joseph Denton shot you."

He winced, feeling the bump on his head. "How long am I here?"

They turned towards Brianna who was now waking, taking a deep breath as she stretched with a wide yawn. Brianna noticed Craig looking at her. "Oh, you're awake," she yawned again.

"Good morning, sleepyhead," Emily said to Brianna. "Our patient is looking much better this morning although I have seen plenty better!"

"What happened to Joseph Denton?" Craig wanted to know. "The last thing I remember is when he pulled the trigger on me."

Brianna started to explain. "After he shot you - or at you - and you fell, Emily went for him. He couldn't see her and -"

"No!" Emily responded. "I never touched him. I had been out of the way while you fought him, Craig. There was another spirit there."

Craig took a swig of water from the glass next to his bed. He winced as the cool water hurt the tooth that moved out of place when he caught the bullet. "Who?"

Emily shrugged. "I didn't get a good look, but it was male."

Brianna's face lit up as she remembered. "Yes, it was male," she added. "I'm sorry I thought it was you, Emily."

"Was it Shane Denton?" Craig asked, although he couldn't understand why Shane would have tried to hurt his own brother. "But, more importantly, you have caught Joseph, right?"

Brianna shook her head. "He went over the railing and into the water." She paused. "It's a long drop to the river below. They are still looking for his body."

A couple of hours later, a stiff and sore Craig Ramsey walked alongside Emily and Brianna towards Shane Denton's room. As he approached, he noticed the police guards were missing from the door but said nothing. They were released from duty after the news of Joseph Denton's deadly drop in the river.

"Can I help you, Father?" the nurse at the reception desk called out to him.

"Father?" Brianna said, but Craig shushed her as he recognised the nurse.

"I'm here to see Mr Denton," he responded. "I meant to see him yesterday but-"

"Mr Denton has been transferred," the nurse told him. "I thought you would have known."

Craig smiled. "People never tell me everything I need to know," he grinned, hoping his injured tooth wasn't too noticeable. "Which hospital?"

The nurse looked at some paperwork nearby, paused to read it, and looked back up. "It seems he's been taken to-"

"Gemini Research Centre," Craig said, finishing the nurse's sentence and surprising her.

She couldn't hold back the surprise on her face. "Yes! Did someone tell you after all?"

"I had a feeling they would be interested in Mr Denton," he responded, turning to walk away. A dark cloudy expression covered his face as he walked away.

Brianna hurried after him. "Project Gemini?"

"Yes," Craig growled. "The government bastards have him, and they have figured out what a weapon he can be."

As Brianna drove them home to Craig's place, Brianna told Craig about how the mobile phone towers were all working again. He nodded, not appearing to take it all in, although she knew he was mulling things over in his head.

"And," she said, with a happy note. "Today is the first day in just over a month I haven't received a phone call about a mobile phone related traffic accident."

"That's something," Craig answered, looking out the window at the people walking along the footpaths.

"I wonder if Sally Green's interview and the video clips on social media have made an impact," Brianna spoke, adding a slight upward note to the statement so it almost sounded like a question.

Craig looked at a group of people playing some game on their mobile phones, walking along the footpath as they did, completely oblivious to the pedestrians and vehicles they almost collided with. The game involved catching video game creatures and was location-based. He shook his head, a sarcastic look coming over his face. "Yeah, and if I flap my arms really hard, I can fly to the moon."

People never changed. Just like Narcissus and his fatal obsession wih his reflection, they loved their technology; it was an addictive obsession tainted with doom. And, he could do little about it.

But Craig Ramsey had other things on his mind. He hadn't been completely unaware of things after hitting his head. Craig remembered flashes of Joseph's assailant, and there had been something familiar about his saviour. He looked at his phone, flicked to the messages screen, and saw an unread message waiting for him. It was from Tyrone. His heart beat faster in realisation as he pondered if he should open it or not. At last, he made his mind up, read it, and dropped the phone from his trembling remorseful fingers. Colonel Ryan was right.

Never turn your back on the living for the sake of the dead.

Acknowledgments

Thank you for reading Dead Cell. I hope you enjoyed reading it as much as I loved writing it for you. It's been a wild ride while writing it.

I have special thanks for my beta-readers. Helen Odins is a good friend of mine who I first met in 2005 when we worked together selling mobile phones. She's a voracious reader and a quick proofer. Kris Verity is a writer friend of mine, and you will see her work in the future. Her comments on the characters verfied my interpretation of Inner Muse's thoughts.

Dead Cell is based on a short story idea that came to mind in 2012. The original adversary was Joseph Denton, a trained assassin with superb abilities that killed drivers for the same reasons. I won't name those reasons in here because I know some people jump straight to the end to find out what happens. If you did that, ha ha! You missed out.

Not long after completing publication of Twelve Strokes of Midnight, I decided to look at this idea closer. Who would the hero be? I went through a few different versions there. Emily Fraser was originally a male spirit. I won't divulge his details because I see him coming up in a future book with the same characters.

As you know, Tyrone is in a new predicament, and Colonel Ryan hinted that a big storm is coming in the future. Craig Ramsey's work is not finished, and there are some bumpy times ahead for him and Brianna Cogan.

My wife Katrina and I are preparing for our

firstborn child, and we're both looking forward to the adventure. In between helping with nappies, feeding, burping, and whatever other things come up, I will try to write more about Craig, Brianna, and Emily. As for how the stories appear (novel or short story) I can't say at this time. But there is more, and I hope you will join the journey.

Please feel free to visit me on Facebook at http://www.facebook.com/ChrisJohnsonAuthor. Drop me a note. Say, "hi", and tell me what you think. Better still, come along to GoodReads, Amazon, and Smashwords to write a review.

Until then, take care!

About The Author

Chris Johnson was born in Rockhampton, Queensland, Australia, at a very young age to parents who, for reasons unknown, treated him like a child in his very early years. He later ran away as a young adult and now lives with his wife and a spoiled cat in Brisbane where he works as a stage mindreader. His other work includes "The Trick" and "Twelve Strokes of Midnight".

Chris Johnson can be contacted through
http://www.facebook.com/ChrisJohnsonAuthor
and
http://ChrisJohnsonAuthor.blogspot.com.au

www.ingramcontent.com/pod-product-compliance
Lightning Source LLC
Chambersburg PA
CBHW060948120726
47910CB00002B/536

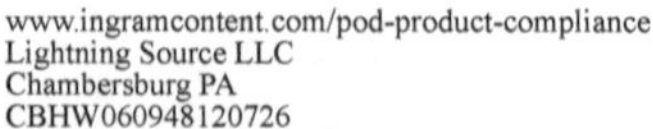